Plotting for Beginners

Sue Hepworth & Jane Linfoot

snowbooks

LONDON

Published in 2006 by

Snowbooks Ltd.

120 Pentonville Road

London

N1 9JN

Tel: 0207 837 6482

Fax: 0207 837 6348

email: info@snowbooks.com

www.snowbooks.com

British Library Cataloguing in Publication Data

A catalogue record for this book is available from the British Library.

ISBN 1-905005-12-1

ISBN 13 978-1-905005-12-3

Plotting for Beginners

Sue Hepworth & Jane Linfoot

To Dave,
of course

and to Chrissie Huntley,
my kind of heroine

SH

To Anna,
India and Max

JL

I went to the woods because I wished to live deliberately, to front only the essential facts of life, and see if I could not learn what it had to teach, and not, when I came to die, discover that I had not lived.

Henry David Thoreau

Becoming a writer is akin to the menopause: it is a deeply unsettling transition. (Though in the former case, hot flushes are rare.)

D.J.Rowland

La coeur a ses raisons que la raison ne connait pas.

Pascal

April

Tuesday 1st April

Gus has gone.

As a mark of tenderness he let me drive the car to the airport.

"Well I suppose you'll be doing it all year when I'm not here so at least I can supervise your last practice."

"Cheeky sod," I said.

As I turned onto the A6 I said "Do you want me to run through everything again?"

"Yes, just to calm me down."

So as I drove I explained again about checking in and then talked him through all the procedures and destinations—customs, security, gate numbers, Heathrow, Denver.

When we reached the security barrier we gave each other the biggest hug of our lives.

"Just make sure you come back in one piece," I said. "I don't want to get an email from Dan telling me you've been savaged by a bear."

"Will you be OK?" he said. "You know how long I've wanted to try this, don't you?"

"Of course. Go on, you'd better go."

We kissed each other as if it were the last time (hark at me, I sound like Ingrid Bergman in *Casablanca*). Then he walked off to be searched.

"I love you," I called after him.

"Love you, too."

I watched him go through the arch and collect his bag. He turned round and caught my eye and grimaced. Then he put down his holdall and held out his hands in front of him and made them shake, pretending to be even more nervous than he was. Then he smiled and waved again, picked up his bag and went.

I walked back to the café near the entrance, the one that smelled of apricot and almond cookies. I treated myself to a celebratory pot of earl grey tea because there was no-one to complain about the "extravagance." And it felt like an occasion, so I bought a pack of shortbread fingers too. I saw an empty sofa, which felt like a sign—a sofa is just what a newly liberated writer needs. I got out my notebook and described the scene...the waitress flirting with the Jon Snow look-alike in crushed corduroy suit and exquisite arty tie, and the business woman who thought no-one could see her flicking her nose-pickings under the table.

On the way home I played my Fred Astaire tape. I sang along to all the songs and joined in the taps on the steering wheel, and there was no-one to moan about the choice of music, or the taps. And when I got home I watched *Neighbours* and no-one complained.

What fun! I have a whole year of this ahead.

The above is what I was *expecting* to write here tonight. This is what I *am* writing...

I wanted to go to the airport starting on the A623 via Chapel-en-le-Frith, but Gus preferred the "far superior route" via Buxton. There was no third way. Balls to compromise. Compromise just means that at least one person is unhappy. Sometimes it's both.

Once I got there I was dying for a cuppa but Gus said Thoreau would have waited for a drink till he got back to Walden, and I should do the same.

We had a long-married, businesslike hug at the barrier.

"Just make sure you come back in one piece," I said. "I don't want to get an email from Dan telling me you've been savaged by a bear."

"Will you be OK?" he said.

"Of course. Go on, you'd better go."

"Well," said Gus. "Just think. The next time you drop me off here I'll be on my way to Australia."

"What?" I said.

"If the Rockies goes well, I'm planning on doing the same in Western Australia."

"*What*?"

"It's another type of wilderness, and I thought—"

"If you're planning on going to the bloody Rockies for a year and coming back and then going to Australia for another year we might as well be separated."

"But isn't this year a kind of separation?"

"What?"

"You were so adamant you weren't coming with me. I did wonder if a trial separation was what you were wanting."

"You wondered what? Are you mad?"

"I just thought—"

"OK. Why don't we? If you're planning on doing your Thoreau crap in every wilderness in the world for the next ten years, why don't we treat this year as a trial separation?"

"I only said Australia, I didn't say—"

"They're calling your flight number. Go on, piss off. See you next March."

He strode off without looking back. I stood there with my arms crossed and watched him go.

I had been planning to listen to my Fred Astaire tape on the drive home, singing along and doing all the taps with my hands on the steering wheel but I didn't feel like it. I scrabbled around on the passenger shelf, looking for something to suit my mood. I ended up putting on a Loudon Wainwright tape of Sam's that was lurking in there. The first track was *I'm Alright* (without you). I joined in very loudly.

I've just rung up to cancel *The Times* and order *The Recorder*. There'll be no more monthly flipping between the two. And I'm having something really smelly for tea— maybe a kipper. Tonight I shall read in bed till midnight and no-one will carp about the light. (Do I detect a fish motif? Is this what Bodmyn Corner means by subtext?)

It's wonderfully quiet here.

Now it's make or break.

Double or drop.

Wednesday 2nd April

When I woke up this morning to silence and the blissful freedom of an empty house, and I thought of my computer sitting waiting for me to go and start writing, a holiday mood swept over me.

And then I remembered what happened at the airport.

I still can't believe I said it. I still can't believe I said that about the trial separation. Where did it come from? I love the man, goddammit. Well, I'm fond of him. How could I not be? But we have always wanted different things, and now that the children are gone our differences have come out in starker relief.

I can't believe I said it.

But what I really can't believe is that he didn't try to argue me out of it.

I've always wondered how people our age who have been married forever, how they agree to separate—when there's no-one else involved. It has crossed my mind maybe once a year that as Gus and I are so incompatible we'd be better off apart, but I've always thought that once you actually voice the idea of divorce as a possible option, the marriage has lost its innocence and even if you don't split up, the idea would always be hanging in the air, tainting everything. Well now I know how people do it, how they take that first awful step of mentioning it, though the hordes of fifty-somethings who are splitting up can't all be having rows at airports.

It's typical, isn't it? My very first untrammelled day as a writer has been taken over with inescapable, swirling thoughts about all of this. Well, I've decided. He's going to be away for a year anyway, so it's a good opportunity to see how I manage. I'm going to go for it. There'll be no retracting from *me*.

from: daniel howe
to: sally howe
subject: dad

The eagle has landed and is asleep in my spare bed. I am going to drive him up to the cabin tomorrow when he has got everything on his huge long list of supplies. Don't worry, Ma—I'll sort him out and get him installed and teach him all about bears, and spend a night with him before I head back to Denver. Love Dan.

When Dan got the job in Denver I was gutted. Not that I told him that; I was exceptionally well behaved. I said "Wow!" and "How exciting!" and "What a great opportunity!" and "So near to the Rockies—you'll be able to drive up for the day and go snowboarding." But when Gus and I left him at the airport that dreary January day, I snivelled all the way home. What's the point of having children if they live a ten hour flight away?

Thursday 3ʳᵈ April

When I was down in the village today, Mrs Mountain— busybody suprema—asked me if I would miss Gus while he's away.

I wanted to say, "It would be a lot easier to miss him if he hadn't gone and left me with blocked drains."

But I didn't. I said what a respectable, middle aged, middle class woman should say when her husband of 31 years has just flown off to spend a year on the other side of the world without her, and when she's decided not to tell people that it's a trial separation.

"Yes, Mrs Mountain."

Nor did I tell her that I'm glad Gus has gone away because it means I can get on with writing my novel, undisturbed. Trying to write with a houseful of newly retired husband is impossible.

There you are, relishing your empty nest after waving the last fledgling goodbye as he flies off into the world. There you are, eager to embark on all the projects you have been saving up until there's sufficient personal space to be able to think, about to launch into becoming the new creative you— and then what happens? The bloody bald eagle decides he's had enough of hunting for prey and plumps back down in the nest wanting all your attention.

Early retirement. Hmmph. Women reach fifty and think they're on the verge of liberation and excitement, and their broken down men just want to stay home and fart. Or, in my case, go and live in a cabin in the Rockies and fart.

Friday 4th April

If I were writing a book about my year without Gus then today would contain what Bodmyn Corner—creative writing *maestro buonissimo*—calls the inciting incident (*Write Your Way to Fame and Fortune,* page 43.)

It was about eleven in the morning and I'd done really well—986 words in two hours—when I got to the bit where Pam tells Maurice she lied about the job, and I got stuck and found myself staring out of the window at two giant hares in the field beyond the back wall. I got up to tell Gus to get out his binoculars and have a look. I was opening my study door, mouth open to shout his name, when I remembered where he was and got this sharp 'oh bugger' stab (though why I should think this I have no idea—it must be just habit). Anyway, I sat down again and checked my email as a distraction and got this little beauty from *The Observer* (a broadsheet no less, not some poxy local paper):

```
from: kelly trounce
to: sally howe
subject: re: my true confession
```
If we wanted to use your true confession at some time, would that still be ok with you? And would you want us to use your real name? I think I've had it for more than a year, but it reads very nicely.

I couldn't believe it. Bodmyn Corner (*Write Your Way to Fame and Fortune,* page 256) says beginners should be patient and not pester editors, but it's so long since I sent this off I'd forgotten I'd sent it.

I jumped around my study shrieking "Yes! Yes! It reads very nicely," and twisted my arthritic knee, so I sat down again and wrote a reply.

Do I want her to use my real name? Is she kidding? How

can I be a famous writer with a pseudonym? I emailed her back saying yes to everything, and how much would they pay?

Then I went down to the kitchen and rang (best friend) Wendy and she was suitably impressed and sounded as excited as me, bless her. Chomsky was sitting on the windowsill miaowing and giving me his when-you-have-time-perhaps-you'd-be-good-enough-to-let-me-in look, so I did, and I told him about *The Observer* email as well. I'll be delivering two-hour monologues to Chomsky before I know it.

Saturday 5th April

It's only 7.30 am, and I'm sitting at my desk and raring to go because I slept so well on my own.

Not one night sweat. I lay dozing for a while this morning and it was only when I stretched out my left arm onto Gus's side that I remembered he was 4,000 miles away and it would be this time next year—if then—that he would be back beside me, listening to the World Service and snoring.

Sunday 6th April

The drains, the drains.

Damn the drains. Damn Gus. What on earth is the point of having a husband with a shed full of DeWalt boy's toys if he doesn't *use* them? He knew the drains were squiffy two days before he left, and yet he still didn't sort them out. I shall have to get a man in. I've tried putting bleach down, and I've tried poking about with one of Gus's crow bars, but it's no better. There I was, thinking one of the joys of having the house to myself would be baths with no interruptions, and now I can't even have a bath because the front path gets flooded. Yesterday I found Badedas bubbles on the aubretia. I had a bath an inch deep this morning because of the drains. I can't even have a long hot shower, because the shower has been on the blink since Christmas.

I bought *The Observer* today to see if my article was in. It wasn't. In the True Confessions slot it was a professor of English Literature writing about how he hates Shakespeare. Maybe they'll have mine in next week.

I was listening to *Open Book* on Radio 4 this afternoon. They were just about to launch into a studio discussion with literary agents about what they look for in a submission from a new author, when the phone rang, and instead of letting the machine get it I picked it up, dammit. It was brother Richard.

"I'm overwhelmed with disappointment," he said. "Paul's just rung and told me VSO have accepted him."

"Disappointed? You should be proud."

"Of course I am. But it means that now I'm completely bereft of family. You know I was planning on going to live near him."

Personally I think it's rather sad for a 57 year old to want to move to live near his son. Not that Richard's had any interest from potential buyers. His house has been on the market for 18 months and he's had no offers, and Izzy is hassling him to lower the price just so she can have her share and buy somewhere new and get on with her life (another early retirement divorce.)

"It's hard for you, I know," I said.

"Yes, well, let's change the subject. Did Gus get off all right?"

"He got off. I'm not sure *all right* is the phrase I'd use. It depends on your point of view."

"You're being most abstruse."

"We've decided to have a trial separation." I couldn't help

19

blurting it out. I hadn't been going to tell anyone, but it's a poor do if you can't tell your brother something so huge.

"Not you as well, Sally. I always thought you and Gus were different. I know you've had your troubles, but no, not you. You and Gus are an institution."

"So are the Post office and the NHS and look what a mess they're in."

"But still intact."

"Yes, well, it's possible that Gus and I will be when he gets back. Though I doubt it. I'm already enjoying my empty house." I smacked my hand over my mouth. What was I saying? Poor Richard was beside himself when Izzy walked out. And he's been utterly miserable in *his* empty house.

"You just wait," he said. "And it's just a trial in your case; it's not the same. Whose idea was it?"

"I'm not sure whose idea it was. It just kind of sprang out of nowhere. But it makes a lot of sense. The kids have gone—though Sam being at Uni and only twenty is still technically a dependent, I suppose. Anyway, it's obvious we want different things. I want to write. I want to see the kids and my friends. I want to do what normal empty nesters do and go away for weekends to see all the places I've never seen. Gus wants to be a cross between Henry Thoreau and a hermit."

"What do you mean?"

"Oh come on, Richard. You know he's always had a thing about *Walden*. You know he's always wanted to try to do what Thoreau did—subsistence living in a cabin in the woods. If he hadn't been married to me he would have done it years ago on a permanent basis. Now he's retired he wants to try it before he's too old. I would have done it with him, just for a year, if he hadn't also insisted on doing it in a wilderness."

"But surely you can write anywhere."

"Yes, but I would go absolutely nuts living miles from

anywhere and seeing no-one but Gus. Aren't the fifties the time when we're supposed to do what we want?"

"But a trial separation? Haven't you and Gus ever heard the word compromise?"

"It's not as though we're all going to die at sixty, Richard. There might be another forty years ahead—that's a hell of a lot of compromise."

Tuesday 8th April

When I arrived at Italian class tonight, Maria, our teacher, was sitting at her desk and Jeremy—class lothario—was standing at her side with his arm along the back of her chair. He was talking and leaning right over and pointing to something in her *Buongiorno Italia* book. He wasn't so much invading her personal space as making camp there and setting up a flag. You could see she didn't like it, but he was oblivious.

He spends every lesson leering at her, answering every question, acting like teacher's pet. His accent isn't bad, but he doesn't half lard it up. Sometimes Maria says *"Bravissimo"* to him and sometimes we can see her mouth twitch at the corners and it's obvious that she thinks he's an annoying prat. He looked up when I walked in because Maria called out *"Buona sera,"* but then he turned back to Maria and tried to engage her in a fake conversation about how to conjugate *ire* verbs.

Tonight we were learning members of the family. Once we'd been through all the vocab, Maria stood up and told us, in Italian, about her family. I sat listening to her orderly relatives, even down to the mother-in-law who lives in London (*"fortuna"*) and I thought *I wish I were married to a man called David who taught electronics at the university*.

I could just picture him in his tweed jacket with the leather arm patches setting off to work in the morning and coming home at night and sitting down for his meal with me, and napping on the sofa during the boring bits of the news and just waking up in time to lust over the lovely Lisa on *East Midlands Today*.

I wondered about life with a tame husband, though I know the reason I first fell in love with Gus was because he was so eccentric.

How can a man who has refused to go abroad for the whole of his adult life, who freaks out every time we drive up north for our hols, how can he then decide to bugger off to the bloody Rockies to live in a cabin just below the aspen line, seven miles out of the nearest "town," in a place so remote that the previous incumbents had to buy their own snow plough? He can get on a plane to Denver to spend a year on his own, but he can't go to Venice for the weekend with me. He can contemplate flying to Australia to live in the bloody bush, but he can't come on the ferry to France. If he were reading this over my shoulder, he'd be spouting his favourite quote, "Consistency is an illusory virtue of the unimaginative." Infuriating.

Wednesday 9th April

Last Saturday in *The Recorder* they had something about a married couple who auctioned all their belongings and sent the proceeds to a school in Palestine, so I thought I'd write something about the trouble Gus and I had when we were choosing new furniture after moving here.

It was a case of traditionalist with a penchant for period style (me) meets radical minimalist who thinks that form should always follow function (him). What possible middle ground in clothes storage is there between someone who wants an Edwardian chest of drawers in satin wood and someone who prefers a stack of wipe clean plastic boxes? Or for sleeping arrangements between someone who yearns for a king size cast iron bedstead, and someone who hankers after hammocks?

Then there was the problem of his aversion to visiting cities. Where do you buy sofas in a market town like Bakewell? I thought I'd found the solution by ordering two from a mail order firm. But sofas which appeared to have perfect proportions in the catalogue, when transposed to our sitting room looked like sofas on steroids. We returned them, and sat on the floor for eighteen months.

I wrote all this up, plus more of the arguments, and bunged it off by email to the editor of *The Recorder* leisure section. Easy peasy, and no s.a.e.'s required.

As an isolated writer, it's a good job I go to writing class. It's so nice to go along and be with people who care what they do with their words.

I might need all the support I can get this year. I have told myself that the reason I've not been getting on with my writing is because of all the interruptions from Gus. Now he's gone I have no excuse. If I don't make any headway with my writing this year—now that I'm on my own—I shall know I've just been kidding myself.

Thursday 10th April

I had a day off from writing today because my eyes were sore from too much looking at the screen. I woke up with a bad headache at 5 am, with flashing lights in my left eye. I got a cup of tea and went back to bed and listened to the radio, but the mug of tea just brought on a series of hot flushes.

So I took the homeopathic approach to housework—i.e. as it is so foul, you do it while you are in a bad mood and then you're not wasting a good mood. I cleaned the bathroom and listened to the serial on *Woman's Hour* because there was no Gus to interrupt with *Where are my keys? Have you seen my pruning gloves? What have you done with the secateurs that Nina gave me for Christmas? Etc, etc.*

Admittedly he's not been as bad as Alan. For the first six months after he retired, Wendy kept threatening to run away and become a missing person because Alan didn't know how to entertain himself.

Friday 11th April

I managed to do my 8 till 1 slot, working on an article for *Country Living* on different ways of storing seeds—which includes my patent method of keeping them in condoms for sterile and dry conditions.

After dinner I walked across the fields to the post office in Redmonton for a stamp for my letter to Gus (our village post office has closed down). In future I shall have to go there only at busy times. Today I was the only customer, which meant I was alone in the shop with Billy Bathgate. It would have been all right if I had just been getting stuff from the post office side because there's that barrier over the counter that protects the customers.

Unfortunately I also needed some groceries, such as potatoes, which they keep in a sack on the customers' side of the counter. When Billy Bathgate came round to get some he pinched my bum. I whirled round and glared at him, but then I couldn't think of anything to say. What *do* you say when a chap twenty years your junior grabs your bum, especially when you always assumed said chap was gay on account of his penchant for tartan trews? Also, I couldn't quite believe that he *had* pinched my bum and I didn't want to say something in case I had imagined it. I was mute. He, meanwhile, just started whistling *My Love is Like a Red, Red Rose* and went on loading Maris Pipers into his scale pan.

"I hear Mr Howe has gone abroad," he said as he retreated behind the counter to his scales. (Billy Bathgate is an incomer Scot with a posh and perfect Edinburgh accent, but Bodmyn advises against doing accents and dialect in dialogue so I'll just have to put in the occasional "Och" when recounting what Billy Bathgate has said.)

"Yes, the Rockies."

"Fancy going away and leaving his lovely lady wife behind."

"Can I have a packet of porridge oats, please?"

"Och, you know I can always supply your oats if you need them."

"And a pound of that nice mature cheddar," I said, ignoring his innuendo.

"That's a fetching pink scarf you're wearing, Mrs Howe. I like a woman in pink."

"Actually, it's a lot warmer than I thought," I said, pulling the offending scarf off and stuffing it in my bag. And it *was* warmer—a hot flush assaulted me at the thought of what was going on in his mind.

"Would you like me to bring all this round in my van, Mrs Howe? It seems a lot for you to carry home. You know I'm always happy to deliver, don't you?"

"No, that's fine thanks."

"I can come any time, you know. I could bring things up in the morning when I deliver the paper if you ever need anything. I know you're up early—I caught a glimpse of you last week in your negligee."

And as if all this wasn't enough, when I had paid him

and he was giving me my change he held my hand with one of his and pressed the money into my palm with the other. Then he closed my fingers over the money and gave my hand a little squeeze.

Then as I turned to leave, he said "Are you having trouble with your drains, Mrs Howe? I noticed there was surplus water on your front path yesterday. Do you need me to bring round my drain rods? I'm a wizard with my rods."

Billy Bathgate has thick dark wavy hair, which looks as if it's been sculpted. He wears his immaculate navy Pringle jumper (complete with thistle badge) tucked into his tartan trews. He is also in the habit of breaking off in the middle of a transaction and taking a cotton bud from a drum he keeps under the counter, poking it in one ear, withdrawing it and examining the end, then turning round the bud and doing the same with the other ear. I would rather not think about his rods.

Sunday 13th April

Another *Observer*. Another no show. Maybe if there is nine months between a submission and an acceptance, there's nine months between an acceptance and a publication. If that's the case, I'll have had one article published by next March. Some writing career. Bugger.

Monday 14th April

At creative writing class tonight we discovered the class is finishing due to council cut-backs. What a pain. Some of us were so disappointed we decided to carry on meeting off-piste, at Riverside Books, if they'll have us.

Duncan's going to be "tutor," in return for a book-token. He has filled in previously when the tutor's been ill, and everyone likes his approach. Our first meeting's planned for after Easter.

Tuesday 15th April

Italian class: Jeremy sat next to me (ugh!) and ear-wigged on everything I said to Christine about Gus being away.

Christine and I are useless at Italian. We have to give each other hints under our breath, while Jeremy gets everything right and then indulges in five minute discussions on pedantic details... "Sorry to be so silly, *signora*, but why does *arrosto* not agree with the *patate fritte*?"

Christine and I make wild guesses at translation. Last night the waiter in the book was asking the customer if he wanted *burro*, and Maria asked us what *burro* was. "Is it donkey?" I said.

Normally Jeremy would tut loudly or raise one eyebrow, or intervene with the right answer. Last night he guffawed, which is a suspect word, I know, but in Jeremy's case, it is precisely right. After guffawing, he made some comment about my sparkling wit. Most odd.

Wednesday 16th April

A dreadful night. I woke up at 3, 4 and 5 suffocating and sweating, threw off the duvet and lay exposed to the chilly air. After I'd cooled off it took ages to get back to sleep. When I got up for breakfast I felt appalling.

That free booklet that I picked up in the chemists gives the symptoms of the big M: of the twelve listed, I have eight. Terrific.

It's all the so called minor symptoms that make me want to slit my wrists, the symptoms that all those male medical researchers are unaware of or think are trivial. They can grasp the fact that hot flushes and night sweats and vaginal dryness are a pain, but never mention the other crap: like mood swings—weeping because it's a Wednesday. Like memory loss—where did I park the car? Like loss of concentration—what car? Like confusion—which pedal is the accelerator?

And what if you are one of the thousands of women who have had breast cancer whom the medics won't give HRT to because it's contra-indicated? The bloody booklet just blurts on about healthy diet and exercise and sleeping well and keeping busy and taking rests and basically all the things I am already doing. Wendy recommended red clover tablets, and I've been taking them for two weeks now. I wonder when they start to kick in.

Thursday 17th April

Living on my own has so many advantages. What liberation.

I can eat Parmesan, Stilton or curry without anyone moaning about the smell.

I can watch *Neighbours* without a snooty voice from behind the crossword saying "How can you rot your brain with this pap?"

I could even watch a Fred Astaire film, if any of these trendy twenty-something programme planners deigned to show one.

I can read the paper quietly after Saturday lunch without wearing earplugs to shut out the noise of *Any Questions* and then *Any Answers* blaring out from the radio in the kitchen, while Gus cleans his bike and feeds his political fetish. I wonder how he is managing without 24-hour news.

Friday 18th April

Another day of shame: no writing. I went to Sheffield instead.

I spent half an hour checking my stars in all the women's mags in WHSmith. I started by looking at indications about romance and relationships (something new for me). I wasn't looking for a new romance—just to see what's going on for Gus and me. *Hearth and Home* said, "For Librans there'll be romance close to home," which may be true if you count Billy Bathgate, but obviously can't be Gus. And *Fabulous Fifties* said, "Frissons in the stationery cupboard are unlikely to have the desired outcome." When did I last see a stationery cupboard? My stationery store is limited to one pack of printing paper on the shelf above the ironing board. Oh well, Gus and romance always were mutually exclusive so there was probably no point in looking.

I turned my attention to careers. That's what I should be concentrating on, not worrying about the future of my marriage, dammit.

But I couldn't find anything relating to careers. Where are fifty-something aspirational career women supposed to look for their horoscopes? There may be a gap in the market here. If I fail to storm the bestseller charts, maybe I could become a celebrity astrologer for female baby boomers. I'll have to talk to Wendy about her astrology correspondence course—keep it as a back-up plan.

Having failed to find any planetary encouragement, I went into John Lewis for some solace. I adore John Lewis. Nothing is more calming than half an hour loitering in the aisles. If Holly Golightly from *Breakfast at Tiffany's* had lived in Sheffield and had an attack of the mean reds, she would have gone to John Lewis.

Easter Sunday 20th April

I checked the True Confessions slot in *The Observer*. I wasn't in. Have they lost my article? Should I send it again? Have they changed their minds? Should I email and ask? How is one supposed to know what to do? How can a novice possibly break in?

And why has Bodmyn got nothing to say about this?

Tuesday 22nd April

Sam arrived home from Leeds this afternoon. He had told me that he was spending all vacation on a field trip to Harris and he wouldn't be coming home—so it was a lovely surprise.

He dumped two huge bin liners of washing in the hall and then gave me a hug and an Easter egg.

"Here, Ma. I wanted to get you a Fair Trade one, but Oxfam had sold out, so I swallowed my principles and went to Thorntons. I hope you appreciate it."

"It's really sweet of you to spend your student loan on an Easter egg, Sam," I said.

"Oh, I didn't. Dad gave me some money last time he was up. He asked me to get you it."

I was touched. The egg stemmed from pre-separation days. Then I took the egg out of the carrier bag and was even more touched, because the icing inscription on the egg said "Bestselling Novelist."

"And did Gus tell you to get this inscription put on as well?"

"No. I chose that because I couldn't remember what he'd said until after the woman had finished."

"What did Gus ask for, then?"

"Bestselling Wrinkly."

Wednesday 23rd April

This morning I sat up in bed with my mug of tea and the egg and tried to concentrate on the Bestselling Novelist inscription. I am trying out visualisation as a route to success with my writing. I tried to break the egg to start eating it, but the chocolate was too hard. When I finally managed to stick my thumb in, the egg exploded and all the white icing letters flicked off and scattered under the duvet. Was this a sign? Or was it just a shattering of hubris? Whatever—I scrabbled around under the duvet to find all the letters and eat them, like a cannibal hoping to acquire the characteristics of the person he's chewing on.

I managed to write all morning because Sam didn't get up till one.

When I went down for dinner he—the boy with the vegan principles—was munching his way through a packet of prawn crackers (which apparently have never seen a prawn), a stray tin of spaghetti hoops (that Gus hadn't managed to eat before he left) and the extra Christmas pudding that I bought and never used. *Vegan diet* obviously does not equate to *nutritional integrity*.

Thursday 24th April

No writing because of interruptions from Sam.

We have had two days of fab drying weather when he didn't do his washing. Today it was raining so he did. He turned on the heating at 25°C and strode from radiator to radiator, festooning them with boxer shorts and shaggy trousers and tee shirts, moaning and whinging and asking me why we don't have a tumble dryer like everyone else. I reminded him that when I suggested buying one last year he had climbed on his ecological soap box and blasted me for being environmentally unsound.

By the time I dropped him at the station tonight we had had our obligatory row. It started when I was eating a ham sandwich for tea and he lectured me on the evils of eating meat and I told him where to stuff his veggie-sausages.

Friday 25th April

I got a letter from Gus, and I don't know what to make of it. Of course we'd agreed to write in the days when it was just him going away for a year on his own. In those heady days before the bust-up, he insisted he'd only be writing once a month, and he would not be emailing or phoning, because Thoreau wouldn't have done that. Prat. It was only to please me that he agreed to let Dan equip him with an American mobile, so that if Thoreau-man is dying of appendicitis or he's trapped in the kitchen by a hungry black bear he can call for help.

But why has he written now, when this is supposed to be a trial separation? Maybe he thinks it would be too weird to completely cut off all communication after so many years of being together.

Hello. How's it going back there?
I am now installed. Definite drawbacks to transatlantic transactions in real estate. The cabin is a zillion times more shiny than I wanted, though Dan insisted it was the simplest on offer.

Of course I shall ignore the spa bath, and I simply shan't use the heating system. At least there's a fireplace, so I can have log fires. I've decided to build an authentic cabin instead (lease permitting). With twenty acres it's not as though I'm short of space or wood. The birdlife is astonishing. So far I have seen:

Mountain Chickadee
Black-capped Chickadee
Mallard—can see those on the river at Bakewell
Red-tailed Hawk
Golden Eagle—supposedly common, but even so—Wow!
American Crow—to remind me of you
American Kestrel
Pine Siskin
Black-billed Magpie
Gray Jay
Yellow-rumped Warbler—to remind me of Mrs Mountain in her golfing trousers

Every view I have is satisfyingly devoid of human habitation, although there is a cabin a mile away down the track—I guess it qualifies for the title "next door." I exchange waves as I pass with the guy there, who has more dogs than I have been able to identify. He does a lot of chainsawing on the homestead and always wears ear defenders. The noise of chainsaws and barking carries way up the hill to here. Half way around the world, up a mountain, and I still can't escape the howls of mad dogs. If the guy ever takes off his ear defenders, I may say hello.
I can see why Thoreau wrote that stuff about chairs in his house: "one for solitude, two for friendship, three for company." When I finish my cabin, I may have just one.

Thank you for the spaghetti hoops you wrapped in my fleece. What a surprise. Good job customs didn't search my luggage. I haven't eaten them (would Thoreau have eaten spaghetti hoops?)

yet. As long as I have them I can't miss them. I am saving them
for a difficult day.
Take care, Gus

Good grief! I had no idea that Heinz tins were banned substances.

If he bothers to write next month, let's hope there'll be more news for those of us who don't have a bird fetish. It's so long since he's written to me, I'd forgotten how much his letters resemble round robins.

Wendy's husband Alan drove over tonight to bring me the latest Anne Tyler she'd promised to lend me, and naturally I asked him in for a cuppa. He gave me the book and then when we got in the kitchen he took out a bottle of Rioja from the poacher's pocket of his Barbour jacket.

"A present," he said.

"From Wendy? How sweet," I said, taking the bottle and putting it on the side next to the microwave.

"From me. I think you're wonderful to let Gus go off and do his own thing and not complain." This from the man who last year followed Wendy around saying *What are you doing? What are you doing now? Where are you going? When are you coming back?*

"Oh, well…" I burbled and stopped mid sentence. I could think of nothing to say because he was looking at me with droopy eyelids and a peculiar smirk, and I could feel a hot flush coming on.

"Gus is a very lucky man. I've always thought so. Actually, I'm dying to know what this tastes like," he said, pointing at the wine. "It was in Jane McQuitty's fifty best buys in *The Times* last Saturday. Shall we open it and have a taste? Wendy's out at her astrology group tonight so I'm all on my own, like you." And he gave me another one of those looks, and I wished I hadn't invited him in.

I was aghast. As far as he knows, I am still unavailable. Did he really think I would be interested in a fling with him, my best friend's husband?

This red clover I'm taking must be working. It must have boosted my oestrogen levels so much that my skin has taken on a fresher bloom, my hair has become unusually lustrous, and the rest of my body is emitting some long forgotten pheromones and giving me an aura of rampant sexuality. What else could be the explanation?

I have to say that it's encouraging to think that people still want to make moves on me, even if there are those who view me as a wrinkly. If I were mad enough to want to become embroiled in another relationship, then it looks as though I could.

Sunday 27th April

Another bloody Sunday when I wasn't in *The* bloody *Observer*.

Wendy came over tonight. It was a delight just to see her—as in, to look at her. She always cheers me up.

Wendy is a chameleon. She shops for outfits rather than single items, reads Vogue obsessively, and gets most of her stuff from charity shops. She was wearing her "ethnic Wendy" look with a head turban-wrap thing (vestigial water-carrying headgear), beaded sandals, and huge jewellery. Tonight it was the splashy bright tribal version, though she does do a muted hairy Bedouin yurt look too.

"You look terrific, Wendy. I don't know how you do it," I said.

"For a look like this you have to think volume. Which is a bit tricky for someone my size." (A Patsy Seddon petite—so for volume think millilitres rather than cubic feet.)

35

She brought my birth chart with her. I asked her ages ago if she would get her astrology group to examine my chart and tell me whether I was going to be a successful writer. That was in the BTS (before trial separation) epoch. Now I want to know about my marital prospects as much as I do about likely publication, but as Wendy doesn't know, that's the one thing I can't ask about. Very frustrating...

She sat with me, showing me the diagrams and notes and burbling on in the jargon—a Stationary Direct Mercury, and a Mars Pluto conjunction in the house of publishing, and about Jupiter being in the third house—which, according to these notes she's left me, is the house of everyday mental communications.

All her astrologer buddies decided that it looked very hopeful, and that I could do it and I thought "Yes!"

But then she said that they don't have a lot of accuracy with actual predictions. For example, last year one of them had got a new man and they had predicted marriage and happy ever after, and it had only lasted four months before he left her for the next door neighbour.

"Did you go back and look at her chart again?" I asked.

"Yes, we wanted to see why we didn't get it right."

"And?"

"There was a transiting Neptune opposing her Sun which none of us had noticed, not to mention a Uranus quincunxing her Venus, so it was no wonder he buggered off."

"So which house tells you about partners and marriage?" I asked.

"The seventh. But that's not relevant to you, is it?"

"No, of course not. What about my future writing prospects? Could there be a nasty planet lining up to give me writer's block?"

"I don't know. We only looked at the potential in your birth chart. We didn't have time to look at your transits."

So I still don't know if the planets are on my side for writing, or for anything else.

Tuesday 29th April

Last night was the first writing group meeting at Riverside Books. All the stalwarts were there—Alicia (in yet another kilt), Kate, me, Duncan (naturally, as he's now the tutor), Janet (who is not called Janet but I can't remember her name), and the teacher called Paul who writes about aliens. (I can never make out Janet's and Paul's relationship—maybe they can't either.) Janet was very bleached tonight—denim, hair—and has lost weight so she's now thin to the point of being see through.

Kate was looking very glam in a new pair of jeans and low cut T shirt, showing off her Easter tan from her holiday in France. Do I really want to be friends with someone who is nine years younger than me and looks like Susan from *Coupling*?

We had some new people too so the posters were obviously effective. Plenty of characters for my novel…

Trevor, late 60's, is an ex-pat just returned from Bali, with a stomach like a football and an exotic purple shirt covered in palm trees. He used more banned words than I knew there were—phrases like "incredulous enigma," "shimmering virtuoso," "pulsating facets." I caught Kate's eye at one point, and after that we couldn't look at each other for fear of collapsing. When he'd finished reading, she asked him for a copy, no doubt so she can have a decent laugh in private.

Duncan asked if he had ever considered sending work off.

"Submitting work?" he said with disdain. "I've been

published in three continents, and I've been invited to perform at World Poetry Conventions in Minnesota, Toronto and Auckland."

Several chins dropped.

Gerry (a man with a large voice) was another new bloke. He used to lived in America, has multiple writing diplomas, sounds shit hot (as Kate would say) and is wanting to break into the non-fiction market. He is shaped like a Teletubby and has tiny hands.

Lastly there was a woman whose name I didn't get, so I'm thinking of her as Janet2. She also has a large voice. She specialises in performance poetry and has *VERY DRAMATIC ACTIONS*.

The evening was entertaining but I'm not sure how educative this new group's going to be.

"Riverside Writers?" Kate whispered to me when we left, "It's more like Deep Water."

May

Thursday 1st May

I got the latest issue of *Mslexia* today. There's an article about neurolinguistic programming in the pursuit of success, and a bit by an ex-insurance salesperson about building up your confidence. She suggests, amongst other things, having a scrap book containing things that you want to achieve, such as pasting in headlines like "Booker Prize Goes to Your Name" or "Your Name Wins Columnist of the Year Award," so maybe my self affirming screen saver—"It reads very nicely"—and the visualisation with the Easter egg aren't such mad ideas. Though I'm going to use a knife next year. I don't think an exploding egg inscription counts as positive visualisation.

Friday 2nd May

I dreamed about Gus last night.

I dreamed we were making love. When he is here and we really make love, I wake up the morning after with a glow that coats all the mundane trivia of my life with an alluring softness and I feel waves of affection for his funny quirky ways.

This morning I didn't feel a glow. That's because in the dream, as we were lying with our post-coital arms around each other and chatting, someone screeched "Cut. Onto the bathroom scene." And I looked up and there were people and cameras all round the bed and I shouted "But I haven't seen the script for the bathroom scene. I don't know my lines." Then I woke up in a sweat.

I forgot all about the iffy drains and ran a deep bath to have a nice long soak and relax, and then of course it wouldn't drain. Pestilence!

Monday 5th May

Today I wrote for five hours—from 8 to 1—and cracked on to the end of Chapter 10. Eat your heart out Mary Wesley. Or is she dead?

Another new person arrived at Riverside/Deep Water Writers tonight: Bridget Fellowes. She has grey hair in a bun and wears horn rimmed half glasses.

She seems to think she is at least Andrew Motion if not U.A.Fanthorpe. Kate and I have already dubbed her B.J.Fantasy. She didn't read but was big on criticism. Every time she made a comment she took off her glasses, and looked intently at the person who'd been reading. Her talk was peppered with phrases like "the categorical exclusivity of language" and "tangible experiences which defy classification." Had she taken a metaphorical wrong turn and arrived at the wrong venue?

Last night people were all trying to remember who was who. Paul shouted across the table to the American (rather rudely I thought) "Are you the American?"

Gerry was insistent that he is not (American), but that he is English and lived in America for seventeen years.

He kept shouting in a mid-West twang: "I am not an American! I am not an American!" Then he read a very American piece in a very American accent which did nothing for his case.

He was still insisting "I am not an American" while washing up in the kitchen at the end of the class.

Alicia knows someone who was at Art Class with ex-pat Trev: she says he is a pervert. During his reading I had to curl up and pinch myself to stop myself laughing. And when he read the line "Obscene eccentricity, wriggling profusion" Kate had a bout of fake coughing and then rushed out, gasping, "I need a glass of water."

I felt sorry for her tonight—she looked so tired. She said it was all the late night collection of her teenagers from their frenzy of social engagements.

Tuesday 6ᵗʰ May

At the end of Italian class tonight, Jeremy asked if he could have a lift home. He said he had come on the bus because his car was being serviced.

We were going back to my car in the car park in the dark, after the class, and he insisted on sharing his umbrella with me even though it was barely spotting with rain and it was only twenty yards to the car. He kept knocking up against me.

Then in the car I'd just steered out of the car park when he stroked my arm and said "That velvet shirt looks so tactile. Do you mind if I feel it? Oh, so sensuous. *E il colore e bellissimo. Amo azurro.*"

"Yes, well…" I muttered as I shrank away from him, promising myself never again to wear it to Italian.

"And I like the way you do your hair, Sally. That soft

plait looks bohemian but also rather glamorous."

"Thanks," I said.

I am growing my hair so I can have a plait and look writerly for publicity shots when I get published, but if it has this weird effect on Jeremy I'll have to remember on Monday nights to scrape my hair into a bun. Also to leave my hair unwashed so it looks limp and greasy and brings out the grey.

"Did I hear you tell Christine that your husband is away?" he said.

"Just for a bit."

"So you're all on your own?"

"That's not a problem; I have so much work I want to do while he's away."

"If you need any little jobs around the house doing, do ring me, won't you?" he said.

"That's OK, he sorted everything out before he went," I lied.

"Well, one never knows when a need will arise."

"Mmm."

"And when it does—just call me—I'm sure I could satisfy your needs."

Yuk. Merely recalling it makes me feel I'm drowning in waves of disgust.

Maybe I should have asked him to clean out the drains.

Why do any of these middle aged/elderly males think I'm interested in lurve, sex, coupling, whatever? Why can't they see I'm a dedicated writer with more important things on my mind than entertaining men?

And if I *were* interested and went in for a bit of casual leg-over it might sap my strength. I need to be frustrated and driven to pursue my writing, not sated and fulfilled, don't I? I'll have to see what Bodmyn says in *This Wonderful Writing Life*.

If I were writing a book about this year, I suppose the attention from all these predatory males would be what Bodmyn calls a sub-plot. Or would it be a minor theme? It's in his book *Successful Fiction*. I'll have to check.

Wednesday 7th May

I did another five hours today—same times—8 to 1. Fantastic: Bodmyn would be proud.

Friday 9th May

Wendy and I went for our free make-overs tonight.

We have both been feeling a little lacklustre in the glam department lately, despite what sleaze-bag Jeremy says.

Gus hasn't helped. On his last night at home I was standing with my back to him peeling potatoes and he was sitting at the kitchen table watching me and said "Why is it that when people get to our age, their centre of gravity seems to move nearer the floor all the time?"

It's all very well for Lulu and Cher and Debbie Harry to be over fifty and beautiful, but who knows how many surgeons and beauticians and sympathetic photographers they have at their beck and call? Gus sees photos of them in the Sunday supplements and says "How come they look like that at your age?" and I have to explain about digital remastering and back-lighting and botox (not to mention yoga.)

And then I ask him to say something nice and he says, in an effort to be encouraging, "You're not a bad looking old crow."

Even Nina—last time she came up for the weekend—even she said I ought to take myself in hand and bring my make-up into the 21st century, and I realised she was right when I tipped up my make-up bag and out dropped an original Biba lipstick.

So when I got the invitation to an account-holders' Special Events evening at John Lewis, where you could have a free make-over, it seemed like a sign.

When we arrived at the event and I saw the other guests, I realised that at 53 I am still not grown up enough to be one of them. I was there in my turquoise fleece and my needlecords, and was not wearing make up because there seemed no point if it was all going to be scrubbed off during the evening. Everyone else was dressed up and posh, wearing lipstick and legs.

Wendy was doing her Scottish look: olive green Barbour jacket, tartan kilt, dainty black-laced dancing pumps, tartan wrap secured by a thistle pin, a scarlet jumper in Shetland wool and a toning tam-o'shanter. I think the provenance of this look was pics of Prince Charles.

I tried to persuade her to take off the tam-o'shanter.

"Absolutely not, Sally. It took me ages to get my hair right with this. I'm not going to waste the effort. I'll leave the Barbour in the car if I must," she said.

But I said she needn't bother, thinking that at least the Barbour covered up most of her highland fling.

Before the make-over, we went to a fashion event presented by an image and grooming consultant called Suzanne Bellucci. We packed into the events room with a hundred other women to see this fifty-something goddess of grooming demonstrate how to put together a wardrobe for a holiday. She was that winning combination of attractiveness and imperfection that keeps the audience committed, rather than signing off in despair at never being able to look that good. She was stunning yet she was real. I sat there in my fleece entranced. I wanted desperately to be grown-up, to be chic, to be invited to an event at the House of Lords, as she had been (and *I* think it should be abolished.)

At one point in the proceedings, when Suzanne thingy was putting on a strapless bra, Wendy started to whistle *The Road to the Isles* and I had to shush her up. "Sorry, Sally," she whispered. "I don't realise I'm doing it, you know."

At the end everyone clapped fervently, and the woman sitting next to me hurried off to try on the brown linen trousers that Suzanne had been wearing. Wendy and I, having more taste than money, went to get a free fragrance sample from the perfume department.

Then we had the make-over. Wendy just bought some blusher, but I bought the lot—moisturiser, foundation, blusher, eye shadow, mascara and lipstick. Well of course I bought the lot. Gus wasn't at home to ask me how much I'd spent.

Sunday 11ᵗʰ May

Still not in *The Bloody Observer.*

Not only that, but Brother Richard wants to move in with me.

He rang this morning and threw himself on my mercy (sorry for the cliché, Bodmyn.) He's had an offer for the house at the asking price, but only on the condition that he completes and moves out within a fortnight. So the pea brain said yes without even thinking about where he would live. He's now madly packing and arranging to put his stuff in store, and hasn't time to find somewhere to rent.

"Why can't you stay with Paul?" I asked.

"Paul is busy packing, too. Also, the couple who are buying his flat are already doing improvements on it."

I decided to be assertive.

"You'll have to book into a hotel, then."

"Have you any idea how much it costs to stay in a hotel? My pension won't stretch to a hotel. If you won't have me I'll be homeless."

"Couldn't you stay with a friend?" I asked.

"I must say, Sally, I feel a little hurt that you so obviously don't want me. You're my sister."

He was right—I wasn't falling off the hall chair with enthusiasm at the thought of his moving in, but holy hatstands, I've just got rid of a menopausal husband and cleared my space-time continuum for writing, so why would I want to clog it up again with a menopausal brother, whose wife has left him because he's "so dull" and whose education authority have given him early retirement on the "jaded headteacher" scheme?

Then I remembered that every time Richard comes to stay he spends all his time in Gus's workshop ogling the machinery. He can never grasp—can any of us?—why Gus doesn't use his tools. "If they were mine," Richard says, "I'd *live* in the shed."

And I thought of all the jobs that need doing around the house—not to mention the drains. The last time I asked Gus why he never fixes the loose door knob on the sitting room door, or puts new asphalt on the shed roof to stop it leaking, or puts down floor boards on the joists in the loft, etc, etc, etc. when he has so many tools, he said "You couldn't imagine Thoreau using a cordless hammer drill, could you?"

And it's not a question of me not being liberated enough to do the jobs myself. Some people are practical and some aren't. When practical common sense was handed out I was in the garden playing with the fairies, whereas Richard was standing in the queue with rubber gloves on and his arms outstretched.

He could have been reading my thoughts.

"I could do all the jobs around the house," he said.

Bliss.

"That would be wonderful, Richard. If I sounded a bit iffy about you coming it's because I'm so busy writing."

"You can't be writing *all* the time."

"Pretty much. I'm trying to get on with my novel while Gus is away."

"I won't disturb you. I can keep busy. Don't worry."

So he's coming.

I must be bonkers.

Tuesday 13th May

Wendy popped in on her way to Buxton for a trawl of the charity shops. She was trying out her new spy/French resistance worker look: cream trench-coat (collar up), black tailored trousers, grey brogues, black beret, and hair parted very much to one side. Smile garnished with vermilion lipstick.

I moaned to her about Richard coming to stay. She took off her dark glasses and chewed one of the legs and said "Mmmnn." Then she put them back on and said "As far as I can see—which is not very far in these polaroids—having a man about the house might be just what you need to put off all these ageing lotharios making moves on you." And *she* doesn't realise that her own husband Alan is one of them. Maybe unconsciously she does—hence the spy look so she can follow Alan and see what he's up to.

I was tempted to tell her about me and Gus as I usually tell her everything, but I'm still trying to sort the situation out in my head.

As for Richard, he will love being useful. He's never happier than when he's in his boiler suit, a screwdriver in one hand and a spirit level in the other.

Yes. It will be fine.

from: kate wensley
to: sally howe
subject: telegraph
Hi Sally,
I wrote an article—about my mother's current obsession with aquafit—and then rang the telegraph to see if they could open appleworks attachments and got put through to the readers' enquiries desk. The man said that all e-mails coming through to readers' enquiries are stripped of their attachments. I explained that I wanted to send things to editors, and he asked if I had been commissioned, and I said no. So then he said I should send in hard copies. When I pushed him again about the e-mail question, he said, in clipped tones, that he couldn't tell me any more. In other words, *sod off*.
So I decided to forget the Telegraph and try *The Recorder*. I took ages to pluck up the courage to actually do it, but now it's gone—to the ed, Kay Wharton.
Fingers crossed, Kate.

from: sally howe
to: kate wensley
subject: re:telegraph
Hi Kate
I am SO impressed with your actually daring to ring someone up on a paper and ask something.
I have NEVER dared do that.
Hope Kay Wharton likes your article, though actually we should start calling them pieces, because there's this piece (ha!) in Mslexia which tells you about the jargon that proper journalists use, e.g.-
A Thinkpiece is an article which is your thoughts and opinions on a subject and which you don't

have to do any research or interviews for—ie
just you spouting off.
A Topical hook is something in the news that
you link your piece to. Basically you can write
whatever you like on any topic you like as long
as it has a topical hook at the beginning. eg
I could write a piece about choosing doorknobs
if it were hitched to the rise in house prices
(reported on the telly this week.)
Sally

Wednesday 14th May

The Recorder says a 55-year-old grandmother from
Gateshead has snapped up a £300,000 advance for her first
novel.

I've done another two chapters—whoopee. I've done Plot
Point One at the end of the First Act, and the first part of
Act Two, and now I'm coasting up to the Midpoint. Bodmyn
would be proud of me.

Eat your heart out, that woman from Gateshead.

from: kate wensley
to: sally howe
subject: fitness and tone
Hi Sally
Have had an email already from Kay Wharton saying
"not for us, but good luck placing your piece
elsewhere. Best, Kay."
It would have been a bit too easy if they had
said yes. Next time I'll have a much more throw
away attitude and I'll sign off "Best, Kate"—
that's obviously hip journo jargon.
Any thoughts on the speed of reply or what she
says?
Kate

Hi Kate
What a shame. Your first rejection....but a classy
one, anyway.
I think that the fact that you have received
a reply at all shows that she has taken it
seriously.
I think that's good.
Not sure what the speed of reply means—but it
can't be bad.
Love Sally

Saturday 17th May

In London for the weekend with Nina and partner Tim;
I am having the fabbest of fab times. Gus rarely goes away
for weekends, and hates London.

I love staying with Nina and Tim. It's great to have a
rising young media executive for a daughter who can take
me out and teach me about urban chic.

Nina's grown up persona amazes me. How can a child
who still talked to her dolls at thirteen—how can such a
shy, imaginative child have ended up as an extrovert media
type?

She and Tim have done loads to the flat since I came last
time. They've re-done their bathroom. It looks like a chi-chi
ultra-modern chemist's shop. Everything is clean lines and
sharp surfaces and all the cosmetics are in the same range so
they match. There's a high glass shelf running down one wall
with towels (nothing but white) stacked all the way along.

They've also bought a Smeg fridge.

Nina has to be up-to-the-minute with everything. She

insists that in her business it's essential. I'm not complaining. It means I get the benefit of all her cast-offs. This time she gave me a fab trench coat that fits me well—as long as I tie the belt to itself at the back—and is so much smarter than my six year old navy Barbour jacket with fraying cuffs.

I wore it out on the Saturday night when we went to something called a gastro pub. I don't know what the name signifies. The thing that struck me was that they were mean with their crockery. While we were waiting for our order they brought us hunks of bread and a shared dish of oil and balsamic vinegar to dip the bread in, but not one plate. And the next day we went in a café bar in Camden and it was the same. I ordered afternoon tea and was expected to rest my scone on my napkin whilst I buttered it. So much for urban chie.

Sunday 18th May

The *nth* Sunday not in *Observer*. I felt so fed up that when I got home from London I emailed the woman and asked her what had happened to it. And then I got really panicky and regretted it because you are not supposed to pester editors. Aargh!! Will I be black listed? Is my career over before it's begun?

Coming home to an empty house tonight (after being away) was weird. And I'm not sure it was good weird.

Monday 19th May

This morning my empty house felt not just fine, it felt wonderful. That is until I checked my email, and got this response from the *Observer* woman in answer to my question

"Are you going to publish it soon?"

```
Not yet. I'll let you know if and when we do.
K
```

I have tried to cheer myself up by thinking of this as a temporary setback in the plotline of my life, but it doesn't work. Sometimes when you need cheering up, Bodmyn Corner comes a very poor second to a Mars Bar.

Tuesday 20th May

Last night at Deep Water Writers, Alicia was telling us about the young tutor at her over sixties computing class. Apparently he's so beautiful he makes her gasp.

"The aim is to make us computer literate," said Alicia, adjusting her pearls, "but I'm in no hurry. I'm enjoying Gavin too much." He must be doing wonders for her word processing because whereas she usually reads from an old exercise book, last night she handed out printed copies of her work. Surprisingly, her piece had less sex in than usual.

Paul (the teacher who writes about aliens) read a piece containing a lot of green slime; there was a class titter when he reached the description of a space ship (though I'm not sure it was meant to be funny).

Paul's "friend" pale Janet1 was silent, but kept giving Paul significant looks.

B.J.Fantasy took off her specs at the end, looked Paul in the eyes and said, "I like the grain of the language, but I'm not sure about the symmetry of your parallel cosmos."

Duncan said "Nice narrative pace."

Kate then read us one of her witty minimalist poems—tonight about a camping trip. She has such class. But I noticed dark circles under her eyes.

"Oh God, I know," she said when I mentioned how tired she looked. "The troops just had a tequila weekend which ended with an ambulance call for one of their friends, and sangria dripping from the light fitting."

Florid Trev (the ex pat in Hawaiian prints who likes large words) read out a long poem full of phrases like splurging fountain, erupting infusion, tumultuous waves, and divine cascades. Afterwards everyone was quiet—perhaps shocked by the enormity.

I said it made me think of water. Duncan coughed a bit. Then B.J.Fantasy took off her glasses and said "Although the tonal variation consolidates, the pentameter is distorted, there is an inevitability of sheer recognition of closure—is this convention or mere homogeneous bulk?"

Florid Trev looked mystified.

Deep Water may not be edifying but it certainly beats *Neighbours*.

Wednesday 21st May

from: kay wharton
to: sally howe
subject: re:make do and mend
Dear Sally,
I like your piece very much but it is a little long. Would you prefer to cut it yourself (to around 750 words) or are you happy for us to do it?
Best Kay

The Recorder like my piece, *The Recorder* like my piece! I've just had the setback. Now I have some progress. The plot points in my writing life are coming thick and fast.

I spent all morning shortening the piece and got it down to 754 words and emailed it back anyway—I hope she's impressed by the speed of my reply.

Thursday 22nd May

```
from: kay wharton
to: sally howe
subject: your piece
```
Dear Sally, thank you for this revised version.
We pay £350 per 1000 words. If you email me to
indicate if this is acceptable, I will put your
story into our system.
Regards Kay Wharton

Being in *The Recorder* is enough for me, Kay, but a nice
fat cheque is always welcome—better than a smack on the
leg with a wet kipper.

Saturday 24th May

I'm not in. I have looked through *The Recorder* leisure
section three times, and I am definitely not in. I hate being a
writer. I thought being a freelance journalist would be better
than being a novelist because you would see your stuff in
print straight away. At this rate of progress I shall have my
first novel published and my second ready to go to press by
the time any of my articles are printed in the paper.

Tuesday 27th May

Another letter from Gus—if you can call it a letter. How
very odd. Has he forgotten about the separation? Or does he
want us to be like those ultra-civilised separated couples who
send each other postcards from their new lives?

*I have found my true home. The weather is perfect. The views
astounding. I am doing a lot of nothing, but looking and thinking.*

I finally understand what the great man meant when he said he liked a broad margin to his life.
Birds:
Common Merganser
Northern Goshawk
Killdeer
Blue Grouse
Wilson's Warbler
Common Raven
Dark-eyed Junco
Tree Swallow
Western Wood-Peewee
Northern Flicker
Broad-tailed Hummingbird—unbelievable.

New (authentic) cabin underway.
take care, Gus
ps Nice for you to have Richard to stay. You'll enjoy the company. Tell him he can use my power tools but don't let him touch my antique adze.

A bloody list of birds! What sort of letter is that? It must mean he's enjoying himself. But if he's actually going to bother to put pen to paper, why is it such a piffling impostor of a letter when he never stops churning out words face to face?

He admitted once that he was prone to pleonasm.

"What does that mean?" I asked.

"An army of words followed by a corporal of thought."

"What does *that* mean?"

"Using fifty words when ten will do."

The cow parsley is out along the lane and he's missing it. Serves him right.

Last year the vandals from the district council came and cut the verges while the cow parsley was in full bloom. The lane was ravaged. We were heartbroken.

This morning I was telling Mrs Mountain (who has lived for forty years in the house the far side of the railway bridge) that I'd rung and asked the council not to mow it this year, and she said, "So it's your fault is it?"

"You don't sound pleased. Don't you adore cow parsley?"

"No I most certainly don't. It's a damn nuisance. It obscures my vision when I'm driving down your road."

"But only for a month. And it's so lovely walking down the lane with creamy vegetation as high as your shoulders on both sides. Don't you think?"

"A far as I'm concerned it's untidy stuff that gets in the way."

She's a local. I'm an incomer.

Wednesday 28th May

Richard arrived today, so the whole day was screwed as far as writing is concerned because I spent the day mucking out the spare room for him. It looked so lovely when it was clean and tidy and polished, I almost considered moving in there myself. He got here after dinner, ringing the bell and opening the door and shouting "Sally!"

I rushed downstairs to see him.

"Are you all right?" he said, giving me a hug. "You're looking a bit peaky." He held my shoulders and stood away and examined me. "Your neck is rather red. Do you have an allergy?"

"That's a hot flush, Richard. I'm fine. I think you're imagining the peakiness."

"I felt like death when Izzy left."

"I'm absolutely fine. I'm going great guns with my writing. That's what this year was supposed to be about originally, as far as I'm concerned, anyway. I've not thought much about the separation thing."

"That's hard to believe."

"I haven't really missed Gus. But it's not the same when you've been married forever, and when Gus is the man in question. Since he's been retired he's spent all his time just hanging around at home. Without him here I've been enjoying the peace."

"Oh Sally—always so brave."

He went outside again to unload his car, and I followed to help.

He didn't bring much stuff with him, which bodes well for length of stay, but bodes ill for his entertaining himself.

In Bodmyn's chapter on Ten Steps to Character, he says that when you are beginning to build up characters you should imagine walking round your character's house and noting their possessions. So I decided to practise my characterisation techniques on Richard by looking at what he'd brought with him.

I took him in a cup of coffee and sat on the bed talking to him while he unpacked. This is a list of what I remember (I couldn't exactly take notes while I was with him.)

1. Two suitcases of clothes, one of which was full of what he calls his "work clothes" i.e. three boiler suits (two navy, one green—the latter waterproof), two pairs of old patched jeans, jumpers with darned elbows, three blue and white checked shirts, boots with steel toe caps, a yellow safety helmet, and a fluorescent PVC waistcoat.

The other suitcase was full of drab, boring clothes that you would expect an ex-teacher to have in his wardrobe. 'Nuff said.

2. One carton of books, which includes seven back copies of *Router International;* two Screwfix catalogues—one for normal sized DIY materials, and one called *Big Stuff; Dickies Legendary Workwear Catalogue 2003*—Gus put him on the mailing list for this (it's Gus's main source of clothing, now he's retired); a book of Art Deco stained glass designs; the two volume Oxford Concise (because he says we don't have a decent dictionary); the Christmas edition of *The Erotic Review* (hiding at the bottom of the box), a first edition of *Catch 22* backed in woodchip wallpaper, an old battered copy of *The Phantom Toll Booth*, a book about Bridge, and every book ever written by Nigel Slater except *Toast*.

3. One plastic Curver box of tools. I ought to list them, but tools are so boring, I can't be bothered.

4. One humongous clip file box thingy full of potato recipes.

5. Oddments he says might come in useful. e.g. three nesting funnels made of grey plastic, a dustpan and brush, an anchor painted in black gloss paint, three bicycle inner tubes, a washed out pelleted chicken manure bucket full of beads from a dismantled car bead seat, a length of chain with links four inches long, and a Sainsbury's carrier bag full of plastic caps from fruit cordial bottles.

6. A sports bag containing a tennis racket, spanking white tennis shoes, shorts and a T shirt.

Maybe my short term memory isn't as bad as I thought it was. Maybe I can knock off the gingko biloba.

Friday 30th May

Bakewell library rang to say that my book on Screenwriting had arrived, so I cycled down the Monsal Trail to collect it. It's by Syd Field, who according to the cover is "The guru of all screenwriters." When I have finished my novel I am going to write a romantic comedy, because screenwriting looks so much easier than writing novels. I wish I had realised this before. You only have to write about 120 pages and there are hardly any words on a page, so it couldn't be easier. If my novel bombs, I can make my name in films. Polish up your dialogue, Nora Ephron.

The book is brand new—no-one has taken it out before—which is a special treat. Maybe I'm the only budding screenwriter in Derbyshire.

I stood with my bike outside the library, leafing through the book, and I got engrossed in a section called *Dazed, Lost and Confused? It Could Be Writer's Block*. I had finished that and moved onto a section called *The Nature of Dull*, when I felt an arm round my shoulder and a voice with an unpleasant resonance whispering "*Ciao bella*."

I leapt a foot in the air.

It was Jeremy. The sleaze-bag had sneaked up on me.

"I thought you spent all day writing?" he smirked.

"Oh I do, I do. This is my dinner hour, Jeremy."

"At three o'clock?"

"Well," I lied, "I was so caught up in the plot I lost track of time."

"And you didn't feel hungry? My appetites are not so easy to ignore," he said in that lecherous voice of his, which would be laughably clichéfied if it weren't so disgusting. "How about a coffee?" he asked, taking a step towards the *Wyes Waters Tea Rooms*, next door to the library.

"It's nice to see you, Jeremy, but I must be getting back. My plotline calls," I said, stuffing Syd Field in my pannier.

"Let me help. I'm full of themes and ideas."

"You sound like that woman in the Thurber cartoon—*'I'm so glad you're a writer- I'm just full of themes and ideas.'*"

I looked up from buckling the pannier. Apart from my

father, I'd never met a man who knew Thurber's cartoons and thought they were funny and could also quote them. If Jeremy liked Thurber he might, after all, be worth knowing.

"Who's Thurber?" he said.

Oh well.

I finished fastening the buckle.

"I can help with your theme," he said. He crossed his arms and tweaked his chin as if he was thinking.

"The theme can wait," I said. "It's the plot that's causing me problems." I bent down and unlocked my D ring and hung it on the handlebars.

"Let me help with that, then. I'm a great plotter," he said as I wheeled my bike away from the wall. I was giving him as many non-verbal hints as I could and he still wasn't taking them.

"I know you are, but the only help I need is with my drains. How are you on U bends?"

"Actually, *bella, mi dispiace*. We'll have to do coffee another time. I've just remembered that my brother said he'd ring this afternoon. I'd better get back. *Arrivederci*." And he rushed off. Sorted.

June

Sunday 1ˢᵗ June

Yesterday's *Recorder* leisure section left me out again. I am beginning to wonder if "the system" is just a filing cabinet of things they might print if their backs are to the wall and a deadline is looming, and they have run out of articles sent in by genuine writers.

Monday 2ⁿᵈ June

Richard and I are still in the settling-in phase.

As soon as he gets up in the morning, he reads the paper. It takes him two hours if you include his attempt at the crossword. I grab those two hours to write.

Then he comes up and asks me what jobs I want him to do, and he says things like "I'll soon get that fettled" and "Don't worry—I'll sort it." Then he puts on one of his boiler suits and I don't see him for a while.

After half an hour he calls up the stairs "Can you spare a minute?" and I have to go downstairs and tell him what colour screw I want him to use—brass or silver, or whether or not I want the joint dove tailed, or whether I want him to use new roofing felt or for him to use scraps he's found in the shed. It is all very tedious. I know I should be grateful that he is doing all these jobs for me—and I am—but why can't he just get on with them, instead of me having to go down and make executive decisions? What do I know about the relative merits of different types of joints?

It's not that I don't appreciate all the stuff he's doing for me. But trying to get into the world of my novel and then getting inside the head of one of my characters is impossible when every half hour I am yanked back into the gritty world of carriage bolts and radiator valves.

Tuesday 3rd June

Last night at Deep Water, the man with the American accent (who insists he is not American) made the coffee and left the gas on. Alicia suggested he might be trying to blow us up. Despite his impressive CV, his piece was *boring*.

Florid Trev and Janet1 were missing.

Janet2 did a performance poem about a visit to the hospital. Her gesticulations were expansive and she almost kicked over the lectern.

Florid Trev-type words are spreading like a virus through the group.

Paul, for example, had written a poem that would have been at home in a corner shop greetings card. It was loaded with banned words. In the last stanza he talked about "vicious pictorial thrall." No one knew what he meant by that. (Even B.J. was stumped.)

Alicia was still swooning over "mighty fine stunner Gavin" (computing tutor). She is doing more swooning than writing these days.

I was sitting between Gerry (the man who is not an American) and Janet2, the performance poet. They argued across me for most of the evening about the contents of McDonalds' burgers.

Duncan read a villanelle as an example of a standard form of poem, and suggested we try one for homework.

B.J. huffed and folded up her glasses and said: "As far as I'm concerned, the villanelle is the frequent refuge of the resonantly obsessed."

Someone should strangle her.

Wednesday 4ᵗʰ June

Wendy rang to talk about my transits and my secondary progressions which—to normal people like me—means predictions. She said my progressed Mercury is trine my progressed Uranus which is very good for wacky writing. I'm not entirely sure about this because I had wanted my novel to be deep and meaningful. I mean—no-one ever got a £400,000 advance for a *wacky* manuscript, did they?

Wendy also said that next year my transiting Jupiter crosses my Midheaven.

"What's that?" I asked.

"Oh, the Midheaven is your position in the world. Usually it's someone's career. If they don't have a career it can be their status—you know, like as wife or mother. And Jupiter is a friendly planet. It brings good luck, new opportunities, and new horizons."

"So is it doing this to my writing career or my marriage?"

"It's good luck and new horizons with your writing— that's what you want to know about, isn't it?"

No, it's not just about my writing! I wanted to say. But I didn't. I said nowt.

I told Richard about Jupiter bringing me good luck with my career.

"You don't have a career," he said.

"My writing, you fool."

"That's a hobby, isn't it?"

"No it is not a hobby—it's my second career—actually my third career. Psychologist was my first. Mother was my second. Writer is my third."

"Why anyone should want a career who doesn't have to have one is beyond me."

"You had one."

"Yes, and the only reason I did was to provide for my family, and look where that got me. As far as I'm concerned, having a career is no great shakes."

And there was me thinking he always wanted to be a teacher. In Ten Steps to Character the first step is deciding what your character wants, and I've been puzzling about Richard. I'll have to watch him and decide what he does want exactly.

Thursday 5th

Richard came and said "Can you spare a minute?" so many times today that I exploded and shouted down the stairs "No I bloody well can't."

Then I felt mean. I went down to make my peace.

"I'm so sorry, Richard," I said, putting my hand on his shoulder.

"Hmmph!" he said, shrugging me off.

"I'm really, really sorry. I know I sound like an ungrateful bitch but I find it ever so hard to write when you want to consult me all the time."

"But I need to know that I'm doing the job exactly as you want."

"But you are—you always are."

"What about yesterday when I was going to put those chrome hinges on the fitted wardrobe and you wanted brass ones? And when you wanted a ball catch on the door rather than a latch?"

"Yes, I see what you mean."

I knew this would happen. I knew it would be a pain having him here. What am I going to do?

from: kate wensley
to: sally howe
subject: pushchairs

Hi Sally,
Have sent my Empty Pushchair Syndrome piece off to KWharton. This is part of my research into rejection notices. Also I signed it Best, Kate so it was worth it just for that. I feel like a member of the literary elite having done that.
I sent off my piece at 2.45
I said
— Hello Kay, perhaps you could consider the attached piece for the Recorder Leisure section, Best Kate Wensley.
The reply came at 2.58.
She said
— Thank you Kate, I enjoyed reading your piece, but alas unable to use, Kay Wharton.
An interesting variation I thought. I was a bit miffed she didn't say Best, though.
This is as bad as that game Black Box, where you have to deduce what is happening inside a black box by posting in marbles on one side and watching which holes they come out of on the other.
All the best, Best Kate

```
from: sally howe
to: kate wensley
subject: re:rejected pushchairs
Hi Kate
I think the fact that you got a variant on the
original is worth far more than the lack of
Best.
I got an email from the Observer woman, whose
guts I hate. She said they may not use my true
confession. If they do decide to use it she will
let me know.
Bugger.
Best,
Sally
```

Friday 6ᵗʰ June

Reading Bodmyn's chapter in *Successful Fiction* on scene-setting this morning made me realise that my descriptive powers are crap. I hate doing descriptions. But then I hate *reading* descriptions. I always skip them to get to some action, or preferably some dialogue. And when I'm choosing a book to read I always look at a bit of dialogue and see if I like it, if it sounds realistic, if it's funny or moving. I was talking to Gus about this before he left.

"I detest dialogue," he said, shuddering.

"But dialogue's the best bit."

"When I open a book and find dialogue, it's a stark reminder that there are going to be people in there."

Saturday 7ᵗʰ June

Not in the *Recorder Leisure Section*—wash your mouth out, Howe, for even mentioning the dastardly publication.

Sunday 8th June

Paul came on a quick visit to say goodbye to Richard. He flies off to his voluntary post in the school in Nepal next Friday. He's a sweetie. He brought some cast-off clothes for Richard, which reminded me of when Daniel went to Denver to live, and he gave Gus a suitcase full of clothes. I wrote a piece about it.

Monday 9th June

```
from: sally howe
to: kate wensley
subject: scruffy husbands
Hi Kate
Attached is my latest piece—written as though
Gus is still working. What do you think?
Best ever,
Sally
```

Pearls Before Swine

Whatever else my husband is, he is not vain. Nor does he like spending money on clothes: there are so many more interesting things to buy—tools, for example, and new fancy bits for his bike. Recently, however, even he admitted his clothes were looking tired.

His wardrobe for the pursuit of his white collar profession is made up of M&S basic range classics, and gleanings from Oxfam—all of them bought by me. If I didn't buy him new clothes he would still be wearing the tweed jacket and corduroys he wore for our first date in 1969. Whenever I ask him to try something on, he doesn't ask "Does it suit me?" but "How much does it cost?"

Two years ago, when even his clothes for do-it-yourself were threadbare, he discovered Dickies coveralls (boiler suits) which answered his every requirement—inexpensive, practical, hard wearing, comfortable and had, joy of joys, 9 pockets, three of which are zipped.

He liked them so much he thought of them as smart casual, and resisted wearing them for dirty jobs such as cleaning out the gutters.

Thus it was that I caught him, in his quest for new clothes, drooling over the Dickies Legendary Workwear Catalogue 2003. There was much oohing and aahing and "now that's what I call no nonsense trousers" type exclamations. He imagined he could not only buy new DIY finery from the range, but also revamp the lacklustre wardrobe he wears for his job.

Fortunately, good sense (i.e. me) prevailed, and he restricted himself—as a holiday treat—to a "Grafters Bib and Brace" which has too many alluring features to detail here, but his favourite is the bottom loading knee pad pouches.

All this was a displacement activity, of course; it wasn't his DIY clothes that were drab and in need of a magic wand. Enter our twenty-something son, who was leaving the country. He came home for the weekend to say goodbye, and to discard some items via us to Oxfam.

My husband has always been the grateful recipient of cast off clothes from wherever they have come—son, nephew, the neighbours—he is not proud. In the past this bounty has consisted of a clutch of T shirts or the odd jumper. This time, because our son has lost some weight and many of his clothes no longer fit, and because he is making a clean break from his old life, he left us a large suitcase full of fashion that he wanted to see the back of.

Do the names Hugo Boss, Paul Smith, Kenzo, Nicole Farhi, Donna Karan or Calvin Klein mean anything to you? They didn't to my husband.

"Are these trendy?" he asked, rifling through the suitcase.

"Why do they all have these labels on? Could you unpick them?"

He was in raptures. The clothes would last him till he died. He'd never have to buy another garment. There was a suit, six pairs of jeans, some snazzy black linen trousers and a dozen shirts smarter than anything my husband has ever owned (not difficult, admittedly) and a stack of casual shirts cooler than anything he has seen Brad Pitt wearing on TV. (Not that he would recognise Brad Pitt, you understand.) There was even a pair of DKNY shorts that—once I had removed the cargo pockets stuck on the side of each leg—would look dandy on a 55 year old with muscly thighs.

I gave him the suit, and took out my favourite shirt from the pile—a blue checked one by Kenzo—and got him to try them on. They were a perfect fit. Wow, I thought, a trendy husband, a smart husband. What a novelty. I wanted to invite his colleagues round and pretend I had just signed a six figure contract for my novel, and that I'd finally persuaded him to spend money on clothes.

After a mammoth trying on session, he came downstairs wearing a pair of CK jeans, and something that had been lurking unloved at the bottom of the suitcase and which only a scruff would take out. It was a freebie: an oversized and shapeless white polo shirt bearing the logo Microsoft Windows XP. "It's so comfy," he said.

I am not a label freak, but I do like well cut clothes. I am sitting here in Hugo Boss jeans and a Paul Smith shirt, and I have secreted in my wardrobe a DKNY shirt for tomorrow. I never was a Dickies woman, myself.

768 words © Sally Howe 2003

Tuesday 10ᵗʰ June

In the *Recorder* today there was an article saying that no-one cooks proper meals any more, no-one CAN cook proper meals any more, and everyone is going out to eat on their way home from work. This is typical of the London-centric media where the twenty-something journalist sees a trend amongst his/her friends and then assumes it is the case for the whole of the British Isles, all classes, all ages, all types of family groupings.

When are they going to get in touch with reality and employ a fifty-something menopausal married woman living in the provinces? I could tell them how many people on our road come straight home from work and eat meat and two veg.

```
from: kate wensley
to: sally howe
subject: pearls
Hi Sally
Loved the pearls before swine.
I've been thinking about this writing game.
Things have got tight in the newspaper line
post Sept 11 because of all the redundancies in
the Media. They're all sitting at home writing
novels/self help bks/pieces and trying to flog
them to their mates who are left in post.
All the people working on newspapers want
to do is leave and write novels (preferably
blockbusters)
All the novelists want to do is win the Booker.
Everyone wants a bestseller.
And I'm desperate to get one tiny thing in. How
like a worm does that make me?
Are you going to ring Kay Wharton to ask when
they are going to print yr piece?
Best Bookers
Kate
```

Hi Kate

No, I'm not going to ring her, I'm too nervous. Also, you're not supposed to pester editors. I know there's a recession and publishing is all very tight. You make it sound as though there's a war on and we are trying to get our pieces behind enemy lines. Very soon you will send Kay something she can't refuse. And I'm looking forward to another Deep Water writer slipping something past the barricades! Aha!

We do have an edge on all these ex journos though because we have fresh voices from the provinces. I wonder why none of the editors realise this. Last evening I counted seventeen hot flushes—and that was just while I was watching Neighbours.

Best ever,
Sally

Wednesday 11th June

I called in to see Wendy today on my way back from Bakewell. She was in the garden—I've not seen her Wendy-as-country-gardener look before (faded denim dungarees, flowery wellies, and a royal blue ribbon in her hair which toned with the tiny flowers in her Liberty Tana Lawn blouse).

"Thank God you've come," she said, putting down a mammoth trug containing three mangey foxglove stalks. "I loathe gardening. Let's have a cuppa."

Over the past few weeks she's been pestering me for suggestions for a birthday present for her twins who will be 21 next month. Now she has found the solution—there's a company called Tremendous Treats who sell experiences.

She has bought the twins a day each driving a Porsche. I told Richard about this.

"What an excellent idea. Do you think they do a day where you can try out exotic woodworking tools?"

Thursday 12th June

I'm still reading *Fortune's Rocks*, and boy can Shreve do descriptions.

I can't.

For limbering up in the description department, Bodmyn suggests taking an everyday object, looking at it for five minutes, and then writing a list of 21 adjectives that describe it. I was in the middle of reading this advice when Richard burst into the study.

I had been luxuriating in the thought that he would be busy all morning, because Richard had decided to clean the kitchen. Actually, I had thought he would be busy all week, because his idea of cleaning the kitchen is not a quick wipe round with the dishcloth, à la Sally. His version of cleaning the kitchen is what Ma used to call "bottoming the kitchen," i.e. cleaning the cooker and cleaning behind the cooker, mucking out the fridge, and then emptying all the cupboards and washing the shelves, before replacing the items not past their sell by date, which then means a trip to the Co-op because of the lack of remaining comestibles.

When Richard disturbs me he usually pokes his head round the door and says apologetically, "Can you spare a minute?" This morning he thundered into the room and threw onto my desk a wet poly bag containing two prehistoric bewhiskered carrots he had found languishing in the back of the salad drawer.

"I don't know how you can live like this," he said.

"Two old carrots? Throw them in the compost bin if they upset you."

"It's not just the carrots or the salad crisper—the recesses of your kitchen cupboards look like something from one of those TV programmes where they call in environmental health inspectors."

"Germs are good for you. Build up your resistance."

"Oh yes? Tell that to the woman in the paper today who died of e. coli. Mother would turn in her grave if she could see the state of your cupboards."

"Well isn't it a good job that you're here to sort them out?" I said. Maybe if I changed my tack I could get rid of him, and get on with my writing.

"Hmmph."

"You're such a star, Richard. Thanks for doing the kitchen. And all the other jobs you're doing for me around the house."

That seemed to mollify him. He went away again, and I did Bodmyn's exercise for getting the descriptive juices flowing.

21 adjectives:

1 hairy
2 wrinkled
3 long
4 warty
5 knobbly
6 lined
7 cold
8 stubby
9 gritty
10 snappy
11 crunchy
12 wet
13 rough

14 fresh
15 round
16 juicy
17 washed
18 succulent
19 tasty
20 matt
21 orange—nearly forgot

List extension for extra Bodmyn points: earthy, delicious, nutritious, natural, crisp, damp, hearty, useful, traditional, ubiquitous, unfathomable.

Friday 13th June

I decided to practice for when I am a famous novelist and have to keep up appearances for book signing tours and photoshoots. (Suzanne Bellucci can be my role model.) So I went to the chi-chi Chatsworth Farm Shop for a free range pork chop.

I didn't wear my old black fleece garnished with cat hairs: I donned the trendy trench coat that Nina gave me. My unplaited hair—though greying blonde—makes me look like Miss Piggy in mid-toss of her primadonna-ish head, only less attractive. So I concocted a chignon and then applied my make-up from the John Lewis make-over.

On the way to Chatsworth I called at the petrol station to fill up the car. I put the nozzle in the hole and turned to check that the display read zero, and squeezed the trigger and petrol spurted backwards all over my hand, my coat and my shoes and then formed a foaming puddle on the tarmac around my feet.

When I went to pay I told the cashier I'd had a fight with the petrol pump and she said "I can smell it. Don't light a ciggy, will you?"

The stench inside the car was so fierce that by the time I pulled into the car park at Chatsworth Farm Shop I was wondering if you could die from inhaling petrol fumes, but once I got out of the car the smell seemed to dissipate.

Inside the shop it was like the set for a Joanna Trollope adaptation. All the women were wearing calf length Barbour coats, opaque tights, and those loafers with little chains across the front. Also, they were wearing make-up and either headscarves, à la Princess Anne, or Alice bands over newly polished hair. I'd always imagined that people pop in there just for treats. But these women had overflowing baskets; they obviously view the place as a supermarket and do their main weekly shop there.

I collected my chop from the butcher's counter, went to pay at one of the checkouts and the dainty, Trollope-type extra standing at the adjacent till leapt back, shiny bob swinging, and whinnied in a horrified tone "I can smell petrol," and the whole shop turned round and stared.

So much for rural chic.

Saturday 14th June

I hung up my poor, petrol soaked coat in the back porch on the airing rack until the stink disappears, but then Richard saw it.

"It's bad enough, Sally, that you don't have a fire extinguisher in the house, without creating your very own fire hazards. Hanging it there is just asking the central heating boiler flame to leap over and ignite the petrol."

So I have hung the coat on the washing line outside.

from: kate wensley
to: sally howe
subject: sweating
Hi Sally,
Sorry to hear about your menopausal problems.
I'm dreading it. I woke up the other night in a
complete panic because I thought I cd feel my
head sweating, and it must be the start of the
menopause.
Had you realised that Kay Wharton and I have the
same initials? Feel quite excited about this.
best bits of love, Kate (KW)
ps Do you think they can tell when a submission
is from an amateur?

from: sally howe
to: kate wensley
subject: re:sweating
Hi Kate
I think that they can tell when it's an amateur
submission. Bodmyn Corner doesn't even acknowledge
the existence of email so I have no idea what is
the correct way to submit by it.
eg should one type "/more" at the end of each
page?—I believe one should, but I never do.
Should one put one's contact details at the top
of the first page or at the bottom of the last
page? Who knows? Etc etc etc.
Best ever,
Sally

from: kate wensley
to: sally howe
subject: butter or marge
Hi Sally,
Re amateurism: I couldn't help thinking that KW
did a civilised reply to me because I signed Best
at the end.
all bests, best love and best butter, Kate

Tuesday 17th June

Pam is a hateful and irritating character, and I wish she would fall under a bus on the way to the interview. Unfortunately she has to get the job or the plotline is buggered.

I'm buggered.

Wednesday 18th June

The words didn't flow today. I turned on the computer, opened chapter 13, knew I had to describe Pam getting ready for her interview, and had no idea what to write. My mind was a blank. The whole thing is boring. Dull, dull, dull.

Maybe I have writer's block. If it is writer's block, I really am a proper writer.

Bodmyn writer's block exercises are more boring than Pam so I switched off the computer, got myself a coffee and sat in the sunshine on the front bench reading *Fortune's Rocks*. For research purposes, of course, examining how Anita Shreve achieves suspense.

Friday 20th June

Another epistle from Gus arrived: he must be sticking to the BTS agreement of one a month.

Settling in. The days pass. Time is but the stream I go a-fishing in, as the great man said...
You ask for more interesting news—is the following what you had in mind?
The guy next door came around to bring some mail, minus his ear defenders. He's called Arnie. He was impressed with the

new/old cabin so far—the framework is progressing. It's made of timbers harvested from the woodland here (don't worry—as you do—Dan negotiated this and it's all legit.) Also technologically legit—all hand felled and hand sawn. Arnie wanted to help by planing the wood up on his machines. I'm not sure he understands what I'm about. He's certainly never heard of Thoreau.

He is so eager to show me his workshop that I've agreed to go, so long as he gets those dogs under control first. I keep thinking I haven't come half way around the world to spend my time looking at woodworking machines. Pleased to hear Richard is making himself useful.

Has your article appeared in The Recorder yet? Remember to save me a copy.

Bird sightings:
Red-tailed Hawk
Peregrine falcon
MacGillvray's Warbler
Spotted Towhee
Rose-breasted Grosbeak
Horned lark
Brown Creeper
Western Tanager
Brewer's Blackbird
Magnificent Humming bird—Magnificent!

Weather—warm days, cold nights.
take care back there Gus

    Birds again, and "take care" again.
    I wonder if he's missing me.

Saturday 21st June

I'm really excited—Daniel emailed to say he has to fly over to London for work next week. And *he* signed it "lots of love." He's only going to be over here for three days and doesn't have time to come up north to see me, but if I go down and stay with Nina and Tim, we can all have a couple of nights out together.

Tuesday 24th June

Last night at Deep Water we had a big discussion about getting facts right, and the need for research.

Janet2 said "Tosh! I just read an article in the Saturday Telegraph Magazine about this author guy who sits in a garage in Northampton and writes novels about deserts and pathology, with no research at all, using only his imagination." She flicked her long hair over her shoulders and looked round defiantly at us all.

Alicia pulled down the cuffs of her blouse to make sure they showed evenly at the bottom of her blazer sleeves, and then said "But Joanna Trollope does a huge amount of meticulous research."

"I really couldn't care," said Janet2. "I don't have time to waste on research. Just listen to this and tell me it would be better if I'd done research."

Then she performed a poem about a modern-day male slave bought in a pyramid in Morocco.

Florid Trev read more of his usual stuff but with less grammar and more punctuation—especially brackets, both random and profuse.

B.J.Fantasy, de-specced, said: "Imagery is the first refuge of the imaginatively illiterate. This work is over-reliant on honing *[or was it homing?]* on the homiletic."

This took the shimmer out of Florid Trev's quadrillion rivulets.

B.J.Fantasy still hasn't read anything. Perhaps she sees herself as resident critic.

No sign of Paul's shadow, Janet1.

The sunbeam on the horizon was Alicia's poem about buying a Male Voice Choir.

In the car park afterwards Kate (looking even more drawn than usual—and not in a good way) said "There's so much bloody copy at Deep Water, the lack of talent doesn't matter." How right she is.

Friday 27th June

This morning I felt like a menopausal country mouse going to London to see my town mouse children. Children? What am I saying? Nina is twenty nine and Daniel is twenty seven.

Daniel was looking really well. The 300 days a year of sunshine that Denver has to offer obviously suits him.

After much discussion the three of them decided to take me to trendy east London to expand my knowledge of young urban chic. Nina said: "You really need to get up to speed on modern metropolitan culture, Mother, if you want to be a freelance journalist."

We went on the tube to Old Street and then walked along the Great Eastern Road. I didn't like it. It felt unwelcoming and wasteland-urban, undomesticated and bleak, but walking along with the three of them I felt bullet proof. Eventually we arrived at a place with a bare lighted window glowing green. We went inside and were faced with a door marked 'Kitchen'. "In here," they said. How did they know it was the restaurant and not the kitchen? Once inside, I saw it was both.

It was one of those places where the designer thinks you want to hear the clatter of the kitchen while you're dining. (I wasn't impressed by that when they took me to the OXO tower.) Why is this a good idea? Is it supposed to feel like home because you're eating in the kitchen? Is it a post modern egalitarian measure to make the chefs feel included in the dining experience? Or is it because they like a portion of people-watching to enliven their hot slog over the wild rice and the gorgonzola?

Nina and Tim debated the décor. Was it seventies or noughties? They thought it was cosy because of the subtle low lighting. Cosy for me means at least one kind of soft furnishing, and I'm not sure that a damask napkin counts.

When I looked at the menu I was startled to find a side order of mashed potatoes costing £4.75. As Richard would say—"They don't know what to charge."

"It's not unusual, Mother," said Nina. The mash must be comfort food (at a price) for the young professionals who dwell in their spartan urban lofts, so far from the home front.

When we arrived there were few diners and the background music was at an acceptable volume. But as the restaurant filled up the music got louder. Surely there should be an inverse proportion between the number of diners and the volume of the music?

The loos were unisex, which I had no problem with, being someone who absentmindedly walks into the gents with embarrassing frequency. I didn't like the fact that the cubicle doors were translucent, though. I felt most insecure.

Sunday 29th June

We went to *The Light* on Shoreditch High Street last night and in a flash I saw why they thought Friday night's restaurant was cosy. *The Light* is housed in an old engineering workshop from which the renovators forgot to move the old equipment. Some of it is still suspended from the ceiling. The walls are bare brick and white tiled. The room is cavernous with a high ceiling, and lit by tiny halogen lights on long leads, like Christmas fairies in a blast furnace. I loved the feeling of space. It wasn't full, just happily busy: there was no jostling, as you'd get in *The Derbyshire Heifer* on a Saturday night. And although every other person was smoking, the smoke rose up to the rafters. The furniture was chunky students union, circa 1968. There were long refectory tables with drinkers sitting on them. Nina thought the room was draughty, but my hot flushes kept me warm.

I was the oldest person there: everyone else was in their twenties. I noticed a lot of bare midriffs and several one-shouldered vests. I could do asymmetric. A one-shouldered vest like that would make a feature of my mastectomy. Gus once said I shouldn't use a falsie—that being asymmetrical was original and therefore attractive.

He has been the model of sensitivity about it. Ever since I first found the lump he has been concerned and caring. When they actually diagnosed the cancer I can remember him asking me solicitously how I felt, and being incredulous when I said I was "a bit fed up."

"A bit fed up? A bit fed up is when you have too much homework or your soufflé sinks."

But that's all I was. I knew lots of people who'd had mastectomies and were still here six or seven years later. It never crossed my mind that I might die. And I knew that old Eeyore would be there, supporting me through it all, even as he was 'secretly' thinking that the diagnosis was my death warrant. And he has been supportive, bless him.

I looked around the bar at all the other interesting styles, such as the man whose jeans extravagantly crotched at knee level. But colour there was none. I was wearing my cornflower blue linen jacket, while everyone else was clad in brown, beige, grey or black. It was as dull as pension day in the post office. I did spot a splash of vibrant green across the room, and then noticed the balding head above it. He was obviously the token middle-aged man: his back was turned or I would have waved.

I needed a pee and was worried because the bar décor was so uncompromisingly industrial I thought the ladies would consist of a row of galvanised buckets. But they were traditional.

When I got back to the bar, Daniel asked me if I wanted a tequila slammer and I had no idea what he meant. It sounded like a Mexican prostitute with a penchant for sadism. But it turned out to be a drink. You lick salt off your hand, then drink a slug of tequila, and then bite into a slice of lemon. I rather liked it. It was bracing and refreshing, like a sharp spell of frost after an autumn of fog and rain.

At midnight we walked back to the tube and as we waited for the train, the quiet platform made me wonder how safe we were, and how 'the children' felt.

"Do you ever get nervous?" I asked them. "If I wasn't here, would you be scared?"

Monday 30th June

Nina and Tim left early for work and Daniel and I had breakfast together before he went off to a meeting. I had spent two days with them and not mentioned Gus, because I didn't think I could manage it without spilling the beans of the separation. This morning I felt sufficiently composed to talk about him without giving anything away.

"Have you been to see Dad since you took him up there in

April?" I asked—nonchalantly, I hoped—while spreading marmalade on an old piece of Peshawar naan I had found in the bread bin. (Smeg fridge or no Smeg fridge, Nina's shopping for basics leaves much to be desired.)

"Yeah—forgot to tell you. I saw him the day before I flew over. I drove Emily up to see him." He emptied the rest of the left-over vegetable biriani—that he'd found in the famous fridge—out of its foil container and onto his plate.

"Emily?" I said, gulping my tea, and scorching my throat in the process.

"You remember Emily. She was in my year at King George's. The one you said looked too good for her own good." He busied himself with the curry. "Oh this is excellent. Even cold. It's great to have some Indian food again."

How could he? How could he drop a hot babe bombshell into the same sentence as a separated Gus and carry on eating?

"The one with long red hair?" I choked. "What's *she* doing in Denver? And why did you drive her up to see Dad?"

"She's doing a PhD."

"And?"

"Oh, she's not doing it in Denver. She's at Sussex Uni. She was just on a quick visit to see her sister who's working in that bookshop I told you about—The Tattered Cover. You know, the one with the old armchairs and the air conditioning and—"

"Daniel! Why did you drive her up to see Dad?"

"She wanted to give him an in-depth interview. For her PhD."

"For God's sake. Is she doing something on Thoreau, or what?" An in-depth conversation about Thoreau—she'd be irresistible even without the film star body and that hair. Anyone willing to talk about Thoreau could do what they wanted with Gus. He'd be a sitting Spotted Towhee.

"Naw, she's doing something about—hang on—I might be able to remember the exact title." He stopped eating, lowered his forkful of cold curry to rest his wrist on the table, and shut his eyes. "Hang on. What was it?"

I sat there hot and shaking.

"Oh yes," he said, opening his eyes, "the male menopause in post modern literature and contemporary popular culture: a comparative analysis."

Then his mobile beeped. He dropped his fork and said "That's my reminder. I'd better go, Ma. Sorry. It's been so nice to see you but I'll have to dash. I might be over in September."

And he gave me a hug and grabbed his cases and left.

July

Tuesday 1st July

I went to Italian class tonight but was distracted all evening. Italian prepositions are a nightmare anyway—just when you are thinking that Italian is the easiest language in the world, the teacher introduces you to prepositions to stop you getting cocky.

But the prepositions had nothing to do with my inability to concentrate. All the way back on the train from London yesterday I was thinking about Gus in his deserted cabin being visited for the day by red hot Emily, intent on asking him her deeply personal questions. By the time we got to Luton, I could see them lying together on the grass in the great outdoors—under a tree to shade them from the Colorado sun—while Daniel went for a walk on his own so as not to intrude. By Market Harborough, Gus had brought out blankets and pillows because the dead leaves were so scratchy. By Leicester, Emily had decided to be a participant observer of some typical male menopause-type behaviour. And by Derby, they were at it. Only when I pulled into Chesterfield station did I think that Gus might be having problems knowing that Dan was in the vicinity and could come back from the putative walk at any time. It was looking beyond the station buildings and seeing St Mary's twisted spire that did it.

"What's the matter with you tonight, *carissima*?"

I stopped the fierce scribbling on my jotter and looked up. Jeremy's eyes showed concern.

"You're obviously worried about something. You've not joined in all evening."

"Oh nothing."

"Come on. You can trust me," he said, laying his hand on my arm.

Maybe I could ask him what he would be likely to do, given a similar situation to Gus's, skirt around the subject... maybe... possibly. "Do you like women with red hair, Jeremy?"

"I like all women. Redheads, brunettes, blondes turning grey especially."

What a prat I was. I turned my attention to Maria and her prepositions.

Wednesday 2nd July

Hooray! A smiley Sloane from *The Recorder* picture desk just rang. What a wonderful distraction from all of the crap swirling round in my head. They want a photograph to go with my piece about Gus and me choosing our furniture. She rang to ask if I was willing, and then to tell me the name of the photographer who would be contacting me.

So they really do want to print it—and they want a photo as well. My first step to publishing fame and fortune.

Thursday 3rd July

I'm feeling better today. Gus is not a womaniser. I don't know why I was getting so worked up. He's a child in the market place when it comes to women. The only times in our marriage when women have tried it on with him—Mrs Mountain's daughter at the millennium celebrations in the village hall, for example—he has not had a clue they were flirting with him. Admittedly he was only collecting me from that event, being a non socialiser, but she was pretty full on—pretending the scarf he was wearing was hers, asking him to get a piece of dust out of her eye, asking if she could lean on him while she took a stone out of her kitten-heeled shoe.

On the way home he said "What an unfortunate girl—having dust in her eye and something in her shoe and losing her scarf, all in the space of two minutes." Poor sap.

Anyway the drains are still playing up, and they're a rather more urgent problem than a quick interview with some PhD student conducted within spitting distance of a third party.

Yes, the bloody drains. Richard has fixed everything in the house that opens and shuts, but he still has not fixed the drains. He didn't bring his drain rods with him. His set of rods are in storage with his furniture.

Gus doesn't have a set. He got all his DeWalt things as a retirement present from his job as health and safety manager and he does not have any rods because DeWalt don't make them. Also, I'd be surprised if Thoreau's cabin at Walden Pond even had drains to necessitate drain rods, and as we all know, Thoreau is the benchmark for everything Gus does these days. Although, if Thoreau had lived here, surely he would have sailed to New York and travelled from there to Denver by rail, rather than flying direct by British Airways—I must point this out to Gus some time.

Billy Bathgate (local Celtic lothario posing as village sub-postmaster) does have a set of drain rods but I refuse to let Richard borrow them.

"You ought to get some, Sally," said Richard. "Every householder needs a set of drain rods."

He clumped upstairs and brought down his *Screwfix* catalogue to show me. "Look—they've got some very tasty ones in here." He thrust the catalogue under my nose and pointed. I pretended to look and then turned away to switch on the kettle.

Richard went on. "They're flexible polypropylene. You get a plunger with the set, and a double worm screw. They even double as brushes for sweeping chimneys. Very tempting. And only £16.99. Shall I order some? I'm actually finding it hard to resist buying a spare set myself—these look so seductive."

"I suppose you'd better get me a set."

"Why do you sound so reluctant?"

"I hate spending money on things with no fun quotient."

"But everything in the *Screwfix* catalogue has a fun quotient. If you're worried about the cost, maybe I should get the hose out first—a fierce hosing can be very salutary for recalcitrant drains. A good hosing really teaches them a lesson."

"Oh, Richard, whatever you think."

"The beauty of Screwfix is that if I order them now they'll be here tomorrow!"

He'd just placed the order and put down the phone, when it rang again. It was the *Recorder* photographer. I thought he would be driving up from London, but he is freelance and works for an agency in Mansfield. He wanted to come tomorrow. Tomorrow? He must have been joking—the house is a mess so I fobbed him off.

I said I had a meeting with my agent in London, and I didn't have a window in my diary until next Wednesday. I impressed myself with my quick thinking on three counts—

firstly to fob him off, secondly to use the proper jargon—i.e. window in my diary—and lastly, to mention my fictitious agent.

Next Wednesday seems a long time to make him wait, but when *I've* waited this long to get a response to the piece in the first place, I don't suppose they will spike it because they can't wait a few days for a photo. On Tuesday Richard has some old friend staying for the night and I need to have a clear head for my first press photo. This bloke—Iain—is supposed to be leaving on Wednesday.

Friday 3rd July

How am I ever going to get any writing done? How am I going finish my novel? How will I ever get enough space inside my head to think up more pieces? I'm sure Joanna Trollope doesn't have to put up with all this crap. You would think, wouldn't you, that once the drain rods arrived Richard would at least be occupied on his own for a morning?

When the *Screwfix* delivery man called at breakfast time Richard ripped open the package and started salivating.

"These are little beauts, Sal. I can't wait to get started with these. Give your drains something to think about."

While he was running his hands up and down the polypropylene, and drooling over the double worm screw I crept upstairs and started writing, thinking I could crack on. Maurice and Pam are just about to have a nasty row and I was looking forward to writing the dialogue.

But I'd only just got my emails answered, hadn't even opened up Word to work on Chapter 14, when Richard peered round the door wearing a face mask, his bottle green waterproof boiler suit and his can-you-spare-a-minute expression.

"The drain is clear at that cover in the front garden—half way down the hedge—but the one at the corner is blocked, so I'm going to rod between, and I need you to come and watch."

"You do look very glamorous—in a devil-may-care Dickies workwear kind of way, Richard—but I never dreamed that drain clearing was a spectator sport."

"Don't be silly. I need you to watch and tell me if a blockage appears at one opening, when I rod from the other."

"What kind of blockage?"

"A clutch of sanitary towels, maybe?"

"Chance would be a fine thing, Richard—they'd have to be five years old."

"Well something else unutterably disgusting—dead rat, an extra large stool, a glut of condoms, whatever."

He really knows how to show a girl a good time.

Saturday 5th July

Yuk! What a stink. It turned out to be a dead rat clogged up with a mass of beech leaves. Perhaps that will be the end of it.

Now he's done the drains I shall have to find something else to keep him occupied. He has joined the village bridge club, but that's only one evening a week, and unhappily it's on a Monday night—the same night as my Italian—so I don't really gain very much. Although it's nice for him.

He has been down to the tennis court on the rec on Wednesday and Sunday mornings between 10 and 12— tennis club days—but so far he has only managed to have one game, and that was with Mr Coyle, who uses a walking frame—even while playing tennis. According to Mr Coyle, the rest of the tennis club is away on a group holiday in

Amalfi—courtesy of Saga—getting in with their hols before the schools break up. I am wondering whether to ask Richard to do the front wall, which is dry stone, limestone, and which is falling down. Gus had been planning to do it before he got caught up in the trip to the Rockies. He was very keen on doing it, probably because he considers stonewalling his kind of thing.

"I can imagine if Thoreau had lived in the Peak District," he said, "he would have had a go at walling."

Maybe I had better save it for him, just in case he comes home to stay.

Aargh! I've just remembered something. I was going through the conversation in my head that I had with the photographer and I seem to think he said the picture desk had asked him to get a shot of me and Gus looking daggers drawn over a piece of furniture, and he asked if Gus would be home and I said yes.

So I have a giant problemo. What am I going to do? I need a man. I don't want to miss having my pic in the paper because I don't have a substitute for Gus.

Sunday 6th July

I asked Richard if he would pretend to be Gus. Unfortunately, Richard is like that man in the Thurber cartoon who doesn't know anything except facts.

"That would be fraudulent," he said, looking shocked.

"No it wouldn't. If Gus were here, he would be having his photo taken."

"But he's not. You are asking me to pretend to be someone else, which is fraud. I will not be implicated in something so dubious."

"Rubbish," I said. "You'd just be Gus's body double—

like film stars have for scenes showing parts of their body that they feel are less than perfect."

"This is real life, Sally, not a film. When are you going to cotton on to that? I'm telling you it would be fraud."

"Oh come on, Richard, it's only like when a secretary PPs a letter for a boss. If Gus would do it anyway if he were here, you would just be a bodily PP for Gus."

That made him think.

"Could they do something to disguise my identity?"

"You mean like one of those shots of criminals on the telly, where the picture is clear, but the criminal's head is all messed up and blurry?"

"I think the word you're looking for is pixilation."

"Whatever you call it, it would look weird. This is the leisure section we're talking about, not the crime reports. What about having your back to the camera? Like in those documentaries where they have a darkened profile and use an actor's voice to protect the informant's confidentiality?"

"Certainly not. No, I can't think why I even entertained the idea. It's bogus. You'll have to manage without a man."

That's what this year is about, and I consider I'm managing pretty well. All I need is a two minute stand-in for a photoshoot.

Monday 7th July

Tonight's Deep Water highlight was Florid Trev reading a poem bursting with rude imagery (am I starting to sound like B.J.?)

Florid Trev always makes sure he sits next to Alicia, and during his reading she looked as if she was going to be sick. When he reached the climax of his poem and shouted "Ejaculation!" Alicia lurched away from him and her hearing aid popped out.

B.J.Fantasy stroked one side of her specs and said, "Your sense of the erotic, Trevor, is huge and attuned."

Duncan was speechless.

I glanced at Kate but she was slumped in her chair with her eyes drooping. I'm not sure she'll last out until her holiday.

Tuesday 8th July

Richard's old school friend Iain arrived today. He has been living in Italy—near Padua—since early retirement, but his wife died two years ago, and Richard says he's been unsettled since then. He has a married daughter in Brighton with a child and an aged mother in Edinburgh, and he seems to be spending the summer travelling between the two. Richard invited him to stop over here to break his journey.

Richard was still mucking out Sam's room for him to sleep in, and I was writing when I heard the gravel crunch on the drive, through the open window. I got up from my chair and looked out. The man getting out of the car was tanned and tall. About six foot three? He had thick grey hair and a lean face. And his clothes were fab: ivory linen shirt and chocolate brown linen trousers. He looked as though he'd just stepped out of a Boden catalogue. Yum.

"Richard!" I whisper-shouted across the landing. "I think Iain's here."

"You go and let him in, Sally. It's too embarrassing not to have his room ready. I've nearly finished."

I went downstairs and out the front door, and I don't know what came over me—maybe it was the surprise at Richard having such a tasty looking friend—maybe it was the excitement of the press photographer coming tomorrow—

maybe it was the scene in the novel I'd mentally just stepped out of (Maurice's boring golf club friends were descending in droves on Pam's birthday party)– but when he turned his head from shutting the car door I came out with a Thurber cartoon caption *"Ooooo guesties!"*

Then my neck went hot and then my face, and I knew I had turned bright red. Hot flushes are worse than blushes. They take you over completely and unsettle you. How totally cringe-making. Why had I said it? I wasn't back in the sixth form common room with Jackie and Gill, gurgling over my book of Thurber cartoons, for goodness sakes.

But before I could retrieve even a splinter of stately middle-aged presence, he beamed and said, *"I brought a couple of midgets—do you mind?"*

Another Thurber fan! How over the top, fantastically delightful.

We shook hands and smiled and he didn't have one of those wimpish wet fish handshakes like the curate has—it was warm and firm and I found I kept my hand there a bit too long. Not quite long enough for him to be unfurling my fingers to release his—but verging on it. Bloody hell.

"Let's go in. Did you find us OK?" I said.

"Yes—you know what Richard's directions are like— every last detail. Truth be told you spend more time reading them than you do driving. I'm assuming you're Sally? There's just a hint of resemblance around the eyes."

"Sorry, yes, of course. And I take it you're Iain and not some other random friend of Richard's coming visiting."

"I'm not random."

No, if he were a number, he'd be prime.

"You've got a lovely spot here," he said, waving his arm in a huge arc which encompassed the garden and the surrounding fields. Then he walked up to the house and started examining the wall of the new extension. "What wonderful pointing. It has real integrity. So many houses are ruined by poor pointing. You must congratulate your builder."

He was still patting the stonework when the window opened upstairs and Richard poked his head out.

"Pleased to see you're still running your hands over walls, old man," he called down.

"Richard! How are you?"

"Fine, fine. I'll be down in a minute."

Iain and I walked up to the front door and over the threshold. He put down his Gladstone bag (nice tan leather, soft and stylish—no doubt Italian) in the hall and looked around.

"Nicely detailed mat-well," he said, looking down, and then looking up and around "and you've obviously side stepped the problematical circulation issues so often associated with domestic extensions."

I think it was architect speak, but I didn't ask. I didn't want him to think me a dumbo.

"Do come in and have a coffee, or would you like tea?" I asked.

We went into the kitchen. On the way past the hall mirror I saw him glance at his reflection and adjust a lock of hair at the side of his forehead. He sat down at the table while I blundered around with the kettle. I felt as though he was watching me and it made me nervous.

Chomsky came in and miaowed and leapt up onto Iain's knee. Iain adjusted his legs to accommodate Chomsky and stroked him with long, firm, smooth strokes.

"I like your interior palette—I like the confident use of modulated tone," he said, looking round at my terra cotta kitchen walls. It was so nice to have a man in my kitchen who not only noticed what colour something was but who also appreciated my taste, but oh my God, why was he talking like that? Maybe he was nervous as well, and nerves made him retreat into occupational jargon.

I tried another Thurber caption to make him feel at home: "*I wouldn't rent this room to everybody, Mr Spencer. This is where my husband lost his mind.*"

He cracked out laughing, and at that point Richard came into the kitchen and said "What's so funny?" and punched Iain on the arm. "Good to see you. You're looking impossibly suave, as always."

I thought it odd that Richard should recognise suavity, but then Iain oozed style so I guess even Richard couldn't miss it.

We had a pleasant evening—Richard cooked aubergine parmigiani and I made lemon meringue pie—and Iain provided a bottle of Pinot Grigio. The evening was warm and we ate outside on the patio.

We talked about Italy in general and Venice in particular and then Richard mentioned my writing.

"How fascinating. I get *The Recorder*. I can get it in Padua, but it doesn't have the supplements at the weekend, so I don't know this leisure section you're going to be in," said Iain.

"Well, I might not be in it again—thanks to Richard. I'm not going to be very popular when it's just me in the photo and not Gus as well." I explained about the subject of the piece—arguments over furniture—and how they wanted a photo of me and Gus and that Richard had refused to stand in for him.

"Oh, Richard has always been po-faced and proper, haven't you Richard?"

"I, I, I—" he spluttered.

"When did you say the photographer is coming?" said Iain. "Tomorrow? I'll be Gus if you like."

What a star. All I have to do now is persuade the

photographer to restrict shots of Iain to views of the back of his head. Even then, Iain will have to wear a hat, because Gus is bald and Iain is not.

Wednesday 9th July

The photographer came.

As soon as I woke up I felt jittery. I tried to sit down and describe in writing how I was feeling, because Bodmyn suggests that at times of emotional extremity one should put down one's emotions in words, as practice for describing one's characters' emotions. But I couldn't. I was so emotional: I couldn't even hold a pen without shaking, let alone hit the correct keys on the keyboard.

So I got Richard to take Iain on tour of the fleshpots of Bakewell with instructions to bring back special biscuits for the photographer from *Bloomers* deli (to get him in a good mood) and also some pot pourri to make the house smell sweet. Meanwhile I spent all morning titivating the house (and myself).

09.30—Started by tidying the bedroom. (Photographer due to take photos of chest of drawers in there.)

10.30—Realised I should be cleaning behind the chest of drawers, in case it had to be moved. Vacuumed the bedroom and then moved on to the rest of the house.

Polished table in dining room—nice smell of polish made me realise that pot pourri a waste of money. (If I cleaned more often I would know this.)

11.30—Spent an hour trying to decide what to wear, trying on clothes, none of which would do, then ironing fresh ones. By this time Richard and Iain had arrived back, there being not many fleshpots in Bakewell, and I hauled Richard upstairs to ask his advice. He said I should borrow one of his boiler suits, as anyone looks fetching in one of those.

12.00—Rang Nina to ask her what I should wear, but was told by her office that she was in Berlin for the day. What's the point of having a rising young media executive for a daughter if she's never available for consultations on my own career in the media?

12.01—Put on make-up whilst visualising that I am Suzanne Bellucci—elegant, poised and with a warm inner radiance suffusing my interesting and alluring face.

12.33—Decided to wear the thing I got out first—my favourite blue velvet shirt (also beloved of sleaze-bag Jeremy) that Nina bought me in Munich.

13.00—Richard came up and tried to calm my nerves by saying that I didn't need to spend time fretting as no-one looks at photos of women over 30 anyway.

13.27—The photographer arrived thirty three minutes early. He was called Steve. I plied him with coffee and best Ashbourne ginger biscuits while Iain did an excellent job of pretending to be Gus and being utterly charming to me about the fact that I'd not found time to give him dinner. He explained to Steve that he is in sensitive work that made it impossible for his face to be identified in public, so that Steve agreed to take a shot that had a full frontal one of me, and only a back view of Iain's head.

13.30-15.30—How could it take two hours for a photoshoot when all that is required is one measly photograph?

I tried to persuade him to make the photo backlit because it's so much more flattering for women my age, and Iain whispered "Come off it, Sally. It's hardly necessary."

Anyway, Steve said it was impossible. So then I asked him if he could take the shot from a bit further away so my wrinkles didn't show, and he said the bedroom wasn't big enough to get sufficiently far away.

At this, Richard started shaking with laughter and Iain

leaned in close, and I got a whiff of subtle aftershave as he whispered in my ear, "Don't do yourself down."

I didn't ask Steve if he would do a spot of digital remastering, because he obviously didn't care about making his subject look her best. He seemed to have us down as a novelty shoot. All he cared about was getting the most innovative shots, or the technically best shots or something else photographery that had nothing to do with making me look glam.

Why couldn't they have sent Testino? Or Jane Bown? Why is it that I get a photographer who lives in Mansfield? At this rate if I get famous and want Jane Bown to take my photo I'll have to go to London to get it done. I hope she's still alive by the time I'm famous.

Iain has gone. He's a bit of all right. I'm certainly not thinking of getting clogged up with another man having just broken free of thirty years of shackles—time off for good behaviour—but if I were thinking of it, Iain is definitely a bit of all right.

Saturday 12th July

If the photographer had not been here to take my pic, I might think I had imagined Kay Wharton accepting my piece, because it's another lousy Saturday when I am not in the lousy *Recorder*.

You'd think there'd be space—the Saturday papers get fatter and fatter.

Sam came home this afternoon from Leeds. He's working right through his summer vacation in a wholefood co-operative. He's here for one night for Wendy's twins' birthday party.

Sunday 13th July

Sam got up at 2.30 and had to catch the 3.30 train back to Leeds. Who knows when I'll see him again? Christmas, probably. Until which time he'll send me an average of one text a week. Oh well.

Monday 14th July

from: kate wensley
to: sally howe
subject: lost pieces
hi Sally
are you going to ring Kay Wharton to ask when they are going to print your piece?
best photoshoots
love Kate

from: sally howe
to: kate wensley
subject: re:lost pieces
Hi Kate,
No I absolutely cannot ring The Recorder—I'd be terrified. Ringing is what agents do, not measly menopausal novices.
Love and best,
Sally

Tuesday 15th July

from: kate wensley
to: sally howe
subject: ringtones
hi sally
why do you make me correspond with this Kay Wharton if she's so awful? it would be easier if she were called Tiffany.
best first names, love kate

from: sally howe
to: kate wensley
subject: re:ringtones
Hi Kate

I know it seems pathetic, especially as in my distant past I used to be a bona fide professional. But this feels like being twenty and starting all over again. Plus there's the total loss of confidence courtesy of the big M.

Re: first names, have you noticed that women journos on broadsheet features pages all have posh names à la Vanessa, Candida, Rosamund, Portia, Virginia, Cassandra, Miranda, Lucinda, Philomena. Maybe I should change my name to Susanna? Maybe that's why they haven't printed my piece...

Love and best,
Sally

from: kate wensley
to: sally howe
subject: new first names
hi sally

Perhaps you should be called Jocasta. I once thought of being Giovanna. I thought it sounded incredibly artistic, energetic, petulant and impetuous. It still sounds posh frock. But perhaps the sort of posh frock whose English wd not be up to scratch. (ok there too then)

Idea was abandoned when someone pointed out that people (the reading public) hate reading things written by foreigners. I wonder what the xenophobes make of Milan Kundera, Thingy Ishiguru and Hanif Watsit. Probably wouldn't even remember their names.

love and best italians, giovanna

from: sally howe
to: kate wensley
subject: jocasta

Hi Giovanna
I don't like Jocasta. I'd rather be Daisy.
Love and best
Daisy

Saturday 19ᵗʰ July

A letter from Gus:

Hot days, cool nights.
Cabin progress very slow, but enjoying it all the more for that.
I'm getting there.
Your kind of news (?)
I found some traditional pegging details in a book Arnie lent me,
and have been experimenting with them. For sure Arnie won't
be needing that book any more. He's a machine man through
and through.
I have also been down to town with Arnie. Even though I told
him that Thoreau said "I never found a companion that was so
companionable as solitude," he didn't take the hint.
Arnie is ex National Guard. His yard (he calls it his plot) is
organised with military precision. (apart from the dog shit, which
is clearly out of hand)
He wears his ear defenders for shooting practice as well as for
chainsawing. He does a lot of both. I haven't heard the guns as
he mainly uses a silencer (thankfully for me or it would be like
living in a war zone). I don't know why he bothers with the ear
defenders but under the circumstances I'd rather not upset him
by asking. Don't get the wrong impression—he seems like a great
guy.
The cabin frame is in now in place. I get great fulfilment when I

104

study its stoic skeletal form. I am building a hearth and chimney.
Though in this heat it's hard to imagine why.

Terrific bird sightings:
Townsend's Solitaire
Violet-green Swallow
Warbling Vireo
Williamson's Sapsucker
American Pipit
Ruby-crowned Kinglet

take care, Gus
ps Has your article been in yet? You didn't say.
pps Daniel's friend Emily is an interesting girl. Refreshing to find
someone young who's read Walden. Had some long conversations
during the week she was here. She wanted to know all about
my experiment and even helped me erecting the cabin frame.
Intelligent and practical—a rare combination. Just surprised she
spent so much time in the jacuzzi. Ashamed to say she tempted
me to try it. I feel my integrity tarnished.
ppps Why do people wear jewellery in their nether regions? e.g.
navels

Jacuzzi? Walden? The week she was here? The *week* she
was here? How come she was there for a week? Daniel said
he took her up for the *day*.

I have emailed Dan three times today and got no reply.
I have rung him at home—as soon as I thought he'd be
awake—these time differences drive me barmy—but even
at six and seven and eight in the morning (his morning) I got
his answering machine. So I rung him at nine at the office,
where they said he was in Hawaii—a week's vacation and
then a week's conference. They did not have a number that I
could reach him on. Aargh!

Monday 21st July

Too fed up to go to Deep Water. The thought of a young slim redhead who likes Thoreau is enough to make me want to slit my wrists, whether or not she has body piercings in her "nether regions."

Tuesday 22nd July

Slit my wrists? What am I saying? We're supposed to be on a trial separation, so what am I whittling about? I shall devote myself to my writing.

I have told Richard to go ahead with mending the wonky front wall. I can't think of anything else for him to do bar extending the kitchen. He is thumbing through his Screwfix catalogue as I write—looking for specialist walling tools.

Up till now I have told him not to touch the wall, because Gus wanted to do it. Now I don't care about Gus. Serves him damn well right for buggering off to the Rockies and entertaining women with his cabin frames and his jacuzzi. He can rebuild Emily's wall if she has one.

At the front of our house, just behind the famous wall, there's a tall and bushy and rebellious hedge of Escallonia, which is covered in tiny pink blossoms. It looks like an impressionist greeting card I sent Wendy, except that in front of the blossoms there is no deckchair occupied by a languishing lady in a billowing frock, who rests her parasol over her shoulder as she reads her book.

Richard was doing some weeding under the hedge this morning and crawled right under it to retrieve an old Co-op carrier bag that the wind had blown under there, and discovered that there are loads of pieces of stone lurking under the hedge, so he now has something to fill in the gaps of the wall. Except he's not going to fill in the gaps, because, being Richard, he is going to dismantle the whole thing and rebuild it from scratch. And why would I want to argue with that? It'll keep him busy for weeks.

```
from: kate wensley
to: sally howe
subject: end papers
Hi Daisy
Missed you last night. Deep Water breaking up
for the summer. We presented Duncan with his
book token and he read a lovely poem he'd written
about orchids.
B.J.Fantasy excelled herself when she suggested
that Florid Trev would do well to look to the
silence of the blank page. She still hasn't read.
Perhaps she is in her blank page period.
Next meeting second Monday in September—trust
you can make it?
Best dates, love Giovanna
```

Wednesday 23rd July

Richard has dismantled the wall already. Now he is in the shed making wooden frames, which is apparently the next step in the Wonderful Wall Building Programme.

He is such a happy soul to have around when he's got a job in hand. I just went down to take him a glass of orange squash. He had taken off his checked shirt and his grafters bib and brace, and was wearing cut off denim shorts, his big work boots, and a bare chest. The doors of the shed are flung wide, and he's listening to Radio 4. He gulped the drink down in one go and picked up the saw he had been using and said "This is what tiggers like."

Thursday 24th July

Something has happened to Richard.

Now he is building the Wonderful Wall, I never see him. I take him a drink out at coffee time, and again in the afternoon, and I think he comes in for his dinner about one, but apart from that I don't see him.

It is bliss. The house is empty and quiet, and if I could only stop thinking about Gus I'd be able to get on with my writing undisturbed.

Friday 25th July

Richard is still engrossed in the wall. There has not been a single can-you-spare-a-minute interruption today. It's most odd. With all the other jobs he has wanted me to go down and admire his handiwork. I can't understand it.

I would be back into my Bodmyn Writer's Lifestyle Pattern if I didn't keep nipping down to the sitting room to flick through the photo album looking at pictures of Gus.

Saturday 26th July

I wish Richard would come up and disturb me. I'm stuck on Chapter 15. And it is sunny and hot outside and I am sick of being inside in a room that faces north and gets no sunshine. No-one has rung and no-one has emailed and I would delight in any distraction at all—not from my novel, but from thoughts of Gus and the bloody redhead.

I'd even welcome Richard wanting me to watch him clear the drains again. Even Jeremy appearing at the door and trying to seduce me would be better than nothing. Strike that. I do not want to see Jeremy… but that's how sick I am of these intrusive, obsessive, crushing thoughts of Gus and Emily in the jacuzzi.

Monday 28th July

At last I understand. Richard is not calling me down to admire his progress, because everyone in the village is doing it instead. Every time I went out to take him a drink today there was a different person standing admiring the WW. It's obviously a terrific ice-breaker. If this goes on, he can dispense with the bridge club and the tennis fraternity as social entrés, because by the time he has finished the WW he will know everyone in the village.

This morning it was the woman with the two Red Setters who lives in the last house in the village, and this afternoon it was Fred, the retired builder.

```
from: kate wensley
to: sally howe
subject: les vacances
hi daise
too stressed to hold down shift key for caps

yesterday took 4 cats up motorway to harrogate
for hols with granny.
horse and stick insects go to holiday quarters
tomorrow.

arrangements for departure are not advanced. so
far in preparation I have bought some apples for
the journey, which have since been eaten.

andy is cleaning out the car. he has just come
to tell me that some cat wee from yesterday has
gone into one of the grooves that the seats
slot into. we agreed that seat grooves are the
```

responsibility of the transport manager (him).

if you don't hear again assume we have gone,
best airwicks, love giovanna

Wednesday 30th July

I've just emailed a piece to *The Recorder* features editor,
Daphne Vicars.

In this morning's paper there was a news report about
some research into how often married couples tell lies to
each other. I've been messing about for ages with a piece
about lies and compliments and fudging. Gus doesn't tell
lies. He is always coming out with comments that are less
than flattering about my appearance, like "From this angle,
with that shopping bag obscuring your legs, you look quite
slim."

And Richard does it too, so I rewrote the piece, using
material from him as well as Gus. The news report in *The
Recorder* provided just the right hook.

Fingers crossed. I might stand a chance if only because my
piece will arrive in Daphne Vicars inbox the same morning
that the report is in the paper.

Now I'm taking Richard out to lunch to say thank you
for all the stuff he's been doing. Actually it's a sort of sotto-
voce reward for getting on with the WW and not pestering
me.

Later:

It would have been a pleasant lunch if the new barmaid
in *The Derbyshire Heifer* wasn't young with long red hair. I
see redheads every bloody where.

When we got home at two-ish, the Red Setter woman was
loitering by the gate, pretending to look at the WW. Richard
jumped out of the car and chatted to her while I parked

and went inside and found—guess what? A message on the answering machine from someone saying she was Daphne Vicars. I couldn't believe it was really her, and thought it was Kate playing a practical joke, but then remembered she knew nothing about Daphne Vicars or the piece. Daphne V said she'd emailed me and got no response, so she was ringing me. She thought my piece was "very amusing," and she wants to run it tomorrow.

I listened to the message again—oh music to my ears—and then I went to the front door and shouted to Richard "Can you spare a minute?" so that he would come and listen to it, too, to make sure there was absolutely no mistake.

That verified, I checked my email and got what we social researchers call triangulation: an email from Daphne V—she thought my piece was "delightful" and she told me their terms (which I already know, of course—from my friend Kay Wharton.) I tried to email her back but my server wasn't serving, so I gave up and raced around the house in a frenzy for twenty minutes instead.

When I went back to the email and tried again it worked. But then I worried about her not seeing my email confirming that I accepted their terms. It felt too scary to phone her in person. She sounded so posh and so London. She would hear my hesitant, menopausal Northern tones and suss I'm not a trendy thirty-something from Fulham, and she might change her mind.

But I phoned. I sat on my chair with both feet firm and flat on the floor to ground me, like it said in *Mslexia*, in the piece about pitching for a commission. The switchboard put me through to Features and a woman spat down the phone, "Hold on a minute, please," and then threw the receiver down with a clunk. I held on. I held on for five minutes, tantalised but unable to catch the animated conversation adjacent to the telephone (Bodmyn is always telling writers to eavesdrop for interesting dialogue). Eventually someone picked up the receiver again and took my message. She said she would get back to me.

She didn't, so I listened to my voicemail from Daphne V again, just for encouragement.

Tonight it is like being six years old on Christmas Eve.

Thursday 31st July

5.50 am
What a night.

I took Chomsky to bed as a comfort but he kept sitting on my head so at half past midnight I took him back down to the kitchen. Then at 2 o' clock I woke up with a hot sweat and dying for a pee, but then was too excited to settle back to sleep.

I did eventually nod off, but then woke up from a dream in which my piece had been published, but edited so much it was unrecognisable as mine.

Even flinging my nighty and the duvet off and doing deep breathing made me feel hot and flustery.

I lay there for what seemed like hours, feeling ruined and cursing Gus for being four thousand miles away when I needed someone to soothe my brow and make me calming cups of camomile tea. Will he ever do that again?

In the end I gave up trying to sleep, and padded into the study to listen to Daphne Vicars on my voicemail again. Only three times. Then I went back to bed and tried to doze but Billy Bathgate should be here soon with the paper so I'm sitting waiting in my dressing gown (carefully buttoned right up to the neck).

It's in! It's in!

It's 6 am and too early to ring people and tell them. If Daniel was where he should be—in Denver and not in numberless Hawaii—I could have rung him, because in Denver it's still last night (11 pm).

I emailed Kate and then I remembered she's away.

So I've been to show Richard. He was still asleep, knocked out by all his hard work on the WW. I woke him up. He tried to open his eyes to see the page I was shoving under his nose.

"Look Richard! Look at my name! Sally Howe! In big letters at the top!"

He managed to grunt "Most impressive" before falling back into a stupor.

It's hard to describe how I feel. It's as if I'm in a giant bubble of vibrating air—just like I felt on the morning that Nina was born.

Later:

Once it got to breakfast time I rang everyone in the world—well, all right, Wendy and Nina and Sam.

Then I was desperate for more copies of the paper, but didn't want to buy them from the post office: if I asked Billy Bathgate for extra copies, he'd arrive on the doorstep with a special delivery, bursting his tartan trousers with curiosity. So I drove down to Bakewell where I reckoned I could buy them incognito.

I managed to buy five copies from the newsagent and get back to the car without being spotted by someone from the village. I sat there in the Co-op car park and opened one up at the relevant page, and there was my piece, and I thought "Gosh, it's not just in the copy at home—it's in this one, too."

Tell Me Lies

It comes as no surprise to learn from recent research conducted by Relate (The Recorder 23/6/03) that ninety percent of married people claim they regularly lie to their spouses.

Personally, I am committed to plain speaking and integrity, but last night, as I was clearing the kitchen sink and my husband was slurping his supper-time bowl of yoghurt, I decided—yet again—that total honesty in marriage is overrated.

It had been one of those days that start out well but become more and more disheartening, until by bedtime one is longing for the oblivion of sleep. When he heard me sigh over the scrambled egg pan he asked me what was the matter.

"I'm fed up," I said. "I feel old and ugly and fat and tired. My career is going nowhere. And I'm a useless mother."

"Oh come on," he said. "only some of those are true."

I hear him schmoozing people outside the house all the time, so I know that white lies aren't beyond him. I wish he would toss a few in my direction. It's sometimes more worthy to give encouragement than to relentlessly deliver the bare faced truth.

But I need to polish up my own ability to encourage, particularly when he is doing jobs around the house. He can fix a noisy tap, adjust a sticking door, make bedsteads, bookshelves and stained glass. He can cope with plastering, plumbing and electrics. I am the envy of all my friends, and he is the bete noir of their husbands.

The trouble is he works on praise power, and I don't give enough. When engaged on a job, he will shout, every half hour "Can you spare a minute?" Whether I am making a soufflé, shaving my legs or talking to my sister on the phone, he interrupts me to admire developments since my last site visit. He wants me to praise the crafting, comment on the smoothness of the joint, the invisibility of the mend, the handsomeness of the wood grain, the ingenuity of the design, whatever.

I am not up to the task. I appreciate all of these things, but feel that one sentence should be sufficient. I cannot get excited about practicalities when they are works in progress. That's what I keep him for.

And because I am not au fait with the constraints of physics, engineering, or the cost of materials, I have unreasonable expectations, namely, perfection. After 33 years of marriage I have learned to modify my hopes, and now I desist from even hinting that between the ideal and the reality falls the shadow— but if there is even a millimetre of misgiving in my tone, he will sense it.

Knowing how dispiriting he must find it to work for me, I have considered buying a lie detector and practising to deceive it.

This summer's project has been easier for both of us. He is building a dry stone wall between our front garden and the road. He is making a grand job of it, and I have been pouring on the praise, but wondering why he is only calling me out at coffee breaks. Then I discovered I have a supporting cast: everyone who walks their dogs up our lane stops to admire his wall, amazed that it is the first such wall he's built, and gosh, without any training. The retired builder stops every day on his walk around the village to give tips and pats on the back. Even locals driving by in cars slow down and open their windows and shout "It's looking great!"

Next he's going to mend the wall at the back, at the bottom of our garden, which means he won't be in a position to receive supportive feedback from assorted villagers. But an arrangement of mirrors to beam his image to the front gate might look a little odd. So it's back to solo applause: I am limbering up in the approbation department.

I hope he'll reciprocate, and whilst he's building the wall he'll practise his compliments. He's not beyond hope. Last week he said: "You don't look too bad if I don't let my eyes stray too far."

Most of the time I'm happy to be married to a truthful man.

It's just sometimes I wish he was Kurt Vonnegut, who said "Live by the foma (harmless untruths) that make you brave and kind and healthy and happy."

741 words
© Sally Howe 2003

Hooray! Hooray! Hooray! At last I'm a published writer.

Result.

August

Friday 1st August

You'd think that a heat wave would make one more likely to have hot flushes, not less likely, but I haven't had one for a month. This red clover is cracking stuff. Shame it doesn't sort out emotional problems as well.

Even if I'm still churned up about Gus, at least I feel OK about my writing. When the novel is getting tricky, and I can't decide whether to put plot point two at the end of chapter 16 or chapter 17, a little smirking voice in the back of my head says "Who cares? Last week I was in *The Recorder*."

As for Richard, he's still engaged full time with the WW. Except for the time he spends fielding compliments from all his fans, a fan base which seems to have enlarged since the influx of trendy clothes donated by Paul. Dog Woman, the woman with the Red Setters, is always within growling distance when I pop out with his cuppa. I wonder if she always spent all day walking up and down the lane and I never noticed, or if she limits her route to Goose Lane just since Richard has been working on our frontage.

Objectively, he's not unattractive. He's getting a nice tan, he's fairly muscly, in a wiry, gnarled sort of way, and he has nice brown eyes.

I ought to call Dog Woman 'Pippa' I suppose, as that's

her name, but her dogs are so lively and annoying, like two badly behaved toddlers with attention deficit disorder and she merely appears to be an accessory of them. They are overwhelming: jumping up with muddy feet on every human within ten paces, barking, slavering and yelping. If this were a film they'd steal every scene. And not in a good way. Plus they are red-haired, which is one more bloody thing I have against them.

Saturday 2nd August

The Recorder Leisure section contains something by every writer in the known universe bar me. But I refuse to be downhearted. I know now it's possible to break in—the proof is pinned to my notice board.

I am tanking along with Maurice and Pam and am on track to get the book finished by the time Kate gets home from her hols. She has promised to critique it for me.

The only current domestic glitch is that every morning, before I can start work, I have to deal with my sweet peas.

I went mad with them this year, knowing Gus wouldn't be here taking over half the borders with his horrible municipal bedding dahlias. It's excellent having the garden all to myself. If we stay separated, I'll always have a garden to myself. But oh, if we do go our separate ways we'll have to sell the house, and then who knows what size garden I'll have?

My sweet peas are Annie Gilroy, Matucana, Dorothy Deckford, Aunty Molly, Flora Norton, Gypsy Queen and Lord Nelson. I have eight wigwams-full plus enough to cover a ten foot length of trellis. They look less like sweet peas in those tasteful, delicate photos from *Country Living* and more like the impenetrable thicket round the Sleeping Beauty's castle.

They take up an hour every morning—what with tying up the growing stems, picking the blooms and then arranging them in vases. If I were a character in my book, Pam would be saying "Ooh, she's a martyr to her sweet peas." It's nice to be able to have so many sweet peas that you can give them away to friends, but it's getting silly. Yesterday I picked four bunches. Today it was six.

Richard was watching me picking sweet peas in my nighty at eight o'clock this morning, before it got too hot to do anything outside but sit immobile in the shade. As I went back and forth, bringing in bunches of different colours, I pointed out that hardly any florists stock sweet peas.

"Aha!" he said, "How much could we sell them for?" His mind went wild. "If I'm still here next year—" (Oh God—perish the thought, Richard) "—we could plant the whole of the garden with row after row of sweet peas. You could make a fortune."

"Fine," I said. "But we would need to sell them to upmarket restaurants and hotels, not just to florists. And we'd have to take samples round this year so that the scent would seduce people into making orders. Would you take charge of sales?"

"You're the extrovert," he said. "You'd have to do the marketing."

"I see," I said. "I'd plant them and tend them and pick them and market them. What would you do?"

"I would arrange the canes."

Sunday 3rd August

Finally—I made my blackcurrant jam. The blackcurrant crop has been huge this year, and I have been picking them and ramming them in the freezer, waiting for the cookware shop in Bakewell to have their summer sale, in the hopes of getting a proper jam pan. Yesterday I snapped one up for £20. Excellent.

I was all ready to start on the jam at ten this morning, neatly synchronised with the *Archers* Omnibus. The blackcurrants were thawed and ready, the sugar and jam pots waiting, the *Archers* theme tune was dying away, and then Richard muscled into the kitchen.

"My back is aching so I thought I'd have a day off from the wall. Want some help?"

"I can manage, thanks. Why don't you go and sit in the sun with the crossword?"

"I'll just help get things organised, shall I? What you need is a system. A production line. You have no sense of order, Sally."

By the time the jam had reached setting point he had taken over, and by the tenth full jar I was sitting in the corner reading *The Observer*.

I wouldn't mind so much if he hadn't talked through *The Archers*. He wouldn't like it if I went and stood in front of the telly when he was watching his bloody cricket.

We—He?—made 20 pots of jam, and yet the freezer is still brimming with blackcurrants.

Monday 4th August

I came down for breakfast at seven o' clock this morning and Richard was already standing at the cooker over a steaming pan, dressed in apron, T shirt and shorts (it's still too hot for boiler suits even in the early morning).

Also he was wearing his wellies, "To prevent jam splashes from scalding my legs, Sally. Safety is the watchword. The kitchen is a veritable Bermuda triangle of danger."

Gus has never been as bothered about health and safety at home despite it being his job. If he *had* been bothered about it, the trial separation might have come a whole lot sooner.

"Could you fetch me some more jam jars?" said Richard.

It didn't matter that I was barely awake, nor that I was still in my nighty drinking my first mug of Yorkshire tea; no, when Richard's in the middle of a job, that's all that's important. I was dragooned into going out to the shed for more jars. Then I had to wash the bloody things.

I had originally picked the fruit, washed it, weighed it, then frozen it, then sorted out the jars, and there he was, merely presiding over the pan.

"I really can't take my eye off it, Sally. It's far too dangerous." He could relax just a bit, you'd think, and be more like Gus whose approach to H&S could be described as broad brush.

"You know," he continued, "we should go into jam production and sell it to the tourists as a locally-produced, wholesome preserve."

Come home Gus, all is forgiven. He knows the value of a quiet beginning to the day. There's a man who likes a broad margin to his life. I wonder what he's doing now.... it's ten-thirty, bedtime here, so it will be three-thirty in the afternoon, Mountain Time.

He's been gone four months. When you've been with someone for 30 odd years you don't miss them in the short term. Your whole being is imbued with them. It's like a saturated solution. When they go away and stay away it's like dye coming out in the wash. Only after a few washes do you see the loss of colour and the material fading. (I'm sure if I were Anita Shreve I'd be able to think of a better image than this; I'll have to work on it.)

Tuesday 5th August

Onto my penultimate chapter. Maurice and Pam are coasting along to the crisis.

Dog Woman/Pippa was talking to Richard when I took him out his mid-morning drink.

"Would you like some sweet peas?" I asked, thinking to charm her. She helps to keep Richard occupied so I figured I ought to be agreeable.

"It's a shame my Floral Art class has broken up for the summer. Yes it is."

"Yes, you could have dispensed Sally's fecundity amongst your pupils," said Richard.

"Oh, do you go to the flower arranging class in the village hall?" I asked.

"I teach it. And it's Floral Art. Floral Art."

I distinctly heard the capital letters.

"Yes," she said. "I suppose I could take some sweet peas off your hands. I understand you have to cut them every day to keep them flowering. That's what I understand. Yes I do. Though it's difficult to achieve any kind of balance with sweet peas—even dynamic balance."

Not exactly gracious. I went back out with some sweet peas—the sickly sugar pink ones that I wish I hadn't grown—and as I handed them over to her someone shouted up the lane, "*Ciao bella!*"

The shout was so loud and so sudden that the three of us swivelled round in unison. The dogs thrashed around and barked and pulled their leads fit to wrench Pippa's arms out of their sockets, so much so that she dropped her Aunty Mollies.

It was Jeremy. I wanted to dart back inside the gate and out of sight behind the escallonia, but there was no way I could pretend I hadn't seen him.

He was with two other men. They were all kitted out in hiking boots, shorts and hairy legs, with rucksacks and maps in clear plastic wallets hanging round their necks. They were striding up towards us, and when they drew level, Jeremy said to the others, "You go on, chaps, I'll catch you up."

I stopped to pick up Pippa's flowers from the road. He squatted down next to me and handed me a stem, and looking up through his floppy fringe, he said, "How lovely to see you Sally. You're looking well. Are you going to introduce me to your *caro marito*?"

I leapt up.

"Richard's not my husband. Jeremy, this is my brother Richard—and Pippa. This is Jeremy."

I was flummoxed, wanting to escape but not knowing how to do it tactfully. I looked down at my hands and saw the sweet peas, which reminded me how many there still were in the kitchen, and I blurted out, "I don't suppose there's any point in my offering you some sweet peas when you're on a hike, is there?"

Then I realised that he might think an offer of flowers was significant.

"Not really, but I'd love to see your garden."

"What about your friends? They'll leave you behind."

"That's all right, they're going to stop at the pub for a quick one."

"My computer's on and I'm actually mid-sentence, Jeremy. I just broke off to bring Richard a drink."

But he was already striding up the drive. I scuttled after him with my heart in my Clarks slip-ons and my brain racing for exit lines, and I remembered a bit in the screenwriting book where it says you should enter a scene as late as possible and leave it as early as you can. I wondered if the screenwriting guru knew someone like Jeremy.

There was nothing for it but to give him the briefest of tours round the garden.

"These are the changes I made last year," I said, pointing to my herbaceous perennials. "I'm working towards undulating borders rather than straight and square."

"I've always liked your undulations, Sally," he said, putting his arm round my waist.

"And that bit over there," I said, stepping out of his reach and using an icy tone, "That bit there is going to be a pond. Richard's going to dig it out for me in the winter."

"You can have some of my frogs if you like. They're very sexy, my frogs."

"What?"

"In the spring, when they start to ribbit. Always turns me on, when they climb on top of each other and ribbit."

"Do you remember in Italian class, Jeremy, you asked me to let you know if there was anything I needed while Gus is away?"

"*Si, bella*?"

"Well are you any good at cleaning out gutters? I've got a ladder, but I'm terrified of heights."

He looked at his watch. "God, is that the time? Better fly. The chaps will be calling mountain rescue. Sorry, Sally. Lovely to see you. Ciao." And he went.

Thursday 7th August

Richard fielded a phone call today and said I was in. I wish he hadn't. It was Angelina Bond, an extremely annoying woman I went to school with.

"Sal-gal, how *are* you?" she said. "You didn't send me a Crimble card this year, and I was out of my mind with worry."

Funny how it was August and this was her first call. I

knew I hadn't sent her a Christmas card—I had been doing some serious culling of my list—decided that there was no point in sending cards to people I never wanted to see again.

"Didn't I send you one?" I said. "I can't think how that happened. It must have got lost in—"

"Anyway, I'm so pleased you're still alive. So many people start popping off their twigs in their fifties, don't they?"

"Well, I—"

"Sal-gal, I was wondering what you were doing next week. I was thinking of coming up to see you. Driving up and staying for a couple of days. Will you be there?"

Not *Is that convenient?* or *Do you mind?* Merely *Will you be there?*

"Actually, Angelina, it would be lovely to see you, but I have my brother staying."

"Well, you don't live in a two up two down, do you?"

"No, but I also have a lot of work to do," I said.

I'm too honest. Why on earth didn't I just say I was going to be away?

"Work? I had no idea you were still doing that psychology twaddle—I mean, research," she said.

"I'm not. I'm a writer now. Didn't you see my piece in *The Recorder* recently?" I said, to stub her out.

"'Fraid not, I'm a *Telegraph* woman. But you're writing? That's fab, Sal-gal; we'll be able to swap notes. Have lots of authorly confabs."

"What do you mean?"

"You are speaking to a woman who has five books in her Harrods tote bag and her own personal editor."

"What?"

"Mills and Boon. I've worked out the system. Pin money, supplements Archie's pension. It's ridiculously easy, and what *fun*. I can't think why everyone doesn't do it."

At least she wasn't with Bloomsbury or Black Swan. How did five Mills and Boon books rate against one piece in *The Recorder* and one piece yet to come? Established crass versus novice class—I wasn't sure. But it did occur to me that she might have some useful tips on getting a book published—such as—did she have an agent?

"Sal-gal? Are you there? What do you say? How about next Tuesday?"

Monday 11th August

I miss Gus in bed in the morning. I miss him hogging the loo for hours on end. I miss him sprawling on the sofa with the paper and making scathing comments all through *Neighbours*.

And I hate writing. I hate this driving obsession to be published. It's ruining my life.

I found myself standing next to Mrs Mountain in Bakewell Market this morning. She ran over my foot with her tartan shopping trolley.

"How are you?" she asked.

My foot's OK, I wanted to say, but I hate my life. But when people ask how you are, it doesn't matter if you're feeling a bit fed up or slitting-your-wrists-suicidal, you are supposed to say "Fine thanks."

And worst of all: the awful Angelina is arriving tomorrow.

Tuesday 12th August

I had a post card from Kate in France.

Salut Daisy, Temps up to 40 degrees C. Too exhausting. Today is cooler: put on sweatshirt to celebrate. Go to lake to swim each

day—Manon des Sources meets Baywatch. Miss my screen.
Best sandflies, love Giovanna.

Lucky bugger.

Angelina rolled up at tea time.

"Hello there!" she called up the stairs.

"Sally! Angelina is here!" shouted Richard.

"Just coming."

I saved the writing I'd been doing, and then sat waiting while the computer closed down. I needed to summon all my reserves of patience. By the time I got downstairs, Richard had put on the kettle and was showing Angelina the bench by the back door, the only place we can sit outside in the shade. She was already doing that little-girl-looking-up-into-the-big-man's-eyes trick. Oh how I remember that from the sixth form common room. That's how she pinched Russell Blaney from me. That, and the fact that she is half my size.

"Sweet of you, Richard. But I must get Tiggy out of the car. He's been so upset," she said, turning to me and kissing me on both cheeks. A far cry from Cross Leys council estate. "I'm sorry I'm so late. I had to drive at 30mph all the way— Tiggy gets beside himself if I go any faster.

"Tiggy?" I asked.

"My cat. I couldn't leave him at home. Archie's hopeless with him. He's on a programme, and I have to supervise it personally."

"Archie's on a programme?"

"Tiggy. He's a bit overweight. He had a flea allergy, and the vet gave him a steroid injection. It cured the allergy, but unfortunately, Tiggy ballooned. The vet put him on a diet programme and recommended I take him to Weight Watchers."

I cackled. I hadn't remembered Angelina as funny.

"Don't laugh," she said, in a tragic tone. "It's tough for him. The other cats are doing so much better than him. He's been to ten sessions and he's nowhere near his target weight."

"Weight Watchers? For cats?"

"Yes. Haven't you heard of it? Once a fortnight. It has a very high success rate. The nurses are all very strict."

She turned, and her floaty sundress swirled around. It was pink and low and had shoe string straps. She had her hair pinned up, and I could see that when you get to our age, a little flesh is no bad thing. Unfortunately for her, she didn't have any. This is when we size 14s get our reward. Thin people show the wrinkles and the sagging muscles in their skin so much more than fatties.

Talking of fatties, she brought Tiggy in from the car in a basket mounted on wheels. He was less like a cat and more like a furry version of one of those sag bags stuffed with polystyrene balls.

"I'm afraid you'll have to keep him in your room, Angelina," I said. "Or Chomsky will be terrified."

Wednesday 13th August

Talking to Nina last night on the phone about her work, she said she'd been organising some Christmas photoshoots.

"Christmas? But it's only August," I said.

"Yes, Mother. You know you're going to have to be more on the ball if you want to be successful in the media."

"But I thought the media was about being topical. I can do topical," I said.

"You also have to plan ahead. Get wired to lead-in times," said Nina. "Glossies, for instance—you said you wanted to get something in a glossy. They work three months ahead—at least."

I have some notes I made last Christmas, about Gus and his outlandish views on the festive season. So I've written a piece about it—while Richard's been giving Angelina a guided tour of Bakewell—and I'm sending it to *Hearth and Home*.

Friday 15th August

I missed Gus so much this morning that I even got his old green jumper out of the drawer and sat with it on my knee and alternated sniffs of it with sips of my morning tea. And then I remembered the bloody redhead and threw the jumper on the floor.

Angelina leaves tomorrow. Thank God.

She is exhausting. She never stops talking. I have only managed to survive because of Richard. When he first came to stay I thought he'd be a good chaperone, but I never dreamed he would be needed to intervene between me and a woman.

She has been flirting with him ever since she arrived on Tuesday. Dog Woman obviously feels threatened, because today was the first time I have ever seen her in a skirt. Also lipstick, and I could swear that her hair was more groomed. And perfume—Muguet de Bois—unless the dogs have a new shampoo.

At breakfast time, Angelina said she wanted to visit Chatsworth House. I can't be bothered with stately homes, but I do like the garden, so we agreed on that.

"Shall we take a picnic?" I suggested. "We can sit under the trees and look at the fountain—it'll be the only way to keep cool."

"Picnics are for paupers, Sal-gal. I do not want to get grass stains on my Country Casuals, nor do I want ant bites." She stretched out her leg, pointed her toe at the kitchen dresser, and ran her hand down her shin. "I've taken a lot of trouble achieving an even tan and silky smooth calves. I don't want to ruin the effect with unsightly insect bites."

So we compromised on a stroll round the garden, ten minutes sitting on the stonework next to the hillside cascade, and lunch in the Carriage House Restaurant.

The only advantage of her visit, from my point of view, was the potential for asking her about how she got five books into print, and yet, after two days, I had still not managed to steer the conversation round to books. So I determined to corner her over lunch when her mouth was full and she wasn't talking.

"Tell me," I said, as she was taking a swig of wine, and therefore silent, "about how you got your books published."

"That? It wasn't exactly arduous. It all started when I found an ancient tape on the white elephant stall at the village fete called *And Then He Kissed Me*. Guidelines from Mills and Boon about how to write romances."

"And that was it?"

"It's a formula, Sal-gal. It's not exactly *Mastermind*. Archie was whinging on at the time about the amount I was spending on the beautician, so I thought I'd have a go at earning some pin money. I just followed their instructions, and bingo. They liked it."

"What *is* the formula?" I asked. It's not that I want to write Mills and Boon but I wanted to pump her for anything at all that might be useful.

"They have lots of dialogue, and not much description."

"That sounds all right," I said.

"Unless you count descriptions of the hero's manhood."

"Yuk! I wouldn't want to write about sex."

"That's OK. There's a range with explicit sex and a range without. You could write the ones without."

"You sound established—with *five* published—not just a flash in the pan," I said. I was envious, despite my disdain for Mills and Boon. "What's the secret? I mean—can you give me some hints?" I asked.

"I'll tell you, but it's strictly between you and me and the Duchess of Devonshire. I don't want every fifty-something wannabe writer muscling in. I've got my golden rules. One," she said, sticking up her index finger and displaying her tangerine nail varnish to everyone within spitting distance. "One—always wear a Wonderbra whilst writing. By the way, I picked up your silicone falsie in the bathroom last night. It's a natty little thing—felt much better than the gel pouches I get from Harvey Nicks. Where do you get your falsies from? How much are they?"

"You get falsies free on the NHS if you've had a mastectomy. But can you get back to the point? You were giving me some hints on writing."

"Where was I? Oh yes, one—always wear a Wonderbra—the uplift somehow helps to make my ideas soar. Two," (another finger raised, more hideous nail varnish) "make your heroine a proper heroine—get her into silk lingerie."

"But I'm not writing a Mills and Boon," I said.

"Don't interrupt. These points apply to all sorts of fiction, even—what do you call it?—literary fiction. So, three," (ring finger) "most important point: always keep your readers moist and breathless, and four," (pinkie) "you've got to look after your image—banish grey hair, and always have your highlights done before a publicity shoot."

"Well...thanks...I see."

Fortunately I didn't have to think of a response to all of this wisdom, because Angelina's attention had wandered.

"Look," she whispered, touching my hand and inclining her head to the left, in the direction of the waitress's station. "That's *her*. The Duchess."

She was right. I had seen her photo in *The Peak Advertiser* many times. The Duchess was talking to one of the staff.

"I'm going to introduce myself," Angelina said, getting up from her chair.

"What?"

But she had already swanned over to the Duchess, and I could hear her saying: "Excuse me, Your Grace, may I just tell you how much I admire your choice of décor?"

I had my elbow on the table and my hand covering the side of my face, but I was listening like a spy. Angelina's voice is over-loud, imperious and fruity. The Duchess—as you would expect—has rather more class, so I could only hear Angelina's side of the conversation.

"This is the first time I've been to the Carriage House Restaurant," boomed Angelina. "I'm visiting a friend in Stoneymoor. Sharing a few pearls of writerly wisdom, don't you know?"

Don't you know? Don't you know? Who did she think she was? A character from P.G.Wodehouse?

The Duchess said something—I couldn't hear what. I sneaked a peek, and saw she was edging away.

"One has to do one's bit for the novices, doesn't one? I'm an established writer—she's a mere beginner," said Angelina.

As a small revenge I emptied the last of the wine into my glass, and downed it. She returned to the table.

"Charming woman. Breeding will out. Some people have such class, don't they Sal-gal?"

Yes, Angelina, and some are sadly lacking.

Saturday 16th August

Whoopee! I'm in *The Recorder* today—finally—the piece about Gus and me choosing our furniture—I'm in, I'm in,

I'm in. And it's a whacking spread. Right across the bottom of page 6—a third of the page, what with our photo and all. I have to say—I don't look bad. My writerly plait is clearly visible, resting nicely on my right shoulder, and the blue velvet shirt covers all the problem areas. Nice choice.

Iain did well. His body language is good—even from behind. You can see even from the back that he has folded arms and is looking cross, just by the hunch of his shoulders—I never realised how expressive someone's shoulders could be. What I'm not sure about is whether anyone will realise it's not Gus, because, damn it, we forgot to make Iain wear a hat to hide the fact that he's not bald like Gus.

Thank God Angelina gets up late. I skimmed the paper and hid the leisure section before she got up, and I swore Richard to secrecy, telling him I didn't want to make Angelina feel inferior.

"And they're always talking about writerly jealousy and one-upmanship. That's very sweet of you, Sally."

Angelina said she wanted to set off straight after breakfast but it was eleven by the time we were loading her and the blessed Tiggy into her car. I was just saying good bye to her through her open car window when another car pulled into the gate. It was Iain.

"Richard!" I said. "You didn't tell me Iain was coming."

"Damn, I forgot," said Richard, under his breath. "He rang yesterday from Edinburgh, when you were at Chatsworth. He's on his way back to Brighton."

"Who's this?" said Angelina. She jumped out of the car, straightened her skirt and adjusted her hair. And that was before she'd seen him.

Iain called "Hello. Am I in the way?" as he squeezed between Angelina's car and the viburnum at the side of the drive. He examined his shirt sleeve to check that the plant had left no mark.

"Charmed," said Angelina, stepping forward and shaking his hand before Richard and I could say hello, or introduce her, or even catch our respective breaths.

I introduced them and then said, "But Angelina is just leaving, Iain. Could you pull out of the drive just for a minute?"

"Actually," said Angelina, "I'm a teensy bit early setting off. Perhaps I could have another coffee before I go? Brace me for the journey?"

"Of course," said Richard before I could intervene and shove her back into her car.

We walked towards the house and Angelina pretended to stumble on the gravel drive and put her hand out to Iain to steady herself.

We all sat out on the patio drinking coffee: Iain and Angelina on one bench, Richard and me on the opposite side of the table.

"When I opened my *Recorder* today," said Iain, "there was your piece. Great stuff. I feel honoured to be part of it, even as an anonymous stand-in. Shame I can't tell anyone. Still, at least I can say I have stayed in the house of a *Recorder* contributor."

"What's this?" said Angelina. "Have you got a piece in the paper today, Sal-gal?"

"Oh yes—I forgot to mention it."

"Too modest, more like," said Iain. "But you shouldn't be. It's very witty writing."

"Thank you. Angelina is a writer, too," I said, wanting to turn the attention back on to her. I didn't want her asking Iain to explain his comment. "She writes for Mills and Boon."

"That's not what I call real writing, I mean, I'm sure it's a very special talent in its own way," he said, unconvincingly.

"Absolutely," said Richard, trying to redeem the

situation. "And she's had five or six published, haven't you Angelina?"

"Yes. Actual books. Hardbacks. Not just tomorrow's fish and chip paper. But everyone has to start somewhere, don't they? Even with little domestic pieces in the paper," she said, turning to Iain. He leant back and folded his arms. Angelina wittered on "You shouldn't be ashamed, Sal-gal."

I saw Iain raise an eyebrow. He turned to me and saw me looking at him and winked across the table. He has Bournville eyes. If he were a character in a book they'd be flecked with amber, but he's not, and his eyes are just plain chocolate. Though if anything was melting it was me.

Angelina went on, as she does: "And you mustn't be downhearted if you can't get a publisher for your novel, Sal-gal. After all, it is only your first. Most first novels end up in the back of a drawer, don't they Iain?" she said, placing her hand on his arm and sliding closer to him.

Iain pulled away from her, and looked at his watch. "Gosh, is that the time?" he said, standing up. "We're delaying you, Angelina. I'm sure Sally and Richard have things they need to be getting on with. I'll move my car and we won't hold you up any longer."

She looked rather miffed, but she left.

We had a lazy and civilized time—after she'd gone—reading the papers, having lunch, chatting. It was rather nice having someone as decorative as Iain sitting in one of my deck chairs.

When it started to cool a little at five o'clock we decided to go for a walk.

"Will I need my wellies?" said Iain. "I've got them in the boot of my car."

"Hardly—the ground's rock hard from the heat wave," said Richard.

We walked down the old railway line and back on the

footpath across the fields to the village.

"The tile cuts on that roof are first rate," Iain said as we walked along Gorsey Road.

He had a slim silver digital camera with him and all the way down Main Street he stopped to take pictures.

"It's unfortunate about the laxity of the planning laws during the sixties and seventies," he said. "Villages in this part of Derbyshire don't show such a strict adherence to the vernacular that is apparent in other National Parks—the Yorkshire Dales, for example."

"The vernacular?" I said.

"Yes. The vernacular turns me on. I'm trying to make a photographic record of architectural detail in different localities—lead rain hoppers, flashings, parapets, doors and letterboxes."

I bet he doesn't like the US style mailbox that Gus bought from Chatsworth Garden Centre.

Iain insisted on taking us out for dinner at the Monsal Head Hotel, so despite his vernacular fixation, he's obviously normal, and doesn't think a meal out means taking a couple of apples and a Mars Bar on a hike. Not like some people a few thousand miles away whom I could mention, but won't.

Sunday 17th August

The meal at Monsal was good last night, but I went to bed missing my own unmentionable one.

Iain left after breakfast. As he drives up once a month to Edinburgh to see his mother, I told him to call in any time if he wants to break his journey either on the way up from Brighton, or on the way down south again. He's so undemanding.

Monday 18th August

A letter from Gus...

Good to know I'm corresponding with a Recorder contributor. I knew I should have stuck to one chair, though. Arnie has been a great guy, bearing in mind my general distaste for neighbours. I have to concede we've even had some good talks, though they do have a tendency to stray towards his Power Tools. Enough said. The current, immediate downside to this neighbours lark is that Arnie has gone away, and left me to look after the dogs. For three weeks. It's a full time job. I have to put their food down, call them to the food, then lock them in and clear the runs while they eat. I am in full charge of dog shit clearing. It is taking its toll on a man who came out to find the wilderness. I am back with the mass of men who lead lives of quiet desperation, my life frittered by the detail of dog meals. Did I come half way around the world to look after baying hounds?

Cabinwise (in the little time left after dog sitting duties) I'm cutting and fixing shingles. It's a repetitive yet curiously satisfying activity. I have even cut my daily walks down to four hours to get more done on the cabin. I am working hard to finish in time for fall. Winter will be the time to do less—and enjoy it. By the hearth. With one chair.

Birds seen:
Green-tailed Towhee
Chipping Sparrow
Vesper Sparrow
Mountain Bluebird
Brown headed Cowbird
Hermit Thrush—my avian soulmate

take care, Gus

Huh! He didn't mention sticking to one chair when Emily was visiting, did he? Maybe that's because they were never sitting down—they spent all their time lying on the grass or frolicking in the bloody jacuzzi.

Tuesday 19th August

I came down this morning to find Richard standing at the front door talking to Pippa. She was on the front step, without the dogs, clutching a breadmaking machine.

"I'd be delighted," she was saying.

"Do come in," said Richard.

"No, I must get back—I've left them on their own. No, it's wasted in my house. I can't use it. It's the noise it makes when it first starts turning. Yes, the first part of the cycle. It's a sort of uneven, spasmodic growl, like an Irish Wolf Hound prowling up the path—it drives Ellie and Emmie demented. They have such sensitive hearing. I've tried positioning it in different rooms, and it makes no matter. It upsets them. Yes, it does."

"Are you sure?"

"Please take it. I'm sure. Yes I am."

"Well, thanks Pippa. You can have the first loaf I make."

So far Richard has made three loaves. He's hooked. He even broke off from the WW to take the first one round to Pippa.

Wednesday 20th August

Richard views the breadmaker as an elaborate cement mixer with heat. He is powered up by his baking success:

Pippa apparently warned him that no-one succeeds with their first few loaves and that he should be patient, but every one of his is not only edible, it looks like a proper loaf. He has made another three today: Light Wholemeal, a Milk Loaf and a Rustic White. The attractions of the WW are fading.

"Easy peasy," he said as he turned the last one out onto the cooling rack. "I'm thinking of buying a hundred breadmakers and lining them up in your dining room and making a business of selling specialty bread. Think of it— the 22 million tourists who come to the Peak District every year are a ready market."

I humoured him.

"I've got all those dozens of jars of blackcurrant jam in the shed," I said. "Why not do bread *and* jam? Comfort food is all the rage with urban chic types living in lofts, and yet you never see jam sandwiches for sale on sandwich counters. Isn't the market wide open for them? Never mind tourists, we could ship them out to *M&S* and *Pret a Manger*."

"Excellent idea. Do you have a flip chart, Sally? We'll do some brainstorming later. This could be the definitive way to boost my pension," he said, as he disappeared off to the post office for more supplies. "I'm trying Walnut Bread, Carrot and Coriander, and Caribbean Tea Bread today. Once I've perfected them, and as a first step, I could talk Billy-the-Kilt Bathgate into selling my bread as a local specialty."

Oh what wonderful copy Richard provides. (Copy! Listen to that! The journo jargon keeps popping out, all on its own.) I've just written a piece about him and his money making schemes for the bread, the jam and the sweet peas, and emailed it to Kay Wharton, editor of *The Recorder* leisure section. It should stand a chance. After all, this is what they call the silly season.

Friday 22nd August

I've finished. I've just typed the last full stop. The novel is done.

Now I'll have to print it out and post it to Kate so she gets it on her return.

Monday 25th August

from: kate wensley
to: sally howe
subject: vomit
Hi Daisy
Got your ancient email from July about your *Recorder* piece—well done!
Had to rush back home due to pressing need for teenagers to be in familiar home environment in order to finish coursework that is due in. As I write (10pm) they have been entertaining since early afternoon. There are now seven teens upstairs swigging sangria and planning to make a night of it. I am handing out buckets and asking them to please not get chips or vomit in the cracks between the (exposed maple) floorboards.

Got your book—well done—and have started reading it—so far the only comment I have is that after reading your pieces I am finding this voice lacking. More anon.
Best buckets, love Giovanna

from: sally howe
to: kate wensley
subject: re:home
Hi Giovanna,
Welcome home!
You are not the only person to say that my third person writing is not so appealing. I agree. I am

140

thinking of being an omniscient narrator next.
(What wd you like to be in yr next life, Mrs
Howe? Oh, an omniscient narrator, I think.)
Love and best,
Daisy

from: kate wensley
to: sally howe
subject: narrators
Hi Daisy,
Have just returned with 4 startled cats from
the north. The latest thing in Harrogate (post
aquaerobics) is aquabatics. How very passe we
are in Matlock—we still only have aquafit.

Sangria crew eventually departed at 5pm the next
day. Damage: one sick bucket, provided by me,
crushed by falling drunken person. One wooden
bed frame, crushed in a "we were just looking at
it and it fell to pieces" incident. Now mended
by Andy thanks to skills honed over many years
from Practical Boat Owner.

I didn't realise till recently about all this
narrator stuff. I have so far gone thro' life
thinking there was first person and third person,
and the past, the present and the future. Suddenly
there are indications that things aren't that
simple.
love and best boat owners, Giovanna

p.s. working on holiday diary. I have given
offspring pseudonyms—henceforth teen queens
will be pesto and aragosta and their younger bro
champman.

September

Monday 1st September

I am five months into my writing year and all I have to show for it is two pieces in *The Recorder*—one with photograph, one without, and one finished novel that needs polishing, and which Kate has described as "a good attempt, considering it's your first." Not exactly a resounding endorsement.

She has made lots of suggestions as to how to tighten it up, and I'm going to take it away with me next week when Wendy and I go on our hols. It's a girls' trip. Alan is going on a rustic Italian cookery course in a Tuscan farmhouse. (No doubt in the hopes of meeting lots of bored housewives. Serve him right if it's full of men with the same idea. Hah!)

Meanwhile Wendy and I are using the annual booking that Gus and I have on a cottage in Northumberland. Typical, isn't it? If I'd known when we booked this place that he intended to go to the Rockies for a year I could have gone abroad instead—Venice, maybe. I like Northumberland but when you've been there for fifteen years it gets a bit samey.

Wendy and I are going to take lots of wine and *M&S* ready meals. She has the final exams on her astrology course coming up at the end of the month and she wants to revise for them. I am going to polish up the novel. This is when I could do with a laptop—rather than a six year old desktop—but Wendy's going to talk Alan into lending me his laptop, just for the week.

Tuesday 2nd September

Today is Richard's birthday.

Pippa gave him a book about training dogs—*The Dog Whisperer: A Compassionate, Non-Violent Approach to Dog Training*.

Ominous.

I was stumped as to what to buy him, until the other night when he said: "It's a shame I haven't got more money. There are lots of things I could do if I had more money."

"Like what?" I asked.

"Buy a lump hammer."

We were sitting outside in the fading sunshine after tea. There was I scribbling notes in the margin of my manuscript, and there was he turning the pages of his *Screwfix* and *Wolfcraft* catalogues.

"Are you looking for something in particular?" I asked.

"No, just browsing for titillation."

Every so often he'd say something like "These clamps look impossibly seductive. Look at the ingenious design—you can reverse the heads and make them into spreaders. If I was Tommy Walsh I'd buy the complete set—one in every size."

After I'd decided on giving him tools, I then had to decide what to get. So the next night when I was sitting next to him, apparently amending my novel, I was really making notes on the tools he mentioned as he drooled through his catalogues. But I realised before long that he wants everything in the book. Therefore, rather than risk giving him something not at the top of his wish list, I plumped for vouchers.

When he opened the envelope he beamed. "Thank you Sally. That's a very generous and thoughtful gift."

"What will you buy with them? Tell me—will it be sash cramps, a Dowelmaster or a quick action vice?"

"Oh I shall save them. I don't want to spend them on pure frivolity."

Wednesday 3rd September

Hooray! I had an email from Kay Wharton (*The Recorder* leisure section woman) saying my piece on lunatic holiday schemes—such as the bread and jam sandwiches idea—was just what they needed to fill a space this Saturday. Whilst I am very pleased—of course—that they are going to print it, it nevertheless feels like a back handed compliment. I'm not sure that I want my pieces to be seen as space fillers. That just shows how precious I'm becoming, like a proper writer. Three months ago I would have been delighted just to be in the paper, whether as a space filler or even as a mistake.

Thursday 4th September

What do you know? Another success. If my career trajectory continues in this way I'll be on the Booker shortlist before you know it.

The features editor of *Hearth and Home* rang. She said that everyone in the office had been rolling around laughing at Gus's zany idea on how to spend Christmas, and they would like to give us a double page spread in the November issue (which is in fact the Christmas issue—what?)

Gus and I are going to be in a feel good feature about people who have unusual Christmases.

Feel good for her, maybe, but not for me, because apart from the obvious, there are two minor problemos.

The first is they want a picture of me and Gus. And I didn't tell her that he isn't here and won't be here until next March. (And although I think Iain would be willing to stand in again, I don't think we could get away with another back view photograph.)

The second, and more important problem, is that they have interpreted the piece to be true—when in fact it was just imaginative spoofing.

Christmas underlines our most serious difference—Gus is anti-social, and I love company. He likes it best when there's just me and him at home together. He's also an atheist, teetotal, and is not one of life's natural celebrants. He is allergic to visitors, cards, tree, seasonal food and tinsel. His idea of jolly activity is pottering in his shed, and his only concession to over indulgence is an extra carton of natural yoghurt.

I, on the other hand, love food, drink, family, Christmas trees, lights, carols—the lot.

Our Christmas dilemma is another marital difference about which it is impossible to reach a satisfactory compromise (just like his wanting to live in the back of beyond, miles from anyone.) Whichever way you handle it, someone is going to be unhappy: this is where compromise fails.

Last year—at Gus's request—I tried to make Christmas low key. We did without a tree, for example, and he persuaded me to suggest to the children that they might like to make other plans.

It may seem foolish and trivial to make a fuss about Christmas, but at some fundamental level, Christmas is inextricably interwoven with my notions of home and family. If I don't have a family Christmas, with the house decorated and sparkly, I feel empty and sad—right in the pit of my stomach. I think I could put up with no Christmas if we could go away somewhere, or even if I could spend the holiday washing up at the homeless shelter, but that won't do for Gus. He wants me here at home with him, pretending it's not Christmas.

"It's not fair," he said last year. "We've celebrated Christmas ever since we've been married. We ought to have a year off sometimes. Actually, we should have every alternate year off."

"What?"

"One year Christmas should be on. And the next year it should be off."

"Don't be stupid—it's a season, not a light. We can't just switch it off."

"We can do what we damn well like. Who says we have to do what everyone else does?"

"But I don't want to do without Christmas. I like it."

"We could have a Christmas shed."

I was suspicious. We already have a potting shed, a storage shed and a workshop shed, and I know he harbours an evil imperialist plan to have the garden covered with a vast shed complex.

"A Christmas shed?" I asked.

"Yes. Look, this is what we should do. Firstly, we alternate a Christmas *on* year with a Christmas *off* year. In an *off* year—my year—we would have no visitors and the house would be declared a festivity free zone."

"Where does a Christmas shed come in?"

"You can decorate the Christmas shed as you like. You can hang up all the putrid cards, and have holly and tinsel and all the other paraphernalia. You can even have a bloody tree if you like. You can keep a tin of mince pies in there, and a radio to listen to the obligatory Dickens. If your friends come round, or the children come home for Christmas, you can entertain them in the shed."

"But what if *It's a Wonderful Life* is on the telly? Am I going to be allowed to watch that?"

"I suppose you could if I was out."

"That's big of you."

"Look, Sally, it's perfectly fair. In an *on* year the house would be yours to fill with whoever and whatever you liked. I could slink off to the Christmas Shed to get away from the drunken hordes, and sit in a deck chair and read *Walden*. And I could keep my yoghurt out there—it'd be cool enough."

This is how I remember the conversation going, and it's the essence of what I wrote up for the piece I sent to *Hearth and Home*. And as my concluding paragraph I wrote:

So, that's decided, then. We'll buy a Christmas Shed and get started. The only problem now is to decide whether we start the new regime with an ON Christmas or an OFF Christmas. He says we've had Christmas for thirty years, so this year should be OFF. I say I did without the tree last year, so Christmas should be ON.

The entire piece was a spoof. It was bloody obvious it was a joke.

Not so to Mrs Features Editor.

She asked me if this was an OFF year or an ON year.

"Why?" I asked.

"We'd like to have a picture of you in your Christmas Shed."

"Oh, we don't have a shed just for Christmas," I said.

"So you decorate your normal shed?"

"Well, actually," I said, "it's an ON year this year, which means I'll be decorating the house." This is true. With Gus away, I am going to have a Christmas celebration such as Goose Lane has never seen. "So unfortunately," I went on, "it wouldn't make a very interesting picture—it would look like everyone else's Christmas."

"That needn't be a problem," she said. "Would you be willing to pretend—for the sake of a good story for our readers—that this Christmas is an OFF one, and that you'll be decorating the shed? It would only be like time shifting it a year, just as the photoshoot is made to look as if it's in December but actually takes place in September."

"I suppose that would be all right," I said. I know it was stupid to agree, but at the time it sounded so reasonable: she had caught me up in the idea of providing a good story for her readers.

"So I can send a photographer to shoot you sitting in your deckchair in your decorated shed, then?"

"Yes."

"Would tomorrow, or next week suit?"

"It'll have to be tomorrow. I'm going away on Saturday."

"Fine. Tomorrow. And don't fret about a tree," she said. "Our consumer department has a batch of artificial ones we're reviewing. And I'll get the art department to sort out some decorations."

"Could you send some extra lights?" I asked.

I can't believe what I have agreed to. One minute I'm telling her we don't have a Christmas Shed, and the next minute I'm arranging for them to come and photograph me in it. I should have told her to make sure that when the photographer comes to shoot me he brings some ammunition.

I need to talk to someone about what to do. Richard is away till Saturday—seeing an old Uni friend in Newcastle. But even if he were here, he would say there's no question about coming clean.

Nina is out of the office, according to her colleague. She's flying to the motor show in Frankfurt to organise a satellite link (whatever that is). Why are children always in the way when you don't want them, and never around when you do?

If only Gus were here. He's so useful to talk things over with. He has more common sense than me. He would help me find a way out of this sticky situation. He's done it before. If he were here he would even do a role play with me so I could rehearse what I wanted to say to Mrs Features Editor.

In the absence of Gus I have emailed Kate, my trusty colleague in the guerrilla struggle of freelance writing, and asked her how to salvage the situation.

Friday 5th September

```
from: kate wensley
to: sally howe
subject: your image
```
Hi Daise,
Don't even think of pulling out. This is your first chance to break into the glossies—don't muff it. Lighten up. Everyone will know it's a spoof, and anyway, who reads Hearth and Home? Good luck with the photoshoot—hope the tree is tasteful—can't have you published across Britain sitting next to anything crass. Am relying on you to twinkle.
best baubles, bungles and boobs, love giovanna

It seems like a long time ago now that my mate Pete was here with his bags and bags and bags and bags of equipment.... not to mention the Christmas decorations. He arrived half an hour late looking rather careworn. It's a good job he was late: so was I. It takes a surprisingly long time to tidy up a shed and then decorate it with lights, streamers, tinsel and balloons.

Pete was sweet. He used to live in London and work on *The Guardian*. Now he has a young family, he lives in

Pickering and works freelance. We had a chat about our careers, which made me feel like a true professional. He hates cold calling—just like me. He usually sends his unsolicited emails on Tuesdays—just like me.

Mrs Features Editor had asked him to take some shots of me in my study, writing, as I said I was a writer. That was OK, except that my computer is so ancient it looks naff, and I wished I'd thought of borrowing Alan's laptop before the holiday, as a high tech body double.

Pete's Christmas tree was fine, despite being artificial. We sat it on the work bench and draped it with his lights—huge yellow stars.

It's the next bit of the story that I would like to draw a veil over. I had taken immense trouble with my wardrobe—wearing my violet silk blouse and my Boden navy velvet palazzos (well it was Christmas). But hanging around waiting for half an hour for Pete to adjust his tripods and to position his lighting umbrella, I got really chilly. (The heat wave has fled and this morning was normal English weather.) So I dashed into the back porch and grabbed Gus's gardening jumper—a monstrous mustard Aran, bedecked with cables. It swamped me but was just what I needed to keep me warm while I waited.

Finally he was ready. I sat in the deckchair. Then he asked me—wait for it—to put tinsel round my neck and to wear a Santa hat, and to hold a large lurid bauble. The tinsel was yellow and the hat was scarlet and the bauble was a lurid green—oh, why did they not send a stylist?

There is something that comes over me when a photographer points his equipment at me. I am too easily persuaded. I have this ridiculous unfounded childlike trust that as they are in the business of visual impact, they know what they are doing image-wise, and that no matter how ridiculous or tasteless or yukky I *feel* that I look, the

151

end result will be stylish and beautiful. Why do they let me down?

Now I know that no matter how personable and friendly a photographer is, he *just doesn't care* whether or not a fifty-something female looks her best.

At the end of the session he said, "I expect you'd like to see the pics—shall I email them?"

He was amazed when I said, "No, thanks."

And only now that he's gone have I remembered that when I sat down in the deckchair I was still wearing Gus's disgusting jumper.

Saturday 6th September

The jam sandwich piece was in—filling up space—just as KWh said. It helps to ease the embarrassment of yesterday, but only fleetingly.

Sunday 7th September

Walking along Bamburgh beach this morning with Wendy, she in her Audrey-Hepburn-on-skiing-holiday outfit: tight black capri pants and clinging cerise jumper belted with a black patent belt, tiny leather pumps, coloured popsox and a teensey head scarf. ("I know exactly what you're thinking about my unsuitable footwear, Sally, but could you honestly see Audrey Hepburn in all-terrain sandals?")

The pure, clean sand stretching for miles and the wide blue sky looking so lovely, the *Hearth and Home* imbroglio seemed like a stupid dream.

I was transported back to days spent on Bamburgh beach with Gus and the kids. He was so lovely on family holidays. When the kids were little he was the one—not me—who had enough patience to get their feet properly dry and get out all the sand from between their toes. And when they were horrible grouchy teenagers and stomped off on their own and we couldn't find them anywhere—he knew exactly how long to leave them to stew in their sulks before going to find them. His conciliation skills were finely honed: he could schmooze them back into the fold in record time.

Monday 8ᵗʰ September

It is weird being here without Gus. It's as if he were dead. I have never been to Northumberland without him. I feel as though I'm being unfaithful being here with someone else, even if it's Wendy and not another man. But how weird would it be to never come again, ever? Which is what could happen if the trial separation turns permanent.

Managing to crack on with the revisions needed on my novel. Wendy is just as focussed on her work as I am on mine.

Tuesday 9ᵗʰ September

The pattern of our days here has a certain purity and rigour.

Whichever one of us wakes up first makes mugs of tea, then wakes the other. Then we get into the same bed, prop ourselves up with pillows, and we sit and talk while we drink our tea. After that we go our separate ways. I write and Wendy studies.

We regroup at half past one for a sandwich and *Neighbours*. Then it's out for a walk on the beach, then afternoon tea somewhere that has good cakes—*Topsey Turvey's Cafe* in Warkworth is my current favourite.

This afternoon we drove over the bridge where Daniel almost wrecked the railings when he was learning to drive. Gus used to take Nina and Daniel out for driving practice when we were here on our hols. (There's no way I could have done it.) When they were bored of the beach he would get them to drive round Northumberland in search of Toffos which in those days Gus couldn't live without.

Wendy and I come home when it starts to get chilly, light the log burning stove, bung a ready meal in the microwave and open a bottle.

You would think Wendy would be letting rip with lots of different looks this week—after all, it is her holidays—but she appears to have left most of her fashion at home in her wardrobe. She was Audrey Hepburn again today.

"I'm rather disappointed with the lack of variety in your looks this week, Wendy. Do you ease off when you're on holiday?" I asked her.

"Sod it, I can't swot and pose at the same time. Get used to it, Sally. If I get my Faculty of Astrological Studies Diploma people will have to start thinking of me as an astrologer and not a fashion icon."

Wednesday 10th September

I wanted to go to Craster again and walk across the fields to Dunstanburgh Castle. Gus and I do that walk at least three times when we come up here. Wendy's not interested. She says it's too cold. That wouldn't stop Gus and me. Once we sat on the basalt stones beyond the headland swaddled in jumpers, fleeces and Barbour jackets, hats, coats and gloves— and that was August. We were watching the cormorants and kittiwakes and talking politics. I miss him. I hope that I don't have to go on missing him after this year is over.

I'm going to have to stop thinking about what might or might not happen. Otherwise it will use up all my energy and wear me out. Most unhealthy. I must try to get on and worry about things only when they happen and not before.

Thursday 11th September

I popped into Seahouses for some shopping, and walking past the hardware shop I thought of Gus again. On family holidays he always did the washing up and used to get the kids lined up along the kitchen in a human chain, throwing and catching the crockery to put it away in the cupboard. And I let him. The crockery was blue willow pattern, and if any got smashed we could buy replacements at the end of the week in the hardware shop.

But when I went into Trotters for a stottie cake the Gus glow evaporated. The woman behind the counter had red hair and I almost flung the money at her.

When I got back Wendy asked me what I was so glum about, so I told her about the trial separation and about PhD princess. I hadn't been intending to—I think I've done well to last all these months with only Richard in the know.

"This is huge!" she said. "And absolutely brilliant."

"What? We've been married all this time and you think it's good we could be splitting up now? I don't want to be just another statistic."

"But a trial separation is something most of us only dream about."

"What?"

"A year off from being married. Anything is legit. Even if you have no intention of splitting up at the end of the year, you've got a year off when you can do whatever you like and no questions asked."

"Well, I am getting on with my writing I s'pose."

"Your writing? Don't you fancy something more exciting?"

"Like what?"

"Didn't you tell me Richard had a nice unattached friend who kept coming to stay?"

"Oh, Iain."

"Well? And your stars are looking good in that direction. You've got transiting Uranus coming up to square your Venus very soon."

Friday 12th September

If I ever buy a holiday cottage and rent it out, remind me not to have a visitors' book. I've just been reading the one here. The previous tenants all sound mad. I have made copious notes so I can use it for a piece.

This cottage is one of the best I have stayed in. It is a typical single storey Northumberland cottage, with calming rural views and a sunny back garden. It's comfortable, attractively furnished, well-maintained, and contains everything that opens and shuts.

Or so I thought before I read the visitors book.

"The only thing we could find lacking," says one, "was a dish drainer," as if it were a competition to find the missing item.

The list of complaints is endless:

"Fire very welcome, if a bit hot. Quilts far too much tog. Phew!"

"The pub was much nearer than in the brochure (just over half a mile)."

"The frog jigsaw has two pieces missing."

Get a life.

At least one previous tenant shares my attitude to all these hyper-critical comments "no swimming pool or croquet lawn, couldn't find the stairs, upstairs unfinished…"

Some people use the book to give advice to future guests. Who do they think they are writing for? Lonely Planet? They list their favourite beaches, castles, pubs and cafés. But what's the point? One woman's "good value" pub food is another woman's "microwave fare." The parties can't even agree amongst themselves: "Opinions on *Harvey Haddock's Dining Table* are divided, but I am writing this and I thought it rubbish."

My favourite restaurant critic says this: "If you are not the posh sort I would recommend eating out at the *Nirvana Fish Restaurant*. Mum said it was 'common' so we didn't go there again."

There are nature lovers—just like Gus—who list the species they have spotted during their stay. Though one animal lover goes a little far and talks about "an adorable stray cat which we have adopted and are taking back to London."

When I see tourists walking up Goose Lane in future I shall watch Chomsky with extra care.

Is my delight in walking into a clean, comfortable cottage (made so by someone else's hard work) naïve and undemanding? Perhaps I should sharpen my critical faculties so I can compete with the bloke who wrote—"The wood shed had no hooks for hanging our pheasants."

Monday 15th September

Back home working on my trusty old workhorse desktop.

Deep Water tonight. There were only five of us there—

Kate, me, Duncan, Florid Trev and B.J. Fantasy.

Duncan showed us a letter from a friend of the last tutor, a woman who works for a TV production company. She is planning a series for BBC 4 which follows a writing group and she wants to come and film us for a pilot. What a hoot. Duncan was not keen. Nor was B.J. Fantasy. Perhaps she thinks her cover will be blown. Fortunately Kate and Florid Trev and I made up the majority, so we're going to do it. Duncan said he'd email the woman and tell her that the 29th September is convenient for us. By that time, Alicia and Janet2 will be back from their hols and we'll have enough people to make it sing.

Tuesday 16th September

It takes longer—word for word—to compose a letter to a bloody agent than it does to write a novel. You would think that all you had to do was write a formal version of:

Dear so and so, Here is my novel, would you like to represent me? love Sally

Not so.

Bodmyn (and he's not the only one) says you are supposed to market *yourself* as well as your novel. Best of all is if you're young, beautiful and an Oxbridge graduate. You also need some interesting life events. It helps if you were abused as a child, or were brought up in a cult, or you have sledged solo to the North Pole.

Then you look in *The Writer's Handbook* and carefully select an agent who deals with your type of fiction and send them what they say they want ... synopsis? three chapters? just a letter in the first instance? You get together your little marketing package and post it off.

I have posted marketing packs to six agents, and am agog for the results.

The new term of Italian class started tonight. Christine won't be back from Venice till Wednesday, so Jeremy took the opportunity to sit next to me, and bump his thighs against mine, under the desk, all through the evening. It's getting boring.

```
from: kate wensley
to: sally howe
subject : kind thoughts
hi daise
exciting news on tv front—n'est-ce pas?

pseudonyms fascinated by idea of tv exposure

pesto said her friend jason's mum would do me a
makeover
(jason as in debauched parties above the harlequin
hair salon)

excuse me, who said anything about makeovers

asked what jason's mum looks like and was told
she wears shorty dressing gowns that show her
underwear and a lot of mascara, that she is
usually drunk and hits on the boys at parties

said thanks for the kind thought

(deep water doesn't need a mrs robinson lookalike—
does it??)

best intentions, love giovanna
```

Wednesday 17th September

I wrote and emailed a piece to Kay Wharton about the comments in the visitors' book.

A belated thank you letter arrived this morning from Angelina.

Dear Sal-gal,
So lovely to see you again and catch up.
Don't despair on the writing front. Just remember my tips and I'm sure you'll get there eventually. Try not to take it so seriously, though. It's a game.
After I got my first book published I joined the Society of Authors, thinking they might have some decent dinner dances, but it turned out not to be that kind of club. It's all very intense and highbrow. I'm enclosing their latest Journal. I thought you might like it. It's far too dull for me to waste my time on.
Love
Angelina

Later—I've just checked my email, and Kay Wharton has accepted my piece! I can't believe it.

Thursday 18th September

Richard is very down. After practising his bread making for the last three weeks, he took some samples round to Billy Bathgate and asked if he'd like to try them, with a view to taking a regular order to sell in the shop. Billy Bathgate didn't slice off a corner apparently, or even tear a piece off each. He picked up each loaf in turn, took a bite out of it, then spluttered each mouthful into the bin without even chewing.

After doing this with all six loaves he shuddered and said: "Thanks, but I'll stick to oatcakes and Warburtons."

from: kate wensley
to: sally howe
subject: my post
hi daise,

received two items in post today -
1) promotional stuff for a LOTUS ELISE. I'm not
thinking that I want one of these, but I was v.
pleased that lotus had picked me out as suitable
to be a lotus driver. I don't think they know
about me only reaching 39mph in the espace on
the A6.

2) rejection from editor for poems sent to Poetry
Mag. She apologised for taking so long to reply
but my letter had got lost at the "bottom of
her Mag box". She wanted to use two poems but
"couldn't convince" the other editor to agree.
She hoped I'd sent them elsewhere in the meantime
because she thought they were good enough to be
taken, and hoped I'd send them some more.

She signed off Best Wishes, so she's way behind.
She won't get invited to test drive an Elise
signing off Best Wishes.

some days I think I'm barking up wrong tree.

barking best love Giovanna

Friday 19th September

   Iain arrived mid-morning. I'm not complaining—he did
ring a couple of nights ago to ask if it was OK. He may be an
interruption to my writing, but he's a very personable one,
and he doesn't have that annoying habit of sticking his head
round the door when I'm in my study and saying, "Can you
spare a minute?"

161

Plus he fits in with any arrangements that Richard and I already have so it's not as if we have to change our plans when he turns up. I'm not used to having someone who fits in with what I want with no discussion—it's quite a novelty.

I was booked to go to see *Il Postino* tonight at the Ashington Cinema Club. I was going with Christine from Italian class and I knew she wouldn't mind if I took Iain along.

"Do you fancy it?" I asked him. "It's in Italian so it'll be no problem for you. Some of us will need the subtitles."

"I'll feel right at home. I've been staying with Bec since June, and I feel as though my Italian is getting rusty."

It felt strange going to the pictures with a man—even if it was only to Ashington Memorial Hall. Last time I persuaded Gus to come to the Chesterfield Cineplex with me was seven years ago, to see *Wings of a Dove*. We bought our tickets and went in and sat down, and he got out a torch and a book.

When I called at Christine's house this evening to pick her up, her husband came to the door wearing a bathrobe. "Sorry," he said. "Christine meant to ring you. She forgot all about the film and we got rather involved doing something else." He looked embarrassed.

I wonder if Christine is on red clover.

I walked back down their garden path and as I emerged from their gate onto the pavement and walked back to the car I saw Iain straining to look in the driver's mirror and fingering his hair. I'm not used to men who check their appearance like that.

As we were walking into the village hall I spotted Jeremy getting out of his car in the car park. He'd seen me but I pretended not to notice.

"Iain, do me a favour," I whispered, linking arms with him. "Pretend you're my husband, will you? There's a man who's been pestering me and it would be so nice to put him off."

"I'd be delighted," he said, and he unlinked his arm and put it round my shoulders. "Is that all right?"

"That's perfect," I said. And I must say it felt pretty nice. How long has it been since another man put his arm round my shoulders and his head next to mine? A tingle went down my spine. I'd forgotten what it could be like. Maybe Wendy was right.

I managed to avoid Jeremy's eye throughout the whole proceedings. Afterwards we called in at the *Castle* in Bakewell for a night cap. There was no way I was going to give the village gossips fodder by calling in at *The Derbyshire Heifer* in the village. Going out with Iain was totally innocent but I couldn't exactly get a loudspeaker and explain it all.

"That film is so romantic, isn't it?" I said to Iain as I sipped my spritzer.

"Yes, though to be honest I've always thought it pathetic to get someone else to write your love letters for you, even if the someone else is Pablo Neruda."

"I can think of some people who wouldn't know where to start."

"It's talking heart to heart that counts," he said. "The words don't really matter. I mean, I'm no writer, but my letters must have been adequate. After Serena died I found a shoe box full of them that she'd saved—from years before."

"And did you save hers?" I asked. "I mean, sorry. That was way too personal. Ignore me. Let me get you another drink—I'm driving, remember." And I scooped up his glass and beetled off to the bar before he felt he had to answer.

Huh! I thought, as I waited to be served. There's no way Gus would have kept my letters. He doesn't have a romantic whisker in his beard.

Saturday 20ᵗʰ September

Whoopee! My fourth piece appeared in *The Recorder* today. Next thing you know I'll be getting a column.

Iain seemed impressed. He said he was going to stop at Redmonton to get his own copy from the post office before heading home. "I always read *The Recorder* anyway," he said. "Serena liked *The Times*, but these days I prefer *The Recorder*."

Monday 22ⁿᵈ September

Gus's monthly epistle arrived.

En casa -

These last weeks cabin fever has taken on a new meaning on this Colorado hillside. And desperation. (Was this what Thoreau meant when he said "Most men lead lives of quiet desperation"?) I feel like a pioneer, valiantly struggling to secure shingle after shingle before winter. There was never pressure like this at the office.

And now it's done. The ultimate shelter, perfect in its simplicity. It would take a shallow man to ask for more. With the cabin completed and dog duty a distant memory I am experiencing a state I can only assume to be nirvana.

Bird list
Golden Eagle
Northern Saw-whet Owl
American Dipper
Winter Wren

take care there, Gus

Enjoy your nirvana while you can, baby. The snows will be there before you know it. And you may think your authentic cabin is an achievement, but your woman back home has had four pieces in *The Recorder* and a feature coming up in *Hearth and Home*. Put that in your hand-built chimney breast and smoke it.

At least he didn't mention nirvana when he was talking about Emily.

Tuesday 23rd September

My first novel rejection:

I'm afraid that your novel, Fast Work, does not speak to me, and therefore I do not feel able to represent you. This is just my personal response, and another agent may feel differently. I wish you every success for the future.

Well sucks to her—there are five more agents to go.

At last the WW is finished. Though why I sound as though I'm pleased, I really don't know. It just means Richard will be coming up and sticking his head round the door again every half hour and saying "Can you spare a minute?"

Unless this friendship with Pippa continues. Lately the *Screwfix* catalogues have stayed in a pile on the floor next to his end of the sofa, and he's had his head stuck in his birthday book about training dogs.

"You're not thinking of getting a dog—at least not while you're living here—are you?" I asked.

"Oh, no. Pippa is going away for two weeks in October and she's asked if I'll look after Emmie and Ellie. I'm just mugging up."

My hot flushes have returned. What has happened? Do I need to up my dose of red clover or move on to something stronger? Class A drugs?

from: kate wensley
to: sally howe
subject : more kind thoughts
hi daisy
pesto still banging on about makeovers

strongly suggested her friend Esme's mum who
does a morning of colours and
style advice for only £200

bollocks to £200

have decided to rely wholly on extensively
skilled tv makeup artists

best lip gloss, love giovanna

Wednesday 24th September

I woke up four times in the night drenched in sweat. The last time—at 4 a.m., I couldn't get back to sleep. Consequently I felt dreadful this morning, and also very old.

I was moaning to Richard about this at breakfast and he said: "Talking of death—"

"I wasn't talking of death," I interrupted. "All I said was I was feeling old."

"One thing leads to another. Death will be the next significant life event for you and me, Sally."

"Great! That really does cheer me up."

"Seriously, thinking about death, there's a bit in the paper here about the cost of funerals, and about the problem of where they are going to bury everyone, because the cemeteries are getting full."

"And?"

"*Screwfix* have missed an opportunity. They should do a funeral package, expand into funerals…basic, no-nonsense, and workmanlike, just like their tools. They could promise to do next day service, just like they do next day delivery. If you trust them with your life, why not with your death? Workmen could be laid out in their *Dickies* gear. I'd feel most confident about their service, wouldn't you?"

Thursday 25th September

It's getting really chilly in the mornings. We've got the central heating back on its default setting. But my hot flushes are getting worse and worse. I am taking off my cardigan and putting it back on again all through breakfast. And this goes on all through the day. Next week is my annual check up at the breast clinic. I'm going to beg them to give me some HRT.

Richard's mind is still on funerals.

This morning he said: "I thought it would save money if I built coffins for you and me and Gus. It could be my next project."

"We're in our fifties, Richard, not our eighties."

"Forward planning."

"Where would we store them? In the shed?"

"Yes, but it would be even better to design them with a dual purpose. I could make them double as bookcases until we needed them."

"Mmmm," I said, munching on my toast and wanting him to shut up so I could get back to reading Janina Lemon's column.

"Or better still," he said, "have them on castors under the bed, use them as storage for blankets or whatever, and then when the person dies you could pull out the coffin, empty it and then just roll the corpse off the side of the bed—*plop*—into the coffin."

As if all this wasn't enough, the postman bought another blank rejection from an agent.

Tuesday 30th September

Oh my—we started at half past three yesterday afternoon and finished the shooting (I'm really getting the jargon, now) at eleven. Alicia said they could have done with two crews working simultaneously as they do for *Neighbours*. I had no idea anyone else at Deep Water watched *Neighbours*. Finally I've found a fellow fan.

Anyway, she (Alicia) was put out because Terry the cameraman wasn't as hunky as she'd expected. "Cameramen usually have impressive shoulders because of humping heavy cameras around," she said. "Do you think the boy is undernourished?"

As soon as Elodie (the director) had introduced herself, she made me run up the stairs to show my eager arrival. I had to do it five times because they couldn't get the lighting quite right on the stairs. I thought I was going to expire. I don't run upstairs. I don't even run when I'm late for an episode of *Neighbours*. My poor arthritic knees won't stand it.

I know that the filming of a telly programme is a terrific draw. When they had *Songs of Praise* in Baslow a few years ago it was standing room only, so it must have been the *Songs of Praise* effect that brought back pale Janet1, who was even more see-through than before. When she walked in, Paul (her ex) looked as if he'd seen an alien. He slunk away. His desire to avoid bleached Janet was obviously stronger than his desire to be the latest discovery from reality TV.

Florid Trevor was wearing a shirt with a life-sized palm tree print. He was in overdrive. At one point in the kitchen he was talking to me about art. Did I say talking? Bellowing is more like it. He obviously thought that if he talked loudly enough someone on the crew—two rooms away—would hear him, and he would be fast forwarded to the Turner prize short list.

I was desperate to quieten him down, if only to protect my ear drums.

"What kind of art do you do?" I asked in a tiny voice. That's what teachers do when they want to quieten an unruly class—talk quietly.

"Paintings," he boomed, refusing to take the hint. "Dadaism meets Mondrian."

"Really, how interesting."

He started to fiddle with something around his neck, and I assumed that he couldn't hear me, and was adjusting his hearing aid tuner. So many writers have them. But it was a digital camera: tied round his neck and stowed in his frond-covered breast pocket.

He whipped it out and showed me an image of one of his Dadaism meets Mondrian pictures. It was the size of a stamp, and my reading glasses were in the other room.

"I'm sorry, Trevor, but I can't make it out."

"Pah!" he said, in a Disgusted of Derbyshire tone. "Oh well, have an advance copy of the piece I'm reading out later." The poem was printed on one side and on the back was one of his liney blue and red blurred pictures, obviously placed there so it would be caught on camera as he read.

I was just trying to think of something nice to say about his offering, when Kate came to tell us that Elodie wanted to start the reading and critting session.

Once we sat down I looked around and noticed what everyone else was wearing. Up till then it had been far too hectic.

I'm used to creatives wearing beads, scarves, shawls, artistic multi-layering, cavernous bags and expressive earrings—just not altogether at the same time the way Elodie was wearing them. In fashion terms she was mixing her metaphors (or as Elodie herself might have said—over-egging the pudding. Her speech was over-laden with clichés.) I was waiting for her to shed her excessive backpack but she never did.

But Janet2 (performance artiste extraordinaire) took the jammy dodger. She was dressed like a Corr i.e. with hardly any top held up with nothing much at all, plus floaty bits of skirt that ranged in length from floor to high thigh. Not to mention the Dick Whittington-esque high boots. I could have sworn she also had hair extensions, and this was supposed to be reality TV. I suppose some people will stop at nothing in the pursuit of fame. Fancy asking for a table to stand on to do her piece, though. And fancy setting it to a Corrs number, played on a tape player. Oh dear.

I felt a bit nervous when I was reading my piece to the camera, but it wasn't too bad, even with multiple takes. What was difficult was making the retakes of criticism sound spontaneous. I'd forgotten what I was supposed to be saying by take two, let alone take sixty three. And the other problem was that Elodie's cliché madness was highly infectious. She even had Duncan talking in clichés by the end. We're going to look like the cliché kids.

B.J.Fantasy had a new hair cut. Off with the bun: her hair's now short and spiked with gel. Oh my. Plus she's got new specs—square, metallic turquoise frames.

She was impossible. How could she think there would be time for her to read out three thousand words on the relative use of naturalistic harmonics in the poetry of Seamus Heaney? Anyway, she didn't get chance. Elodie shouted cut after the first paragraph, and B.J. rushed off to the loo. Then when she got back she read out a haiku:

similies are clouds
on the horizon of our
earthly consciousness

I haven't remembered the thing—I have her copy of it for
some reason. It's written on the back of a paper towel. She
must have knocked it out when she was in the loo, which is
quite impressive, even if the haiku isn't.

I can't wait to ring Kate for a thorough debriefing of the
shooting.

from: kate wensley
fo: sally howe
subject : stars
hi daise

great night last night didn't you think?

apart from the no-show on the make-up department
front -
I know it¹s low budget reality tv but even so -
would have thought they could have at least sent
one tiny girl and a powder brush

personal high points:
florid trevor's inverted vicissitudes (whatever
they may be)

terry the cameraman dropping his camera on not-
an-american's foot

did you notice how we split into three groups—
stage hoggers(who need no further publicity),
freezers (led to hide under the table by self and
duncan), and the naturals like you?

o to be a tv natural

best camera angles, love giovanna

October

Wednesday 1st October

I went for my check up at the breast clinic this morning. Everything's fine—no new suspicious lumps.

I told the breast care nurse about the Return of the Hot Flushes (sounds like a band reunion concert) and she still refused to give me HRT, but she did say that an anaesthetist is doing some trials of acupuncture to see if it helps, and would I like an appointment? He's starting his clinic next week. I said yes, assuming I haven't expired by then through over heating.

```
from: kate wensley
to: sally howe
subject: socks
```

```
hi daise
can't wait to hear what your agents say
how could an agent not be entranced by your
central character maurice in his socks with
sandals?
```

```
here all three pseudonyms now reading harry
potter.
if ever you are short of words just take a leaf
out of jk's book—make sure every noun has at
least three adjectives, and every verb has at
```

least two adverbs. you'll be amazed how it pumps
up your word count. 20 thou becomes 80 thou
overnight.

for example....the nice voluntary sector man who
scratchily yet happily wore thick red woolly
socks with his strappy brown bouncy sandals...

best fashion victims, love giovanna

Thursday 2nd October

Still no news from any of the remaining four agents.
Pigs.

What do they do all day? I suppose they arrive in the
office at eleven, have coffee, make a few telephone calls and
then go to a long boozy lunch and don't get back until three.
They then have a post prandial snooze, field a few more
phone calls, and then bugger off for cocktails with their
literary chums. Meanwhile their slush piles totter hopelessly
(i.e. without hope) in the corners of their rooms.

Nina rang me up last night and told me she was pregnant.
I don't think I said the right thing. I *know* I didn't say the
right thing. My first reaction was one of horror.

Why does everyone assume that every woman past 50 is
desperate to be a grandmother? I'm in my writing life now,
not my mothering one.

Friday 3rd October

I am having a bad week.

I feel awful that I wasn't more enthusiastic when Nina
told me her news. It's not that I haven't imagined myself at
some time in the future having a cupboard full of toys in

the dining room. I have. But all that visualisation of me as Grandmother was placed in the *distant* future, along with acquiring a shopping basket on wheels and joining the W.I. If I were St Augustine's mother I'd be saying: "Make me a grandmother, Lord, but not yet."

I am fed up with Gus *not* being here to talk to about stuff going on in my head. I bet he's not ready to be a grandfather, either. I'll have to talk to Iain about it next time he's here. He seems to enjoy his little grandson in Brighton—Becky's child. Maybe the feeling grows on you.

Denial is much underrated as a strategy for coping with life's little pockets of gloom. I know I am facing a new stage in my life, namely ageing, but somewhere in the back of my head I've always had the idea that I am just trying it out, and that there will be something else to try soon.

Nina's telling me I am going to be a grandmother has made me face the unpalatable truth. I can't go back or move sideways: the only stage to try next after ageing, apart from death, is *being old*.

I'm sure that when the baby gets here I'll feel better. In the meantime it seems there's nothing so potent at bursting the bubble of denial as a pram in the hallway—even if it's Nina's pram and Nina's hallway.

Saturday 4th October

Richard was in full moaning whinge mode again about the central heating. I am fed up with him.

When is he going to buy a bloody house and move out? I haven't seen many estate agents' brochures around the place recently. I'll have to bring some home from Bakewell myself and tuck them inside his *Screwfix* catalogues.

Thank God he is going to Pippa's house tomorrow to

look after her dogs while she's away. I shall get two weeks in an empty quiet house.

Sunday 5ᵗʰ October

Richard's gone.

Peace at last.

So why do I still feel down?

I sat and wrote all morning—did a piece about disagreements about the central heating—framed it as a problem particularly assaulting married couples over fifty. By this I mean nature's little trick that women get the big M and an internal heating system which makes the domestic one redundant, whilst at the same time they are shuffling off their child rearing responsibilities and getting ready for new, exciting ventures in the next phase of life.

Meanwhile their coeval men are slowing down and becoming more inclined to sit at home perfecting their technique in a variety of sedentary skills, none of which generates much heat, such as trying to complete the crossword faster than the day before, or keeping abreast of the Test Match, by sitting in front of the telly all afternoon with the curtains drawn and eyes closed.

Monday 6ᵗʰ October

Great day—fab sunshine, blue sky, empty house and good writing.

And yet I still feel crap.

It must be the big M.

The weather today was just like the day I first met Gus. I can see him now—sitting on the corridor floor in my friend Ken's hall of residence, leaning against Ken's door. His muscly, tanned legs were bent at the knee, his feet planted firm on the floor and he was reading a book.

I'd just skidded on a small stretch of gravel in front of the door of Ken's wing, and fallen sideways off my bike, bashing my hip and grazing my hand. Ouch!

I parked my bike and went inside. I turned the corner into Ken's corridor, and there was Gus—a hunky bloke with light brown curly hair, wearing a khaki shirt and sawn off denim shorts. He looked up from his book and smiled. A winner of a smile.

"Is Ken not in?" I asked.

"Apparently not."

"What're you reading?"

"Brecht."

"I don't know Brecht. Read me something—not in German, though." I leaned against the wall and looked down at him. His hair was thick and shiny and he had these weird but very sweet ears, kind of elfish, slightly pointed at the top.

"OK," he said. "Despair where there is injustice and no revolt."

"That's good. Tell me another."

"They're not bloody jokes," he said.

"Keep your hair on. I liked it. Give me another quote."

"Anyone still laughing hasn't yet heard the bad news."

"Unless they're being tickled."

I liked his seriousness, so why did I slip into frivolity? I still do it with him now after thirty odd years—it drives him mad.

"What did you say?" he said.

"Oh nothing. Where is Ken? I told him I was coming over," I said.

"So did I."

"I need him. I'm desperate."

177

"You must be desperate if you need old Ken," he said, laughing.

"Not like that. I mean I need him as a subject. For my research project," I said, bending my knees and sliding my back down the wall next to him, and sitting on the floor. I didn't have my arthritic knees in those days and could manage this move quite gracefully.

"Sounds intriguing. What's it on? I can't imagine what he could be a subject for. A chemical analysis of his sweaty socks? How many hours a person can sleep at a stretch? How to survive when you've spent all your grant in the first week of term? Tell me, go on. What's your subject? Chemistry? Economics? Biology? Maybe I could be your subject."

"Psychology. And the project is a correlation between extraversion and susceptibility to being tickled."

"That rules me out on two counts, so you'll have to wait for Ken. I'm not an extravert and I'm not ticklish."

"Don't be daft! Research doesn't work like that. I need all types."

"As I said—no-one has ever made me laugh by tickling me."

"Is that a challenge?" I said. I was a forward hussy in those days. I tried to tickle him under his arm, forgetting about my sore hand. "Ow. Bugger."

"What's the matter?"

"I fell off my bike and hurt my hand."

"Let me see." He gently took my hand and turned it over. "That looks raw," he said. "Come on. Let's go and find some Dettol."

He jumped to his feet and held out his hand to pull me up. His movements have always been as sure. I love his deliberate way of moving.

"Do you live here in hall?" I asked, taking his hand. It was warm and big and strong.

"You must be joking. Be holed up in here with the motley crowd? Not bloody likely. I'm in digs. Come on, it's not far. We can wheel our bikes if you don't feel up to cycling."

That's how it started.

And he was right about being an introvert, but wrong about not being ticklish.

Tuesday 7ᵗʰ October

from: kate wensley
to: sally howe
subject: last night's deep water
hi daise

will the footage reach the screen??

hope elodie saves the film for the archives so
they can play the bit of you running upstairs
when they are doing "daisy rowland: a literary
retrospective" in twenty yrs time

have done a spot of house tidying in my computer
folders and you now have your very own sub-
folder
are you all right? you didn't seem your normal
cheery self last night

best forward planning, love giovanna

Personally I don't think they'll ever show the pilot episode—how could they wring anything sensible out of what went on last week?

Still no news from any of the remaining agents. Why can't they at least write and say "No thanks"? Last night at Deep Water Duncan said, "Never mind, think of all the famous

179

writers who had to battle with rejection after rejection before they were published."

Then he went on to tell me that J.K.Rowling was rejected thirteen times and William Golding twenty six times etc, etc, etc, and so I stopped listening. I know he was trying to be nice, but when people go on about how many times this or that writer was rejected before they made it big, it's like when you have a broken heart and someone says "There's plenty more fish in the sea." No help.

I was going to email my central heating piece to Kay Wharton this morning.

But at breakfast time (silent without Richard) I was reading a piece in an old *Mslexia* about submitting writing to editors according to the moon.

Apparently the moon whizzes round the zodiac faster than any of the planets. It changes zodiac sign every two and a half days. And if you submit work to editors when it is in some signs you have a better chance of success than when it's in others. So, for example, Capricorn and Scorpio are fruitful signs in terms of success, whereas if the moon is in Aquarius you are advised not to submit, but to spend time tinkering with your computer or looking at your horoscope.

I rang Wendy and asked her where the moon was. She answered me immediately because at that very moment she was sitting cramming astrology. Her exams start tomorrow in London. She said that today the moon is in Pisces. *Mslexia* says that Pisces is the second most fruitful sign for submitting stuff. I bunged off the piece pronto before anything could change.

I opened the kitchen cupboard this afternoon to get out a tin of cat food, and got a weird sad feeling. I stood there scanning the array of tins and wondering why I felt so forlorn, and then I realised it was because there were none of Gus's tins of spaghetti hoops in there. So I drove round to the post office and bought a couple, just to make the cupboard look more normal. More complete.

"Och, so, it's back to the spaghetti hoops, is it?" said Billy Bathgate, who misses nothing. "Is Mr Howe coming home?"

I tried to smile. I wish he were.

Tonight in Italian Jeremy was making constant innuendoes. In the end I told him to piss off. He looked shocked. I simply don't care. I'm too fed up to care.

Wednesday 8th October

I went for my first session of acupuncture today. Good job, as when I woke up I was still in wrist-slitting mode.

The doctor is young and sweet and gentle. I was lying on the hospital bed and as he began explaining what he was about to do, these great tears started rolling down my cheeks. It was so embarrassing.

"Are you all right?" he asked, taking hold of my wrist to check my pulse and looking into my eyes. "What's the matter?"

"Nothing's the matter. It's just what I was telling you before. Not only do I have hot flushes all the time, I also get ridiculous mood swings. There is no reason why I should be crying now. I don't know why I am."

"Are you sure?"

"Really," I said. "Just ignore me, and stick in your magic needles."

He's a babe, and I'm not the only one who thinks so. I was lying in my cubicle with needles in my feet, my ankles and a wrist, and I heard the nurse say to him "It's not the acupuncture that makes all these women feel better, it's your bedside manner."

Thursday 9th October

KayWh emailed to say she liked my central heating piece and was going to use it. Excellent. She said she completely agreed with my analysis. She must be suffering from the big M too. I wonder if that gives me an edge over younger freelances submitting to her.

I only had one night sweat last night. And when I woke up I felt eager to get out of bed and start my day. This treatment seems to be working. Bollocks to red clover.

Also I had no hot flushes this morning until Richard arrived on the doorstep with the dogs. It was pissing it down and they were all dripping, even though they'd only walked the three hundred yards from Pippa's house.

"I thought I ought to knock, Sally. I didn't know if Chomsky was in. I didn't want to frighten him by coming in unannounced."

"Why do you want to come in, anyway? I mean—why do you want to bring *them* in?"

"You don't mind, do you?"

"I'd really rather you didn't."

"But I have a problem. Pippa has left me lots of DIY to do."

"The cheeky madam."

"No, I offered."

"Of course you did."

"Yes, but, well, it's rather difficult to get on."

"What *do* you mean?"

"I mean that every time I start up the drill the dogs go berserk."

"Well, tie them up outside."

"Come off it, Sally—when it's raining?"

"Stick them in the garage, then."

"I can't. It's locked, and I don't know where Pippa keeps

her key. I'm going to have to leave them here, with you. You won't mind too much will you? If I put them in my room?"

"Not in your room, Richard. It's right next door to my study. How will I cope with the noise?"

"The dining room?"

"I'd really rather you didn't."

"Don't be mean, Sally. I want to do these jobs for her. Think of all the jobs I've done for you."

I gave up.

"Go on, then. Just for this morning."

"Thanks," he said, coming inside. The dogs skittered about on the wooden hall floor, and then shook themselves, spraying my azure emulsion something shocking.

"This is not a precedent, Richard."

I left him to it. I didn't want to watch the bloody dogs getting muddy footprints on the carpet in the dining room as well as in the hall.

Pah! Think of all he's done for me? He did all that DIY for me because I let him stay here when he was too mean to rent a house. He did it to say thank you. What does he want to say thank you to Pippa for?

Friday 10th October

Those wretched dogs barked for four hours yesterday when Richard left them here. It made absolutely no difference that they were in the dining room. I could hear them all over the house.

How am I supposed to think with that racket going on?

How am I supposed to write?

Why am I expected to put up with it? It's my house. If I had wanted a dog, I'd have gone out and got one for myself. Bloody dogs. They ought to be fitted with silencers.

Saturday 11th October

I wrote another piece—this time on the subject of conversation over breakfast—how noxious it is. While I am waiting to hear from agents about the novel, I may as well concentrate on writing pieces. If I am in the paper regularly now, I'll be able to get something in the paper about the novel when it's published.

Sunday 12th October

Nina rang for a nice long gossipy chat. I love it when she's out of executive-speak and into girl-talk mode. We sat flicking through the *Toast* catalogue together—Nina at her end of the phone, me at my end (I love *Toast,* but for me it's more drooling than buying).

"I don't know why I'm checking out clothes in here," said Nina, after a while. "I ought to be looking at maternity things in *Blooming Marvellous*."

So then we talked about the baby. It's due in May. The idea of having a grandchild is growing on me. Maybe I do want to be a grandmother. Yes I do. I really do.

Tuesday 14th October

Writing went well today. I tweaked a piece I've been working on about becoming a grandmother and was just about to press the Send/Receive button in *Outlook* to email it to KayWh, when I remembered the moon.

So I rang Wendy.

"Are you going to make a habit of this?" she asked. "Because if you are, I'll buy you an ephemeris and then you can look up where the moon is for yourself."

"Are you having a bad day, Wendy?"

"It's Alan. Ever since he got back from his rustic Italian cookery course we've had nothing to eat but pizza. He makes a different type every night—besides which I am getting too fat for my jeans."

"You mean you are a size 10 rather than a size 8? My heart bleeds for you."

I've always found it trying to have a best friend who is petite.

"Bollocks to you as well," she said.

"Sorry, Wendiflora, sweetie-pie. That was just me being envious. What's that noise?"

"Oh, just me, tapping my teeth."

"You really do sound fed up."

"I'm sick of bloody pizza."

"Doesn't he ever do pasta?" I asked. It wasn't like Wendy to be fed up about something so trivial.

"He says he doesn't want to move onto pasta until he's refined his pizza dough. He's even talking about getting one of those special wood burning ovens installed. I ask you!"

We talked for a while, and I tried to cheer her up, and we agreed to go out on Friday night, my birthday. Then she went to fetch her ephemeris and told me the moon was in Gemini.

"Oh no. *Mslexia* says that you mustn't send your work to anyone when the moon is in Gemini. When does it change to something else?"

"It moves into Cancer on Thursday dinnertime, twelvish."

What was I supposed to do? If I waited until Thursday dinnertime, KayWh would be in the throes of press day and she might not even bother to read it.

I bunged off the piece.

What would Janina Lemon have done? Janina Lemon

185

wouldn't care: she's got a column, and columnists can do whatever the hell they like.

Thursday 16th October

Yes!

Bugger the moon! KayWh has accepted the piece I sent about talking at breakfast.

If I carry on like this I'll soon have a column. The first stage I suppose is to understudy for a columnist when she's on her hols. I've seen it—they put in a sentence in italics— *Janina Lemon is away*.

I'm worried about Wendy. It's not like her to get so upset about what Alan is making for tea. She hates cooking, and she doesn't like food that much anyway. That's why she stays petite. I wonder if Alan is having cyber sex with a bored housewife he met on the rustic Italian cookery course...

Friday 17th October

I can't believe it!

I am the proud owner of a laptop.

It's from Gus. What a sweetie! Why have I been worrying about our future together when he's been sitting in his cabin plotting the most thoughtful present he's ever bought me?

He has a gift for buying nice presents. The first I remember was when we were students and he bought me a ball dress which we'd seen in the sale but I'd decided I couldn't afford. That was in the days when he went to balls. What happened?

For my 50th birthday he bought me a trip to Venice with Nina.

It was Wendy who delivered the laptop. She called round after breakfast and wished me happy birthday and said she

186

had a surprise in the car—would I come out and help her carry it in?

It arrived on Monday at her house. She was fed up the other day—not because of the pizzas—but because she was envious of Gus taking all that trouble with my birthday surprise. Alan never does things like that.

At this very moment I am sitting typing on my sleek and lovely, blue and silver laptop with the radio controlled mouse.

I feel like a proper professional now.

Every morning when I switch it on I shall be filled with awe and wonder, and also it will make me think of Gus and how sweet he is. I thought I'd put a picture of him on my desktop, and then I tried to put a caption underneath the picture saying "With thanks to my sponsor, Gus Howe..." But I couldn't work out how to do it, and by the time I had managed it, it was dinnertime.

When Richard came back this morning, having handed the dogs and the house over to the returned Pippa, he carried up the trusty old Compaq to the attic. My study is transformed. Wendy and I are off out for a night on the tiles. Well, OK then, dinner at The Strand. Sometimes it's nice being over fifty. I'd rather be dining at The Strand than doing what Sam did for his last birthday: going to a gig at the Corporation in Sheffield and spending a sweaty night thrashing around in a mosh pit.

Saturday 18th October

Last night turned out rather differently than I had expected.

Firstly Iain arrived early evening, apologising for coming without phoning first. He said he'd had the idea that Richard was going to be away, and so he wasn't going to come. But then he was overcome with tiredness just north of Sheffield and he thought it would be dangerous to keep on driving all the way to Brighton.

"I hope you don't mind, Sally. Here, I brought you these." And he produced from behind his back a huge bunch of long stemmed anemones. Most mysterious. Definitely not garage forecourt flowers. Why did he have them in the car of he hadn't intended calling?

Secondly, we were all sitting having a birthday drink when Daniel rang up to wish me happy birthday and to make sure the laptop had arrived OK.

"I love it!" I said. "Have you seen Dad recently? When did you arrange it?"

"Oh I didn't. At least—we arranged it back in March before he even arrived in the States. He asked me on the phone and he did a bank transfer to pay me for it, and he asked me to set it up in time for your birthday. I sorted out the specifications and the order."

"Well it was very nice of you," I said, while my heart was sinking, sinking, sinking. It was all set up before the airport row. Before the trial separation. When I thought Gus loved me.

I walked back to the kitchen to join Iain and Richard and slumped in a chair, feeling glum.

"Come on, Sally, cheer up! It's your birthday!" said Richard.

"Yeah, sure," I said, drooping further.

Five minutes later he had taken it upon himself to swell the numbers of my friendly and intimate tête-à-tête with Wendy into a full blown dinner party—himself and Pippa, Iain, Wendy and Alan, he'd even invited Christine from Italian with her husband. We all went to the Strand.

Wendy was being a geisha tonight in a slim and slinky

dress (authentic Chinese silk) with oriental floral designs in turquoise and pink, buttons on the raglan and a mandarin collar. She had scraped back her hair into a bun and added a pair of black chopstick things to complete the look.

She whispered to me, as we sat down at the table "And in case you're expecting me to put my hands together and bow when I get up again, don't hold your breath—I'm doing the sexy without the submissive tonight."

Even seeing Wendy as a geisha didn't cheer me up. I was utterly deflated about the timing of the laptop surprise, and didn't feel like the birthday girl.

There was lots of witty banter flying about but not from me.

There was lots of chatter, but I sat mute. Even Iain (who was supposed to be feeling tired) was on top form—talking to everyone, making jokes, being charming. They all said the food was good, but to me it was tasteless. I know that nothing had changed in my situation with Gus from two days before but I'd just had my hopes raised to be mentally re-instated in a long and steady relationship, and then I'd been flung into the disarray of doubt again.

While we were waiting for our coffees at the end of the meal, Christine and I got into a stupid argument about how to spell *I'd like some game* in Italian.

"Iain, you're the expert. Will you write it down for us?" I asked.

"Sure," he said, "though to be honest I speak Italian better than I write it." He took a pen out of his jacket pocket and tore a page out of a diary. He wrote on it and passed it to me. He'd written *Vorrei della cacciagione*, but underneath he'd written something else.

You look so sad—shall I take you home?

I looked up from reading his writing and he was sitting forward with his elbow on the table, chin on his hand, watching me. We sat there looking at each other, not speaking, until Christine said "Let me see. How do you spell it then?"

I ripped the paper in two and handed her the Italian.

"OK, you win," she said, and lost interest, turning to speak to Pippa.

"Well?" said Iain. "Do you?"

"That's very sweet, but it's my party so I'd better stay."

Monday 21st October

As I was waving goodbye to Iain, the postman arrived with a letter from Gus. A nice twist.

The letter:

It's all right for you Recorder writers sitting in the autumn sunshine. Here the snow has arrived. The first big blizzard brought three feet of it in just one night. It's cold. Thank God for that last big push when I got the cabin shingled and weathertight. You cannot begin to imagine the integrity of it—burning wood you have gathered yourself in a fireplace you have constructed yourself inside walls you also built yourself.

Could you possibly do me some woolly socks like your mother used to make your father? I think they'd do the job. (and don't quote me "Beware of all enterprises that require new clothes"—this is important)

Birds:
Golden Eagle
Winter Wren (rather late –it's a migrant)
Western Screech Owl

take care etc Gus

Not a mention, not a hint about the laptop. Had he forgotten about it? Or was he wishing he hadn't sent it?

But if he's asking me to knit some socks—that must mean something. Separated spouses don't knit socks for each other, do they?

Tuesday 22nd October

I've still only received two replies from agents. What are the rest of them up to? Are they all out of the country for six months at a Book Fair in Barbados?

Pippa came round to see Richard this morning, and she brought the dogs with her. It was ridiculously early: I was still in the shower. The first I knew about it was when I switched off the shower and heard the dogs barking.

I went down for breakfast and there she was sitting sideways at the kitchen table, with her long skinny legs wound round each other six times. She was holding a piece of toast spread with blackcurrant jam and was saying "This jam is delicious. You're very domesticated, Richard. Yes you are."

Richard has some ungodly habits at breakfast time. If it's not making jam, it's entertaining women. Strange women.

Instead of waking up slowly and quietly with my head in *The Recorder* features section, I had to make small talk. I've never been good at small talk, and the only thing I seem to have in common with Pippa is that we both live in the same village.

I left them to it as soon as was polite.

She stayed all morning. The barking of the dogs was so loud that I couldn't concentrate on anything.

Wednesday 23rd October

Pippa was here for breakfast again. This time without the dogs. Personally I'd rather have the dogs than Pippa. At least they can be left in the dining room, and they don't require small talk. I wonder why she was here for breakfast if she didn't call in whilst walking the dogs. Very strange.

I went to the hospital for another session of acupuncture. I think I am in love with the acu-doc. It must be because I associate him with relaxation and calm, and because he's so sympathetic. If this goes on he won't need to use his needles. I will be able to lie down on the bed, he can pop his face round the curtain and smile and I'll immediately fall into a swoon. The nurse can come and wake me up after ten minutes with a cup of tea, and I'll be all set up for another fortnight.

Thursday 24th October

Pippa has been over for tea every night this week and it's getting me down. She is a vegetarian—and a soppy one to boot. I have nothing against vegetarians as long as they keep their scruples to themselves and don't try to proselytise. Unfortunately Pippa does not know her place. And Richard is encouraging her.

At least he has been doing all the cooking, and not expecting me to do it. He's running through his potato recipes. Monday we had pommes anna with nut roast, Tuesday it was German rosti with spicy chick pea rissoles and last night we had home made gnocchi. Tonight he was making a fancy kind of potato gratin with extra cheese, and he served this with sweet and sour leeks. We were all sitting round the kitchen table with a bottle of Valpolicella. The dogs—thankfully—had been left at home. I fancied some sausages to beef up the vegetables, as it were, and turned on

192

the grill. Richard said he'd resist, and so I bunged just two under the grill for me.

"I'm sorry, so sorry. Yes I am," said Pippa immediately. "I'm going to have to go in the other room while you cook your meat. It's the smell. Yes it is." And she unwound her interminable intertwined legs, jumped up, grabbed her wineglass and flounced out. Richard followed her into the sitting room and returned within a couple of minutes.

"That was very insensitive of you, Sally," he said.

"What?"

"Cooking meat in front of Pippa."

"What?" I asked, incredulous.

"You know how she feels about eating meat."

"But no-one's asking her to eat meat."

"You intend to eat it at the same table—and you were cooking it in front of her. She can't stand the smell."

"Then it's a good job she got out of the kitchen," I said.

"I'm disappointed in your attitude. Pippa is our guest." He can be so sanctimonious sometimes.

"She's your guest, Richard, not mine. And I suggest that if you want to keep entertaining her you find your own house to do it in. I put up with her bloody dogs, I put up with her, but if I can't cook a couple of Chatsworth sausages in my own kitchen, it's a poor do."

Friday 24th October

Richard is not speaking to me. It's his loss. Personally I enjoyed my quiet day.

Saturday 25th October

My central heating piece is in *The Recorder*. Excellent.

Wednesday 29th October

Yes! Yes!

I got an email from one of the agents. She wants to see the rest of my manuscript. Wheeeeeeeeeeeeeeeeee!!!

November

Saturday 1st November

This is what the agent's assistant said in his email:

```
Dear Sally,
Thank you for sending in Fast Work to Abi.
Can you please send Abi any more of the script
that is available.
Alistair Daltry
```

from: kate wensley
to: sally howe
subject: slush puppy
hi daise

go girl, you're in

from slush pile to bookshop in one exquisite
leap

easy

entirely excited to be friends with about-to-be-
further-read-by-agent novelist

said you'd be needing that film footage

did they talk figures???

best unsolicited manuscripts love giovanna

from: sally howe
to: kate wensley
subject: re: slush puppy
Hi Giovanna,
Did they talk figures? Who do you think I am—Zadie
Smith? To avoid further misunderstanding, I am
forwarding the agent's assistant's email so you
can see for yourself.
Can you read anything between the lines?
What is the significance of his signing just his
name, without so much as a "Best"?
Love and best,
Daisy

from: kate wensley
to: sally howe
subject: missing best
hi daise
re: agent's assistant's sign off

after extensive consideration have settled on
following explanation(s)

a/   as befits position in literary hierarchy—
agents' assistants sign off with name only
b/ he (alistair daltry) is a bad mannered little
shit
c/ he probably has a novel in the pipeline too
(suspect that most agents' assistants do) and so
is exceedingly peeved when he has to send out
letters to potential competitors asking for more
manuscript - left to himself wd dearly love to
write
- worst wishes, sod off
d/ new cool in sign offs is name only without
the best (as trend seeker, will personally look
out for this)
e/ he is too new in job to know better
f/   all of the above

best before bedtime love giovanna

Sunday 2nd November

Richard and I have been barely talking since the sausage incident.

We are speaking in terms of:

"Is there any post?"

and

"Don't forget it's bin day today."

But we're *not* speaking in terms of:

"How long do you think it will take for the agent to read my manuscript?"

and

"Do you think I should buy this rabbeting bit for my router?"

When I come down for breakfast he is never around. Before the row, even though he gets up hours before me he would be sitting at the kitchen table, and would pour me my first cup of tea when I came down and slumped in my chair. Nowadays I don't know where he is.

I think I was being unkind when I told him it was time he found a house of his own. When the time is right I'll try to smooth things over.

Monday 3rd November

"Sally," said Richard this evening, when I got back from Deep Water, "I fear I may have been taking your hospitality for granted."

"I wouldn't say that." (I was trying to heal the breech.)

"I'd like to make amends," he said. "What's in my mind is the shed. Would you like me sort it out for you? Gus doesn't seem to be very orderly in his arrangements."

What could I say but yes?

Tuesday 4th November

Richard was at breakfast this morning, wearing his boiler suit. It was looking strangely pristine.

"Right," he said after we'd discussed the new bite that's appeared on Chomsky's ear, "I'll get off and get stuck into the shed. Sheds are wonderful, aren't they?"

Then he pulled on his safety boots and strode out.

I wrote all morning and emailed a piece to KayWh about the clocks going back.

I was sitting in my study looking out of the window when Richard came upstairs and said "Can you spare a minute?"

"What?" I said, swivelling round in my chair to face him.

"I've found this parcel under Gus's work bench. I started to open it but then I thought I'd better stop. It's a bundle of letters. I think they're from a woman. I'm sorry, Sally."

My heart started to race.

"What makes you think they're from a woman?"

"They're love letters. I just saw the start of one. I didn't read on."

"Let me see," I said, jumping up and snatching the bundle. I sat down and shuffled through the letters, tears in my eyes.

"Richard! Don't ever scare me like that again! You fool!"

"Do you really not care about Gus having an affair with someone else?"

"These are letters that *I* wrote to Gus from years ago. Look—don't you recognise my handwriting?"

And there were some photos too—all of me. The seven ages of Sally.

When had he put them there? How long had they been in his shed? What a weird place to keep them. I looked at the paper they were wrapped in. It was a page from *The Times*. It was dated March 21st. He had wrapped them up just ten days before he had gone. What a sweetie.

Thursday 5th November

Today I got a rejection from the fourth agent out of six. That means two have still not responded. Meanwhile one other is munching on my manuscript—or not, as the case may be. She's probably forgotten she wanted to see it and has tossed it into the waste basket with all the other upstart provincials trying to break in.

I got a rejection email from KayWh for my piece on changing the clocks. All she said was:

```
Hi S, Can't use this—it's last week's topic.
Catch up, K.
```

I should have thought—I should have written the piece ahead of time and sent it in before the event. Doh! This realisation is very humbling. What's more, the brevity of her reply made me feel like lowly worm in the Richard Scarrey books. Now that's a cheering thought. When I'm a grandmother I'll be able to buy Richard Scarrey books again. And Shirley Hughes books. What a joy.

Friday 7th November

Some mornings Richard is not at the breakfast table. Where on earth can he be first thing in the morning?

I sat at my desk all morning, trying, and failing, to think of something to write about, because my mind was full of thoughts of Gus.

Mid morning I heard Richard's tread on the stairs and then his "Can you spare a minute?" round the door. "I've finished the shed. Come and look."

He took me down to show me the newly tidied, sorted shed.

"Look at these interesting fixings I've found under Gus's bench. This D ring, for instance."

"Oh that stuff. He's always picking up disgusting rusty rubbish when he's out on his bike."

"He has some very tasty titbits. People would pay to come in here and have a look."

I looked round at his fancy storage—old paint containers tessellated horizontally to store mastic cartridges, and butchers hooks hanging from the metal rafters with tools suspended on them. He'd made shelves from bricks and kitchen worktop off-cuts, and lined them with rectangular plastic cartons, filled with hinges, bolts, and etceteras, and all precisely labelled.

So it looks as if we are friends again, which is nice. Plus he had given me an idea for a piece about people and their shed habits.

Tuesday 11th November

Jeremy was up to his old tricks in Italian. Telling him to piss off obviously didn't have the desired effect. Treat 'em mean and keep 'em keen seems to be true.

"*Tuo marito*—I saw him at *Il Postino* with you last month—I thought he was staying away for rather longer," he said.

"Yes. He just popped back for a few days in September."

"Home for Christmas, then, I expect."

I didn't disabuse him of the idea. Why should I tell him there's four and a half months of separation still to go? And that after that it could be a life long separation—although the cache of letters throws the whole thing up in the air again.

"How are you managing, Sally? The evenings must be long and lonely now the autumn's here."

"The evenings are fine. The problem I have at the moment is the gales. The wind blew some tiles from the porch roof and now I have a leak. Could you help with that?" It was all lies—but having Richard around has done wonders for my practical knowledge. I could go on *Mastermind*, now, with home maintenance as my specialist subject.

"*Mia cara,*" he said, "*Non sono stupido*. You'll never get published if you keep coming out with the same old story line. This DIY stuff is becoming too predictable. Can't you come up with dialogue fresher than that?"

"I—"

"You have to keep your readers on their toes, *bellissima*."

Wednesday 12th November

There is no news from the scummy agent who asked to see my book, and no news from either of the other two.

Plus I got another rejection from KayWh today—this time for the shed piece. I don't know why she doesn't like it. And her email was a bit off as well.

sorry can't use. not one of your best. k.

Her latest two emails are the epistolary equivalents of thongs: they offer neither warmth nor comfort and are only big enough to cover the bare essentials. I know that editors are busy people, but why can't she treat me to a few more words? If she sent me two lines, at least I could read between them.

Up until now she has always begun with 'Hi Sally' and signed off 'Best, Kay.' Last time she said 'Hi S' and signed off 'K.' Did the fact that she used just initials indicate she was being more friendly?

And what about this time? It was all lower case and there was no greeting. Is this even more friendly? (I know Kate emails in lower case all the time, but she's in her e e cummings period.) Does lower case with KayWh mean she's decided I'm not worth the effort of holding down the shift key for capitals because I'm a deluded loser who clogs up her Inbox with trashy pieces?

Deconstructing editors' emails is like a psychologist's ink-blot test, except that what you find in the email depends on how many rejections you've had that week.

Saturday 15th November

Gus's birthday. I wonder what he's doing. The autumn colours are so glorious this year after the long warm summer, and he would have loved his birthday walk through the beech woods at Carr Bottom, if he hadn't been four thousand miles away holed up in a cabin unable to get out because of six feet of snow. Stupid man.

It was so odd not having him here to make a cake for that I made it anyway—his favourite kind—a coffee cake with coffee butter icing, and with swirls of dark chocolate all over the top.

And in his honour I made his favourite tea—spaghetti hoops with little bits of bacon and fried onion stirred in—and I got out the best tablecloth and set the table with candles and with a single damask napkin. I sat there eating in lonely splendour. Utterly miserable. Maybe I should give up this writing lark and fly off to the Rockies and live happily ever after there with Gus.

Sunday 16ᵗʰ November

I may be missing Gus but giving up writing and flying off to join him in the wilds? It must have been the big M talking yesterday. I shall stay here and become a famous writer if it kills me.

```
from: kate wensley
to: sally howe
subject: hearth and home alert
```

hi daise (or will you be henceforth addressed as media queen??)

it's out

in the public domain at last

nailed a copy of Christmas hearth and home in harrogate (in asda of all places)

whoever said the north of england is backward had better think again

the bad news is I left the said h&h at my mother's house by mistake

the good news is you look glorious, glamorous and beautiful

no worries

no mean achievement as you're in between iman (as in mrs bowie, talking about long legs in africa) and nigella (cupcake-napkin doing a spot of camera licking)

love the tinsel—love the hat—love the deck chair (at christmas? what was that about??)

star quality shining through

best baubles (chocolate colour only this season
apparently please) love giovanna

ps what the hell colour is that jersey in real
life? best call it gold—love again g

Monday 17th November

By the time I got Kate's email last night it was too late
to go down to Bakewell and hunt for a copy of *Hearth and
Home*.

So I went down this morning at eight o'clock and scoured
the shelves of both newsagents. The only copy I could find
was last month's issue.

So then I went to the Co-op who didn't have it either.
There was nothing for it but to drive into Sheffield and
swoop on WHSmith. There it was. In all it's horrible glossy
glory. And there was me inside, in the mustard jumper.
Ugh!

The only consolation is that this Christmas issue is
wrapped in cellophane and it was a real tussle in WHSmith
trying to get into it to flick through and find me, which
means that casual browsers will be deterred and only the
determined and bona fide purchasers will see the story.

I bought two copies and drove home. I took them into
the kitchen and made some coffee and sat at the table to
have a leisurely look. It was awful. It was WORSE THAN
I IMAGINED IT COULD BE. The picture was the least of
my problems. They had changed my piece so it didn't sound
like me. There was no word in the entire piece that had
more than two syllables, and they had changed the phrasing
around so that the punch lines were all in the wrong places.
To cap it all, on an ON Christmas they had made Gus sit in
the shed with a copy not of *Walden*, but of *Where's Wally?*

Nina rang this afternoon from Heathrow on her way to a

product launch in Munich. She was furious.

"Why did you not tell me about this?"

"I thought I had. Why do you sound so cross?"

"You should have asked my advice as to what to wear. If you had given me warning I could even have come up and been your own personal stylist."

"I wish you had."

"You're not fit to be let out, Mother."

"But the photo isn't the worst of it," I said. "I'm supposed to be a writer—they have me down as a writer—and yet they've completely mauled the piece. Dumbed down is an understatement."

"What do you expect? It's a consumer mag—not *The Literary Review.* Anyway, that doesn't matter. It's your image I'm worried about."

from: sally howe
to: kate wensley
subject: re:hearth and home alert

Hi Giovanna
Writers are supposed to "find their voice."
I thought I had finally found mine. Now I am
distraught because h&h have pulped it.
What's more—I look fat and old in Gus's jumper. (And
I never realised before how big those sleeves
were.) I think I have the opposite problem
to that of anorexics—I am in denial about the
reality of what I look like (as are they) but
whereas they think they look ten times as fat, I
think I look half as fat and twice as attractive.
Denial can be such a boon to the over fifties—
until one is forced to face the facts.
I am thinking of running away to sea.
Love,
Daisy.

from: kate wensley
to: sally howe
subject: h&h limited edition
hi daise

need to see the thing again so sent andy off to
matlock—alldays said there had been a bit of a
mix up with h&h

am wondering if this is anything to do with
you?
have you bribed tnt overnite to dump derbyshire's
h&h allocation?

safeway at buxton came up trumps

personally do not think you look fat on photo

admit your sleeve looks mega baggy—but that's
how sleeves are going isn't it?
baggy sleeves not to be confused with fat

be glad you weren't photographed topless

best coverage, love giovanna

Tuesday 18th November

A letter from Gus:
*Snow, snow, though many days are clear and blue with bright
sunshine.*
*Thoreau may have made eight mile tramps through deepest snow
to keep an appointment with a beech tree or a yellow birch or an
old acquaintance among the pines, but as yet I am not made of
stuff as stern. It is cosier by the fire.*
*Dan struggled up and brought some of what he maintains are
his old boots, but they look suspiciously new to me. (He said he*

considers them essential, but they aren't on my current experiment list of allowable goods—sad to say the purity of this list is being eroded daily through dire necessity) The cold 'snap' goes on and on. Arnie seems to think it's not unusual.

I still haven't opened the spaghetti hoops, though I admit I have been close. How are the socks progressing? (I may end up toeless if you don't hurry. Only joking. I hope. Or you could find something authentic from The Camping Shop in Bakewell to send—I know Thoreau said beware of all enterprises that require new clothes, but have decided that this is an enterprise that requires at least decent socks.)

Bird list
Pygmy Nuthatch
Gray Jay
Mountain Chickadee

Take care, Gus

What a bloody useless excuse for a letter. You'd think he was rationed as to the number of words he's allowed to use. Come back, the man I love to listen to, the man who talks for hours on end so I lose track and find I've not heard a word of what he's said.

Wednesday 19th November

I had another dreamy appointment with the dreamy acu-doc. I'm onto monthly appointments now. I wonder if my crush has something to do with the needles stimulating my parasympathetic nervous system. I remember one of my psychology lecturers—in those wonderful days when I was young—saying that the sympathetic nervous system is in charge of fight and flight, and the parasympathetic nervous system "sustains pleasure at bed and table."

Thursday 20th November

Incredible developments. Truly incredible.

I was completely stuck on the writing front and as it was so sunny I decided to play hooky and cycle down to Bakewell to the library.

When I got back—at about eleven—I walked into the kitchen to find Pippa installed in there, ironing.

"Hello," I said. "Why are you doing that here? I mean... I'm sorry; I didn't mean to be unfriendly. I was just a bit surprised to see you."

"Hello, Sally. Of course you must be surprised. Yes you must. But Richard said you wouldn't mind—you see, my ironing board has collapsed—metal fatigue Richard says."

"Where is Richard?" I asked.

"He's at obedience training."

My mind reeled.

"Obedience training?"

"Yes, with Ellie and Emmie. He thought it would be a good idea. Yes he did. He'll be back soon."

"Oh...I thought you meant...never mind."

Then I noticed *what* she was ironing—one of Richard's boiler suits.

The next minute the front door opened and the bloody dogs crashed into the hall and then immediately into the kitchen. They all but knocked me over in their rush to get to Pippa and in doing so got all tangled up in the iron flex and the legs of the ironing board, and the whole chaotic mess of doggy flesh and domestic whatsits would have fallen on top of me or Pippa if Richard hadn't come out of nowhere and saved us by catching the iron in one hand and the ironing board in the other. That man has brilliant hand eye co-ordination. I thought I saw him surreptitiously kick one of the dogs out of the way, too, but that could have been my imagination.

Pippa grabbed the dogs' collars, yanked them out of the kitchen and shut them in the dining room. Then she came back and stood by Richard, one arm linked through his, and the other hand stroking his arm.

"Thank you, Sweetheart," she said. Then she kissed him on the cheek.

Sweetheart? Sweetheart? Is that what she thought he was?

My face must have contorted in surprise and horror because Richard spoke to me rather than to Pippa.

"Sally, we have some news."

"Ye-e-es? Wh-a-at news?"

I sat down at the table.

"Pippa and I are going to get married."

"You can't get married, Richard. You're already married."

I blurted it out, I couldn't help it.

Pippa glared at me, and looked as if she wanted to kill me, despite being vegetarian.

Richard said: "Obviously we'll wait for the divorce to go through, but that's the intention."

So that's what's been happening. That's why he hasn't been here for so many breakfasts, and why she has been here for the others. They've been bonking day and night and I never realised.

I sat silent, my mouth open, looking at the pair of them gazing fondly at each other, until the iron hissed and broke the spell.

It's taken me all day to get used to the news. Now it's the

evening and the pair of them have gone out to *The Derbyshire Heifer* to celebrate.

I rang Wendy to tell her about all this and to get her views but she was out, so I emailed Kate—I had to tell someone. She emailed back straight away.

```
from: kate wensley
to: sally howe
subject: boiler suit man and annoying dog woman
tie the knot

hi daise
am brain numb today as a pseudonym has been
playing non-stop blondie cd—can only think in
guitar riffs

pippa in your kitchen ironing richard's boiler
suits is surely the ultimate in

a/ territorial trespass
b/ intimacy with handyman

you should have known that two people on one side
of ironing board is indication of significant
relationship

best confetti, love giovanna
```

Friday 21st November

Oh no, oh no, I have just had a horrible thought. Suppose Richard plans to stay on here until the divorce goes through. Suppose he isn't going to move out to live with Pippa straight away because of the village gossip. Perhaps she won't want to have her near-virgin status sullied.

Saturday 22nd November

The last post of the week and there is still no news on the writing front—either in terms of output from me, or in terms of letters from agents, or even KayWh emailing to say her last two emails had been sent in error, being really intended for another freelance—and that she does in fact want to use both of my latest pieces.

Monday 24th November

Richard asked me at breakfast time—one of the rare breakfasts he spends at home these days—and breakfast time is when I am at my most vulnerable and dopey.

"You know how you're always wanting to get on with your writing?" he asked.

"Yes?" (Slurping of tea.)

"And not spending time on housework?"

"Yes?" (Stroking cat.)

"And how you say you abominate cleaning?"

"Yes?" (Chomping toast.)

"How would you like it if I got someone to help with the cleaning?"

"I'd love it—you mean get a cleaning lady in?" (Perking up.)

"In a sense. Though I don't think she'd like to be called that."

"What do you mean?" (Looking confused.)

"I was thinking of asking Pippa to live here. To save her reputation."

"What?" (Waking up.)

"You know how people gossip. I thought it would be nice for her if she could move in with us until the divorce is sorted out and we can get married."

Fully awake!

"I'd really rather she didn't."

"Mmmn. I had a suspicion you might say that. Oh well, it was worth a try. I suppose I'll have to move in with her, then. We'll have to brave the wagging tongues of Mrs Mountain and the rest of the village hall committee."

Now I have recovered from the cheek of his suggestion I am feeling in celebratory mood, because he is planning to move out at the weekend. Pretty quick work for Richard.

Whooppee!

Tuesday 25th November

I nipped round to the post office to catch the last post at 4.30, and when I got back a woman called Hetty Francis from *Radio Peaks-n-Dales* had left a message on the answering machine.

from: sally howe
to: kate wensley
subject: radio peak
Hi Giovanna,
Guess what? Radio Peaks-n-Dales want me to go on their mid morning show to talk about our ON/OFF Christmases. (Stuff that down your windpipe, Kay Wharton.) Apparently the managing editor (sounds very exalted) saw the piece in *Hearth and Home*. They're not going to pay—"we are just a little local radio station and don't have a budget for paying people."
It's all very nice to be asked, but how can I go on and follow up the lie in H&H with more lies, this time speaking, in person, about how I decorate the shed etc, etc. It would be too, too awful. I really want the thing to go away, and

yet in another way it's an opportunity to get
some media exposure.
What shall I do?
Love and best,
Daisy

from: kate wensley
to: sally howe
subject: radio peaks-n-dales
hi daise

my angel

radio peaks-n-dales asks you to guest on their
mid morning show and you ask me
what shall i do???

sometimes you are unbelievable

get your (tiny) bum down there and surf the wave
of fame
if peaks-n-dales have picked this up others will
follow
—a new take on the hoary old festive chestnut—
hope you're ready to become THE national treasure
who spends christmas in her shed

richard and judy here we come

(henceforth will personally accompany you as
sleeve coach)

best mustard cutting, love giovanna

Wednesday 26th November

I braced myself and rang the Hetty Francis woman
back. I am going on the radio next Friday (December
5th). I have agreed to be interviewed about our alternative

way of arranging Christmas. I am mad. There is no other explanation.

At one point in the telephone call she said: "Did you say that this idea started off as a joke?" and I wanted to say *Yes, and it still is a joke*. It's never been more than a joke. We've never actually done an OFF Christmas. It's just that the woman at Hearth and Home got the wrong end of the stick and I went along with the story and it all got out of hand.

But I didn't have the courage to say it.

Finally, I have some sympathy for Tony Blair and his dodgy dossier on Iraq. I can see how it happened exactly. Someone on the cabinet security committee probably said "It's a shame we can't pretend that Saddam Hussein could push the nuclear button within 45 minutes of an attack," and the comment was minuted. Then the next day someone was reading the minutes, and thought the 45 minutes comment was true. And the next thing you know the Prime Minister's press secretary is in front of the Hutton Enquiry wearing a mustard cable jumper and sitting in a deckchair.

It's all very well for Kate. She just eggs me on and sits back and watches the fun. She doesn't have to live with her conscience.

Thursday 27th November

No ideas for pieces, and I don't want to start another novel until I find out if this one is any good. I am dumb. I am glum.

Saturday 29th November

Richard has gone—all of five hundred yards up the road. He's taken everything. When I went down for a coffee just now and switched on the kettle I noticed the depleted contents of the bottom shelf of the spice rack. My red clover, my cod liver oil and the glucosamine sulphate for my arthritic knees are still there, but he has taken his zinc, his gingko biloba and his ginseng. At least we can still see well enough to tell whose ageing pills are whose, as long as we're wearing our respective reading glasses.

Sunday 30th November

Iain rang this morning from Brighton.

"Is that the Sally Howe of *Hearth and Home*?"

I clapped my hand to my forehead. "Oh God, not you as well."

"Bec bought a copy for the Christmas recipes," he said. "Who was the bozo who took that photo? It's a travesty."

"Oh don't. Please don't. I'm trying to draw a veil over it."

"You have no need to draw a veil over anything."

"Yes, well. You haven't—" I stopped myself from saying *You haven't seen me with nothing on.*

"You didn't tell me about this Christmas piece. When did they come and take the pictures?"

"The beginning of September. And I haven't mentioned it because I was so embarrassed about it."

"Why? I mean, to be honest, the writing isn't as good as you usually do, but then—"

"That's it. Apart from the photo, that's it. I didn't write the bloody thing."

"But," he said, "is the substance of it true? Does Gus really hate Christmas? How very sad. I love it—the lights, the tree. At least I did when Serena was…and now, well, I'd give anything to spend Christmas with someone special."

"It must be very hard for you."

"Yes, well. Mustn't dwell on..." he tailed off. Then he said, "I'm driving up north today. I wondered if I could call in."

"You know you're welcome any time. The only thing is, Richard has moved out to live with Pippa," I said, twiddling my wedding ring with the nail of my thumb.

"I think we both know it's not Richard I come to see."

"Oh...well...oh," is all I could manage to say.

"So how would you feel if I stopped over?"

"I...yes, I mean...yes."

I heard him let out a sigh, as if he'd been holding his breath.

"That's swell. I'll see you later. Oh and don't worry about food—I'll take you out for dinner, make up for that lacklustre birthday of yours. How do you fancy Hassop Hall?"

Hassop Hall! Gus is always promising to take me there, but in eight years of living within a mile and a half of the place, we've never been.

December

Monday 1st December

Hassop Hall surpassed my expectations. It's exquisite and classy without a wisp of ostentation. There is so much to like... the drive lit by burning braziers, the grand gravel sweep, the entrance hall with open fire, carpets laid on square stone flags, a grand piano, the dining room with stark white damask tablecloths. You can stuff your post-modern urban chic eateries with their kitchens in the dining areas and their insistence you eat your bread off the table.

The food was fab (I had Haddock Meuniere) and the company pleasant, and as a perfect end to the evening Iain asked the pianist to play *The Way You Look Tonight*.

"When is your mother expecting you?" I asked him over breakfast this morning.

"She's not," he said.

"But I thought you were on your way up to Edinburgh."

"It's *next* week she's expecting me. I said I'd go up and drive her down to Bec's for a couple of weeks over Christmas."

"So...why?"

He said nothing. He just smiled at me, reaching across the table to where my hand was resting next to my mug of tea. He didn't hold my hand. He just laid his hand next to mine. Everything faded except that one small spot where his thumb touched the side of my little finger.

I broke the connection and picked up my mug. I took a nervous sip.

"And I really needed to get away from Bec's," he said, drawing back his own hand. "Have some peace. Cosmo— my grandson—is exhausting. I'd forgotten how energetic two year olds are. And with Bec expecting in January, I'm roped into helping rather a lot. Not that I mind, I mean, that's why I came over from Italy. My son-in-law has to do a lot of travelling for work, so he's not much use on the domestic front. But he is there at the moment—hence—"

"You're here."

"It's so peaceful here with you, Sally. And I love your home."

"I thought all architects were scary minimalists."

"In theory. But truth be told, since I lost Serena, I've found little comfort in minimalism." He shifted in his chair and took a sip of coffee. "Here I feel at home."

"Well, I'm happy for you to stay," I said. "But I think I'd better ask Richard to park his car in the drive while you're here. Halt the tongues of the village gossips. It's not as if there's anything to gossip about."

Not yet.

I wrote in the morning, and we spent the afternoon touring the villages in the Derbyshire Dales looking for weather vanes—as part of Iain's picture project.

It was damp and dull—typical December weather—and filthy underfoot. Iain was sporting a new brown Barbour jacket ("Bought for my new rural persona," he said.) When we got out of the car on Wentworth Lane to look at the weather vane on the farm half way down, he walked round to the back of his car and opened the boot. He had his wellies in there in a zip up bag, sitting primly next to a dustbuster vacuum cleaner and an immaculate safety helmet. It was shiny and yellow.

"Why do you have a hard hat in the boot?" I asked. "I thought you were retired."

"Old habits die hard I guess. And to be honest it opens doors—you never know when you might be invited into a hard hat area."

Old habits? The hat was new. And who keeps wellies in a zip up bag? No man I know.

We had a civilised afternoon tea at the Derbyshire Craft Centre—ace treacle tart—what a joy to be with a man who likes pit stops.

We got back in time for *Neighbours,* but of course I couldn't watch it, nor could I video it without Iain wanting to know what I was videoing. What would he think?

What a bind. It's all very well having pleasant and personable male company for a week, but what a sacrifice to miss five consecutive episodes of *Neighbours.* While Iain was outside washing his wellies (which as far as I could see had one tiny streak of mud on each side) I sneaked upstairs and rang Alicia from Deep Water and asked her to record it for me. Thank God I discovered she's a fellow fan; there are so few of us about.

In the evening I lit the log burning stove and Iain and I watched my video of *It's a Wonderful Life.* Life does feel pretty wonderful this week.

Tuesday 2nd December

This morning we did some more touring. Hang my writing.

It's really odd. Whenever Iain and I go out somewhere together, we get ready and seem to be coming through the hall at the same time but I always end up standing outside the front door waiting for him to come out, so I can lock up.

This morning it was raining and I was fed up of standing waiting for him like piffy on a rock bun so I went back in to see what was keeping him and there he was in front of the mirror, combing his hair. Hmm.

On today's trip in pursuit of the vernacular he alerted me to the wonders of chimney pot detail. What with weather vanes yesterday and chimneys today, the skyline has taken on a new significance.

On the way home I called in at Redmonton post office for Christmas stamps, and Billy Bathgate greeted me even more effusively than usual.

"Och, but it's wonderful to see you, Mrs Howe. I'm glad you don't feel you're too important now to patronise your local shops."

"Pardon?"

"Now you're famous."

"Pardon?"

"This here—" and he turned round and pointed to the *Hearth and Home* article complete with hideous photograph, which he had pinned above his shelf of onions.

"Oh that. You surely don't read *Hearth and Home*, do you?" Then I remembered his prize-winning entry in last year's Art in the Community competition—an exquisite, hand-crafted lampshade. Maybe he *did* read *Hearth and Home*.

"No, but Mrs Mountain does. She brought it in to show me so I ordered an extra copy."

"Oh yes. Mrs Mountain," I said weakly.

"So, I've taken the liberty of ordering you an extra Christmas wreath—I've doubled your usual order."

"But why?"

"Well, Mrs H, with your other half coming home for Christmas, and you celebrating Christmas in the shed, I thought you'd be needing one for the front door and one for the shed."

He just doesn't get it. Any of it.

I said I'd just have the one wreath—for the shed—but didn't bother to put him right on Gus's return. The less Billy Bathgate knows, the better. It's a wonder he didn't mention Iain.

But bugger, I hadn't thought about locals reading the piece in *Hearth and Home*. I imagined all the readers being the great British public—not real people who know me. Does the piece on my "OFF" Christmas mean that I have to pretend I'm not doing Christmas this year and so will have to buy all my Christmas provisions in secret? The very year that Gus is away, I am going to have to curtail the wildest excesses of the celebrations. I had been planning to get some of those outside lights to string up in the silver birch by the gate, for instance. And now I can't.

Wednesday 3rd December

I'm worrying about my radio "appearance" on Friday.

I have decided that for the whole of December—not just for my trip to the radio station—I will wear that make-up I bought when I went for my John Lewis make-over in the spring. I need to work hard on the glamour front. And it has nothing to do with Iain being here.

Also, I realised I needed a new coat for Friday, the idea being that at least I would *arrive* at the studio looking smart. My red duffle is cosy but it's casual, and my ancient Barbour jacket is more shabby chic than a nineties sofa.

Richard dropped in while I was talking to Iain about this. He was walking the dogs. I invited him and Pippa to Christmas dinner and he seemed very pleased. I may as well make the most of Gus's absence and have visitors for Christmas.

Iain offered to come shopping with me, but I didn't fancy prancing around in different garments while he scrutinised my appearance, so I suggested he take Richard on another picture tour instead.

"Weren't you wanting to look at door jambs?" I said. "They're right up Richard's street." They're certainly not up mine.

I bundled them off, and rang Wendy and asked her to come shopping.

She turned up as equestrian Wendy in cream jodhpurs, black riding boots and a pink puffa jacket. ("No I don't need a bloody horse, Sally—this is a look, not a lifestyle!")

After two hours search we eventually found a coat: the right colour (black), and the right price, and an interesting double breasted style, classic but with a dash of the military, suggested by inserts and extra stitching. Unfortunately it was cropped.

I pranced in front of the mirror, wailing "The coat is me, but it doesn't cover my bum."

"So what?" said Wendy. "Buy it." And I did.

But she is thin and I am not. She has no inkling of the seductive but disastrous implications of the cropped top for someone with child bearing hips, of which the doctor said "there's plenty of room in there for a big ten pounder." (Admittedly this was when I was pregnant with Dan, twenty eight years ago, but the comment is still engraved on my body image.)

When he saw it Iain said nothing—an exemplar of tact.

Richard's comment was "You look like Michael Jackson from the front, and a dinner lady from behind."

And he's right.

It is not enough for a shopping partner—i.e. Wendy—to share one's age, one's taste, to understand one's lifestyle, to be honest, and to recognise when one's blood sugar needs a boost. She must also have the same sized bum. Or bigger.

The coat will have to go back.

Another cosy evening by the fire tonight. Iain sitting in one armchair—me in the other. He didn't want to watch *Channel 4 News*.

"I can't be doing with all that politics—a two-minute news bulletin once a day is all I need, Sally."

We chatted about this and that. There were some interesting subjects, such as why Christmas morning telly no longer has Rolf Harris visiting children's hospitals. But sometimes Iain drivels on about dull things like drains.

"Ah, drains. When I was still working I invariably specified Hepworth fittings..." I drifted off here and only cut in again for "...manholes can be very exciting..." where I dipped out again until "...drains are all about falls," he finished.

We read quietly for a bit as well—him with *The Recorder*, me with Anita Shreve.

"It's like honey on my soul, Sally," he said, looking up from the features section.

I was engrossed in Anita Shreve. "Sorry? Honey on your what?"

"Toasting my toes across from a lovely woman. I feel right at home. And safe. Truth be told, I never thought I'd feel like this again."

"That's sweet."

"Yes it is. It surely is. And last night was the first time I—"

I closed my book. "Yes?"

"No. It doesn't matter, I don't want to burden you with it, I—"

His voice had gone low and quiet. He was gazing into the fire and rubbing his hand up and down on the chair arm. I noticed for the first time the dark hairs on the backs of his fingers.

"Tell me," I said.

"Well…"

I got out of my chair and knelt in front of the fire, stretching out my hand and touching his. "Go on."

"I have this recurring nightmare—it's a flashback, really—it's finding Serena in bed, dead, after the brain haemorrhage."

"Iain, that's awful. Awful."

The light from the flames of the fire threw shadows round his cheekbones.

"I have it every night. But, last night," he cleared his throat and ruffled his hair on the top of his head. "Last night was the first night I haven't dreamed it since, well, since she died." He reached up and smoothed his hair in the place where he'd just ruffled it. "That's how safe I feel with you."

Thursday 4th December

Today we went for another tour of villages. Who'd have thought you could spend all day looking at the cracks between bricks and stones? And letter boxes! If he shows me another letter box I'll shove his head through it.

When we got back, I started thinking about the radio appearance. My hair has been driving me mad all week. It needed two inches cutting off the bottom, but unfortunately I didn't realise this until after tea when all the hairdressers in Bakewell were shut. I mentioned it to Iain and he said he thought my hair was lovely.

"No it's not. You're just being nice."

"You're getting nervous about tomorrow, aren't you? Don't forget it's radio, not TV."

"That hardly matters—I'll still be mixing with sharp media types. My hair really does need attention. Look at all the split ends," I said, lifting up my plait and examining the end of it against the light.

"It's OK, Sally, it really is, but if you want me to trim two inches off I'd be happy to do it. I know my way around with a pair of scissors. I used to cut Serena's."

I've always thought one of the sexiest scenes in a film is that one in *Out of Africa* where Robert Redford washes Meryl Streep's hair under an African sun, with soapy water from a jug. Unfortunately I don't have Meryl Streep's bone structure nor her complexion, nor am I still a winsome thirty-something. I look appalling with my hair wet and scraped off my face, so I asked Iain to cut mine dry.

"Really?" he said. "I have my Vidal Sassoon Professional upstairs."

"Your own hairdryer?"

"Sure, why not?"

"I suppose your hair is very thick," I said.

Goodness. A man with his very own hairdryer.

I sat down on a kitchen chair and Iain undid my plait. His hands were gentle but confident. He ran his fingers through the long strands to loosen them and spread my hair out on my back and when his hands glanced my shoulders I trembled. He brushed my hair with strong sensuous sweeps. Then he started to cut it. Every time he touched my scalp I felt a tingle. I was so aware of every contact between his fingers and my skin I even wondered if my hair was standing on end with all the electricity. It never feels like that when Janet cuts it at *Joan's Hair Salon* in Bakewell.

When he had finished, he came round to hold it out at each side and check the length—oh—his fingers brushed my cheek and I thought he was going to kiss me and I drew back.

He didn't.

Then I regretted drawing back.

I'm so confused.

We sat by the fire again tonight and Iain took out photos of his daughter and grandson from his wallet. He told me about his house in Italy and showed me a photograph of it. Serena was stretched out on a sunlounger in the garden, smiling. She looked elegant but friendly.

"I'd love you to come out and stay," he said.

"I do like Italy. I've been to Venice twice and it was more perfect than I imagined it."

"What did you like best?" he said, eagerly. "The architecture? The galleries?"

"The colours. I couldn't believe the colours—corals, ochres, terracottas, creams—all set against the blue-grey shot silk canals."

"Yes, the colours," he said. "It's the colours."

"I like the architecture, too, of course."

"You should come to Italy. I could take you on a grand tour—there's so much I'd like to show you. And getting away from my ex-pat friends in Padua would make me practice my Italian. I want to improve it," he said.

"Maybe." I said. It sounded heavenly—driving round Italy with Iain.

Friday 5th December

I may have been confused in the kitchen when Iain cut my hair, but in the dream I had last night I was pretty sure of myself and so was he.

For my *Peaks-n-Dales Radio* interview this morning I wore Nina's hand-me-down trench coat. It looked fine over her hand-me-down trouser suit. I arrived at 8.45 for a 9 a.m. appointment.

Iain had wanted to come with me—to drive me down—

but I persuaded him to go looking for more vernacular details.

"Wasn't there something in Winster you wanted to see?" I said.

"It's a house Pevsner mentions. It's stone with rusticated string courses."

"Yes, well, you go and look at your rustic string courses, and I'll see you at tea time. I'll probably pop into the shops after the radio session and start my Christmas shopping, so don't hurry back on my account." I thought I might just be able to crash out in front of the lunchtime edition of *Neighbours* if I was lucky.

At the radio station the receptionist asked me to take a seat in the foyer while she buzzed Hetty Francis. I leafed through a back copy of *Hello*—which is something I only see every six months in the dentist's waiting room. I thought I was fairly clued up but was shocked to find that I knew none of the people pictured on the front, and was just about to go and ask the receptionist who Gareth Gates was, when a young woman drifted up to me and said "Sally Howe?"

"That's me. How do you do?" I said, standing up, while throwing down the mag on the coffee table and gathering up my coat, my umbrella and my handbag, all in one ungainly fumble.

"Have you had your colours done?" she asked. "You look so different from your picture in *Hearth and Home*."

"Oh, that!" I said. "That was all a terrible blunder."

"Really?" she said as she gave me an incredulous once over. She was young. She looked about 25. She was probably thinking *Why on earth do they want this old codger on the show?*

We went upstairs to a waiting area with five brightly coloured Ikea arm chairs arranged around a coffee table, and a drinks machine in the corner. Then, as I drank the tea she had fetched from the machine, she gave a quick run-down on what I should expect. Once on air, Frank Dreyfuss would ask me a few questions about Christmas, my attitude, Gus's attitude, and how we had decided to solve our differences—the whole story. I would be on air for about ten minutes. It sounded easy.

She left, saying she'd be back at half past nine to walk me to the studio. I finished my tea and looked around for another magazine. Plonked on the top of the pile on the coffee table was—yes, you guessed it—the Christmas issue of *Hearth and Home*.

It was only when I saw it that it really came home to me what I was about to do. *But there is still time to get out of it,* I thought. I got up from my chair, threw down the magazine and turned to walk out. But before I could make it to the stairs, Hetty Francis came running down the corridor and grabbed me by the arm.

"Sorry, Sally. Bit of a crisis. We need you, like, *now*."

She was burbling about a weather report and lost transmission on an outside broadcast, but I wasn't listening. I was panicking about the fact that that there was now no escape from the mess.

We pelted down the corridor and into a large room with glass walls. There were two humungous computer screens, phone lines everywhere, and a woman wearing headphones sitting behind a computer saying "Get her through. Quick. Get her *in* there."

Hetty Francis bundled me through a door into another room where Frank Dreyfuss was sitting behind an oval table. He had several computers, and a big mike, and he was wearing headphones.

Hetty shoved me in the solar plexus and I fell backwards into a chair on the opposite side of the table to Frank. Then she rammed some earphones on my head and turned on the mike in front of me and said:

"What's your name?"

Didn't she know who I was?

"What's your name?" she barked.

"Sally Howe."

"What did you have for breakfast?"

"I didn't. I was too nervous."

She looked through the glass wall at the other woman who made a thumbs up sign, and then she said "OK, Frank. You're on."

Not only was there no chance to get out of the broadcast, there was no chance to feel nervous.

Frank Dreyfuss started talking into his mike.

"How many of you are dreading the festivities to come?" he said. "And how many of you can't wait to get stuck into one long round of partying? And how many of you live with someone who has the exact opposite view of Christmas to you? My guest this morning has solved the everlasting problem of Christmas conflict. Her name is Sally Howe, and she's from Stoneymoor, near Bakewell. Sally, tell me, do you like Christmas?"

"I love it."

"Then what's your problem?"

"My husband hates it."

"And how long have you two been married?"

"32 years."

"Tell me, then, what he's like at Christmas?"

And it went on from there. I had no time to think, no time to be nervous, and then it was all over. Frank Dreyfuss was taking off his headphones and leaning across the table to shake my hand.

"Sorry about the hasty introduction. Everything's up the Khyber this morning. My EPNS is buggered, we lost our syndicated weather; you name it, it's stuffed. Hasty introduction? I should say *lack* of introduction. Have you ever worked on radio?"

"Er, no. Why?"

"You handled it like a pro. All that scurrying at the beginning, no warm up, no intro, and you weren't a bit phased. Most impressive. Like a pro."

When I walked out of the studio, all I wanted to do was go home and unwind on the sofa with *Neighbours*. I was having withdrawal symptoms.

When I pulled up into our drive, though, Iain's car was there. The table light was on in the sitting room, and so was the telly. I peeped in the window. He was watching *East Midlands Today*: the lovely Lisa was delivering the regional news.

He turned round and saw me and waved. I waved back and went in the front door.

"Don't let me disturb you," I called from the hall as I took off my coat.

"I'll switch it off," he called back from the sitting room. "You come in and tell me how you are. I heard you on the radio. I sat in a lay-by and listened. You were excellent. Real presence." He was in the hall now smiling at me.

"No, Iain, you go back and watch the telly. Go on, you're missing your news."

"I'm not a great one for the news. To tell you the truth, and I hardly dare admit it to you—a writer—but I'm waiting for *Neighbours*. I know it's appalling, but I got hooked on it at Bec's."

Oh my.

After we'd watched *Neighbours*—which oddly didn't feel so wickedly indulgent nor as much fun as usual—we shared some lunch. Then I went upstairs to lie down and recover from the excitement of the morning. Iain meanwhile said he wanted to do something to repay my hospitality. Were there any jobs around the house that needed doing?

"There's just one, Iain. I've always wanted the paint stripping off that built-in cupboard in the kitchen—the one in the alcove. Could you do that for me?"

"Lead me to the blow torch."

I gave him the keys for Gus's shed and told him to take what he needed.

I was lying in bed listening to the afternoon theatre on Radio 4 when I heard Iain swearing and banging around in the kitchen. This was followed by a burning smell drifting up to the bedroom.

I got out of bed and scuttled downstairs calling "Everything all right?"

When I got in the kitchen the burning smell was intense, and Iain was grim faced.

"It's so embarrassing. I'm so sorry, Sally. I've scorched your wood."

"My God, so you have!" I said, not very tactfully. "Och well, dinna fass yoursel'" I said in a weird mock accent untraceable to any known region—I do this when I don't know what to say to cover up what I'm feeling—intense irritation in this case—"dinna fass yoursel'" I said again "— I'll get Richard to sort it out next week."

Iain cooked tea tonight to make up. He's an excellent cook. Bloody good job.

We sat next to each other on the sofa and watched an old *Friends* video. My kind of Friday night. The fire was warm and so was Iain, and he was getting closer and closer on the sofa and Ross was on the brink of kissing Rachel, and I was just wondering what it would be like to kiss someone with no beard after thirty years of snogging through facial hair, and then I wondered what Iain's naked feet looked like—whether they'd be sexy like the rest of him or whether he'd have squidgy toes—and what he would think about

231

my falsie, when suddenly I was overcome by a hot flush and that unbearable suffocating feeling that comes with them. I pulled away and jumped off the sofa and rushed to the front door for air, and Iain seemed to take it personally and when I returned to the sofa the mood was broken. Bugger.

Saturday 6th December

Every night I dream of Iain and me, and they're not domestic dreams. Then I come down to breakfast in the morning and sit respectably with him over my toast. It's weird.

More jobs around the house today. I got out the Christmas tree lights late this afternoon to check that they were all working, as I want to get a tree next week. I thought Iain might like to redeem some DIY pride with a bit of electrical fiddling. And there was certainly the opportunity because when I plugged them into the extension they tripped a circuit. It was a dark December afternoon—half past four-ish and impossible to see anything with no lights.

"Iain—the electricity consumer unit with all the trip switches is in the cupboard under the stairs. I'm hopeless. I can never tell which one has gone off. Will you come and show me?"

I led him to the cupboard and we squeezed inside, crushed up against the Dyson, the newspaper recycling box, and fifty pairs of Gus's old cycling shorts hanging on the back of the door with a load of coats. It was a tight squash in there and in the dark my sense of smell was heightened. The air was heavy with a cocktail of Iain's Dunhill aftershave and the distinctive whiff of his new Barbour jacket.

I took the torch off the hook that Gus keeps for emergencies and switched it on. We were standing cheek to cheek, with me holding the torch and him looking at the board of switches, and it was one of those defining moments. I could feel it. My hand holding the torch was shaking.

Iain turned round to face me and put his hand on mine. "You need steadying," he said. "And also, maybe this."

He kissed me, and I kissed him back, and I was thinking how exciting it was kissing someone who shaved, and wondering where it would end. And just as I was on the point of stopping thinking and starting to enjoy it, somewhere in the far reaches of my consciousness a door banged shut.

Then there was a voice.

"Hello? Ma? You there?" shouted Sam. "What the fuck's going on? And whose is that car in the drive next to Richard's?"

I was expecting Sam home from Uni *next* weekend for his Christmas vacation, not today.

"Sam!" I called, emerging from the cupboard. "What a nice surprise!"

Sunday 7th December

Iain left for Edinburgh after breakfast. It seemed the best idea. He said he'd keep in touch by phone. Oh my goodness: I hope he meant talking and not phone sex.

Sam seems to have brought absolutely everything home this time—more than he usually brings home for the Christmas vacation. He said he was worried about burglaries.

It took three trips to the front gate to empty everything out of the taxi that had brought him from the station. It just shows that they can manage to transport themselves and all their clobber if they really want to. Oh God, I'm starting to sound like Gus, who—every time he took any of the three of them to or from Uni—repeated, in excruciating detail, how he travelled to Manchester Uni for his first term on his own, on the train with his motorbike, with guitar and four suitcases. On arrival at Piccadilly Station he then loaded the baggage into a taxi, gave it the address of his digs, and followed behind on his bike. And now here am I repeating it in his absence, talking bollocks. Threads of Gus are inextricably interwoven round the neurons and axons in my brain. Separation or no separation, whether he's here or on the other side of the world, no matter what else is going on in my life, I can't imagine ever being free of thoughts of Gus.

Sam is a chip off the old block. The first thing he said this morning was "What d'you think's going to happen when they vote next month?"

"What vote?"

"Blair's moved the vote on education to January. He's virtually saying 'Back me or sack me.' Haven't you been watching the news?"

"Well—"

"There's no chance that the lily–livered, wash-out backbenchers who backed him on the Iraq war will stand up against him on education. They're pathetic, the lot of them. Seriously, Ma, why don't you know all this? What have you been doing all week?"

Monday 8th December

I got an email from *Hearth and Home* to say that *SWISH Radio* (*SWISH* is a mnemonic for South West Sheffield) wanted to contact me. Kate said the thing would snowball and she's right.

I rang the contact woman at *SWISH* and have agreed to go on air on Thursday for their afternoon phone-in. I'm not worried: I know what to expect now: lies, lies and more lies. A loss of all scruples. That Kate Wensley is a bad influence, and no mistake.

I rang up Chatsworth Farm Shop this afternoon and ordered a free range turkey for Christmas dinner. With me and Richard and Nina and Tim, there's enough people to make a turkey worthwhile. Last year there was only Gus, Sam and me, and Christmas dinner was a minimalist affair. Sam ate Quornburgers, Gus had a bacon sandwich, and I had a duck breast. I'm really looking forward to sharing a decent sized bird.

I'm sure I can find a decent veggie recipe for Pippa and Sam, but if not they can always savage some of Richard's festive potatoes.

Deep Water was fairly lacklustre tonight, but Alicia had brought the *Neighbours* tape for me so it was still worth going.

Tuesday 9th December

Last night I lay in bed drooling at the thought of the turkey leftovers on Boxing Day. But these visions were soon overcome by the imagined disgusted groans from the veggie contingent, not only at the size of the massive bird on the Christmas dinner table, but as they opened the fridge door later that day and were confronted by the carcase. I saw myself on Christmas night, not playing games of Balderdash with everyone, but sitting alone at the kitchen table carving up the turkey in order to secrete cold cuts under a plain tinfoil wrapper, to save the tender minded veggies from offence.

I have chickened out. I phoned the Farm Shop and cancelled the turkey and ordered an organic free range chicken instead. It was easy, and the Chatsworth man was soothing and sweet.

I was thinking about going shopping with Wendy and how—before the coat fiasco—I had thought she was the perfect shopping partner. It gave me an idea for a piece on ideal shopping partners which I duly wrote and emailed to KayWh.

I thought I'd be enjoying the run up to Christmas rather more than I am. Every year, for example, Gus and I have a row about the Christmas tree and I was looking forward to a conflict-free purchase. This is what usually happens:

He says "Can we afford one?"

I say "Don't be stupid."

He says "Why do we have to have it cluttering up the sitting room?

I say "Gus, it's not exactly vertical. Can you please adjust it?"

This year I asked Sam to come with me to fetch the tree.

"You shouldn't be buying a real one. Don't you care about the environment? You should go artificial," he said.

"But they're plastic—which comes from oil, Sam. A non renewable resource. At least I shall recycle a real one. The district council runs a special scheme."

"Hmmpph."

"Anyway, I hate artificial trees—they're naff. And this is the one Christmas I get to enjoy myself without Gus moaning on about it. Don't ruin it. It's one of the perks of having him gone for a year."

I managed to sway him: his rampant opinions do spring from a tender heart, and I was sounding genuinely upset.

"Oh go on, then."

He put the roof rack on the car, and I drove us to Chatsworth Garden Centre.

"Why have you come here?"

"They have the best selection."

"But I don't want to support the aristocracy. Rapists,

pillagers. Their wealth is built on the sufferings of the ordinary people."

"Sam—"

"No. Absolutely not. I'm sitting here. And don't expect me to help with carrying it, tying it on, getting it off, carrying it into the house or setting it up. I don't want any part of it."

Then I remembered. "Sam, it's all right. This garden centre has nothing to do with Chatsworth Estates. It's owned by someone else. It's called Chatsworth because it's on their land—that's all."

So I got my tree. Sam did all the honours. What luxury to drive in our gate, get out of the car and put the kettle on while he unloaded it and carried it into the house for me. It's five feet across and eight feet high and it's standing at one end of the sitting room blocking out the light and looking like a giant house plant, because with all my media engagements and my writing there's no time to decorate it.

Wednesday 10th December

Hooray! I am re-instated as a *Recorder* contributor! KayWh has just emailed to say that they are going to use my piece on finding the perfect shopping partner on the leisure section shopping page.

On the home front, as opposed to the writing front, things are not so sweet. I am getting sick to the back teeth of Sam's continual moans.

"Why did you buy this cereal?" he asked, at dinner time, as he munched through a casserole dish full of chocolate cornflakes.

"I bought it for you. You don't think I bought it for me, do you?"

"But it's made by Cutworths's—that's the multinational

who are flooding underdeveloped countries with baby milk."

"So what shall I get for you, my precious one? Muesli from the wholefood shop?"

"Yuk! No thanks. I'm a vegetarian not a health freak."

"I thought you were a vegan."

"Changed—I'm a veggie now."

"So what am I supposed to get by way of cereal?"

"I'll make do with the Co-op's own brand cocopops. At least the Co-op have heard of Fair Trade."

Thursday 11th December

The visit to the SWISH radio studio was calmer and more civilised than the one to *Peaks-n-Dales*. The introductory routine was similar. Then at the appointed time they showed me into the ops room with the glass walls and they sat me down in the corner. Finally, during a break for the news and a trail (I've even got the jargon, now—it's "trail" not "trailer") I was led through to meet Johnny Hazlewood, showed my seat, and they tested the sound level on my mike.

Then Johnny H gave a short introduction and asked me to tell the listeners about our ON/OFF Christmas compromise, and about the shed, and then invited people to call in. "Our lines are open now—give us a call."

The first one was instant: an old codger called Albert.

"Good morning, Johnny. Good morning, Sally. Your story about Christmas in the shed reminds me of Christmas during the war, when the bombers were flying over Sheffield every night. People say Leeds is so much finer—those buildings in the centre, you know, they say they're champion—but they never had the bomb damage we did."

"Yes, Albert," I said. "But why does my Christmas in the

shed remind you of that?"

"Well, we went down the working men's club and had our Christmas party under the billiard table during an air raid."

"That's so interesting, Albert, and a lovely example of people not letting the war get in the way of their enjoyment of the festivities."

"OK," said Johnny, winking at me. "Onto the next caller. We have Fred Baines on the line from Grindleford."

"I know 'ow you feels, sweetheart, being sent out to the shed. Me wife makes me go outside to me greenhouse for a smoke. But it's no 'ardship. I reckon it's good for the tomatoes. I always 'ave a bumper crop. I'm ripening the last of 'em inside now on me windowsill in the porch. I'm planning on having 'em with a nice bit of 'am for me tea on Christmas Day. No 'ardship."

He sounds like Bert Fry on The Archers, I thought. This phone-in lark appeared to be a doddle. All you had to do was get the listeners talking, and then appear to listen.

The next caller was called Adrian.

"Can you tell me whether you have heating in the shed?" he asked. He sounded camp.

"Er, well," I dithered. Christmas in the shed with no heating didn't sound convincing. Then I remembered something Richard had said. "Yes. One of those small ceramic heaters you see advertised in the colour supplements."

"I don't expect it's as warm as in the house, though, is it? What effect does the lower temperature have on the needle drop? I'm wondering if you can recommend a type of tree that doesn't drop needles? I adore my tree, but my friend always complains about my needle drop."

"Oh, needle drop. Yes—I always get a Norwegian spruce. They have attractively textured needles for a slightly more rustic look."

"Which is very appropriate if your festivities are in the shed," interrupted Johnny. "Thanks, Adrian. Now on line two we have Pearl Dinsdale. Pearl, what's your question?"

"I was just wanting to say that when there was an air raid in the middle of our Christmas party my mother says 'Sod the Germans—they're not spoiling my party. I'm staying here and they can bomb me as hard as they like.'"

I wondered why they were all talking about the war. Was it only pensioners who listened to Johnny Hazlewood?

"And now we have Sarah from Dore," said Johnny.

"Hello Sally. Hello Johnny. Do you have a view on fairies on the top of trees, Sally?"

Did I have a view on fairies? Of course I bloody did—I was on the radio, wasn't I?

The next woman was called Emily. She said that she and her husband were arguing over what to put on the tree.

"He wants silver baubles and I want red ones. At the moment we're not speaking."

My heart bled for her.

"Well, Emily. From where I'm standing—or sitting—I think you're lucky to have a partner who cares about Christmas enough to argue. Why don't you take a leaf out of our book, and each do your thing on alternate years?"

"Right, thanks Sarah," said Johnny. "We just have time for one more caller. OK. Mrs Mountain from Stoneymoor. That's your village, isn't it Sally? Over to you Mrs Mountain."

Mrs bloody Mountain. I never dreamed anyone I knew would listen to local radio. What the hell did she want?

"Good morning, Mr Hazlewood. I would like to know why Mrs Howe, who says she is having an OFF Christmas this year, which means Christmas in the shed, why, if that is the case, I saw her son carrying an enormous Christmas tree through her front door yesterday afternoon."

Bloody hell. Bloody hell. I had the biggest hot flush I'd

had in months. I looked beseechingly at Frank, but he just smiled and raised an eyebrow.

"That was for my shed, Mrs Mountain."

"It looked mighty big to fit in your shed, I must say."

"Yes, well," I said. "I wonder if you have a story about the war, Mrs Mountain. Several of our callers have told us about how they spent Christmas during the war. Have you a favourite Christmas story?"

Bingo. She launched into telling us about the year her brother put washing soda crystals in the sugar bowl at the Christmas party for a joke. I have no idea what happened, because I was panicking and hoping no one would ring in and tell the listeners that my husband was away in the USA, so what the hell difference did it matter how I was spending my Christmas this year.

But Mrs Mountain was the last caller. Thank God.

"Great value," said Johnny. "You headed that last one off at the pass pretty smartish. Nice footwork."

As I left through the ops room, the producer got up and walked round to the front of her desk and shook my hand. "We've had a record number of callers this afternoon, Sally. Well done. If you do anything else that's interesting or off beat, I'd love to have you back for another phone-in. Keep in touch. And Happy Christmas, wherever you're spending it."

When I got home Sam was out somewhere so I had no-one with whom to debrief.

There was a message on the answer phone from Iain, phoning from Edinburgh—thank God Sam was out! "Sorry I missed you. But to be honest, Sally, it's not past tense, it's continuous present. I miss you all the time."

I lay in a lavender and bergamot foam bath, thinking about him. I dozed off into a world of foreign holidays and fancy restaurants and easy evenings by the fire and came to my senses when the water was cold and my fingers were as wrinkled as walnuts.

Friday 12th December

Richard popped in at breakfast time (with the blessed dogs) to show me what he's bought Pippa for Christmas: an electric toothbrush.

"I'm surprised that DeWALT haven't designed a toothbrush attachment to fit onto an electric drill," he said. "No batteries, and it could give variable speeds. It might be a bit unwieldy, but the unwieldiness would be offset by the raw power. Worth the trade off. Plaque would be running scared."

"You ought to write to DeWALT and suggest it," I said.

"I might just do that. Look—I bought one for myself as well. I thought Pippa and I might clean each other's teeth as a sort of post modern grooming."

There was no answer to that.

from: kate wensley
to: sally howe
subject: celebrity status

hi daise
brill phone in—caught you on car radio
just had a thought (admit, rare thing at this
time of year)

daise's christmas book—how to decorate your shed
and other festive hints—next year's christmas
best seller from celeb daisy rowland? definite
commission potential?

best way to prevent needle drop is to hang out
in the greenhouse love giovanna

It's all very well for Kate. There I was, my reputation hanging by a thread, meanwhile she's enjoying the fun from the safe anonymity of her Espace.

Tell me again why I'm doing all of this? Exposing myself in this way?

Saturday 13th December

What a treat to see myself in print again. My piece is right across the top of the shopping page. Score!

Mrs Mountain can go and swing from the railway bridge.

Iain liked my piece.

"I think you're so clever the way you turn everyday happenings into entertaining prose. But you know, I was also thinking—"

"Yes?"

"You should come shopping with me. I might turn out to be the ideal shopping partner. Why don't you come down to London and I'll come up on the train from Brighton and we'll hit Oxford Street?"

"That's very sweet. But I don't think I'd trust you to be honest about what suits me."

"You always look nice—whatever you're wearing."

"That's exactly what I mean."

After that we talked about Italy: where I would like to go, what he would like to show me. We started to plot a trip of most desirable places—like fantasy league football. I can't see it happening—but it's fun to mess about.

Sunday 14th December

Strangely, the Christmas season isn't the same without Gus moaning on about it, without him sitting in the corner complaining about consumerism and how he hates having people visiting, and about the amount of money that I'm spending.

At breakfast time in Christmas week, he always sits at the breakfast table reading out the black and tragic Christmas stories from the paper. *Woman dies on sleigh bell ride*, *Christmas lights cause fatal fire*, *Santa falls off chair and slips a disc*. It seems weird without him doing that every morning, so I am collecting all such clippings from the paper and I'm going to enclose them with my New Year letter to cheer him up.

Monday 15th December

I have felt awful all day—tired and headachy—is it the big M, or is all this media attention proving too much for my artistic sensibilities? Whatever, I'm going to give the Deep Water Christmas party a miss and go to bed.

Tuesday 16th December

There was a note on the kitchen table this morning from Sam. Iain rang last night after I'd gone to bed. No message.

I felt better this morning. I got up early and wrote a funny and highly politically incorrect piece about the trials of Christmas when you have an ecologically-minded veggie in the family, and I emailed it to KayWh. She emailed me back immediately saying she wished I'd sent the piece earlier because she loved it but had no space left before Christmas. She obviously wasn't just being smarmy, because she said she'd forwarded the piece to Daphne Vicars, the chief features editor for the *Recorder* (not just the leisure section.)

Fingers crossed.

It was obviously my day today because just before dinner time, someone from the *Today* programme rang me from London. I just typed that as if it was the most normal thing to happen on a Tuesday morning. Can you believe it? They want me on *Today*, tomorrow. I have to be down at some place in Matlock for 6 a.m.—a remote studio for the BBC—where someone will meet me and fix me up in a room in an office with an ISDN line. I will be on some time between 6 a.m. and 8.30. That's all they can say. I'm going to be on National Radio. The BBC. Watch your step, Mariella Frostrup.

Then what happened was someone rang me from *Midshires TV*. I was so blasé they must have thought I was pissed. They want me to make an appearance on their evening news programme on Friday.

Will the media circus never stop?

Tonight was the Italian Class Christmas party. We had a combined effort with the other language classes that meet on Tuesdays—Spanish and German. Everyone was supposed to go in fancy dress, dressed as a character from the country whose language they are learning. I went as Lucretia Borgia. Jeremy went as Catullus and wore a toga.

He said "I was hoping you were going to come dressed as Lesbia, Sally, and then I could have recited some love poems to you."

"What?"

"*Vivamus, mea Lesbia, atque amemus, rumoresque senum serviorum omnes unius aestimemus assis.*"

"Sorry, Jeremy. The only Latin I can remember is *Longa sunt valla hostium*—the ramparts of the enemy are long."

His toga appeared to be held together by a single kilt pin. I had an urge to unfasten it and see his confidence undone, but managed to restrain myself. Knowing Jeremy he wouldn't have been embarrassed but would have enjoyed the chance to flaunt his rampart. I see him as a baddie in a Mills and Boon explicit.

from: kate wensley
to: sally howe
subject: deep water christmas

hi daise

shame you couldn't make the deep water bash last
night
you weren't alone—what is it about december?
people who have zero life for other eleven months
develop frenzied social calendar
personal phone hot with excuses

self and bj fantasy only revellers—with twenty
four mushroom vol-au-vents, a kilo of pistachio
nuts and a bottle of sparkling water

all bj wanted to talk about was you and your
radio appearances

compelled to break up party when bj began
comparative analysis of christmas literature
from the seventeenth century to present day—
otherwise wd not have been home before new year

best nutshells love giovanna

Wednesday 17th December

~ Not much of me was on *Today*. The ISDN line went
down and disconnected me mid-sentence. Mariella Frostrup
need not worry.

from: kate wensley
to: sally howe
subject: yr non-appearance

hi daise

up with living dead this a.m. so as not to miss
you on today

bad luck it was in the last minute of the prog

on the plus side a/ no time to fluff your lines
and b/ at least a million listeners heard your
name (twice) and your voice saying the words
shed and fairy lights before you were cut off

gets a star rating on the venetian blind scale

best be brief love giovanna

Thursday 18th December

Gus's December letter arrived:

*Thank you for the Christmas parcel, which I have opened
already. You know how I feel about Christmas. Thanks for the
thermal socks too, which the mailman brought earlier. The socks
now mean that at least for fifty per cent of the time I can feel my
feet. The fair isle waistcoat is just what I needed. I haven't taken
it off since I put it on. I haven't seen it much since then, as lately
I keep my polar jacket on day and night.*
Snow report: still white and deep.
*I was thinking that if you see any left-over pickled walnuts
reduced in the Co-op as they usually are at this time of year
perhaps you could get them for when I get back.*
Bit of a surprise on the Richard front. Poor sod.
*I opened the spaghetti hoops on my birthday. They didn't taste as
good as when you heat them up for me. Take good care, Gus*
*p.s. Dan came today with his friend Matthew. The intrepid boys
struggled through the drifts to bring me a Christmas parcel—a
handful of paperbacks and some supplies. He'd been to the
English shop in Denver and brought some PG Tips and four tins
of spaghetti. They didn't have hoops, but who cares? It's manna
from heaven.*

This is the first letter when he hasn't mentioned birds. Is that because there aren't any, or because of cold-induced apathy? He must have been feeling miserable to talk about coming home. And he said *take good care* not just *take care*. That must be significant.

Fancy yearning for pickled walnuts—he never asks for things. I'm glad Dan was able to get through the snow. Poor Gus. Still, no matter how miserable he is he won't be missing Christmas.

Iain rang tonight.

"Sally, why haven't you returned my call?"

"Oh, I'm sorry. It's been frantic here. The local media won't let me alone. And then there's all the shopping and cooking, getting ready for Christmas, and the parties."

"Do you have mistletoe in your hallway there?"

"Yes. Why?"

"Stand underneath it and shut your eyes."

Sam walked into the hall just then and stood in front of the mirror. He has impeccable timing that boy. He grimaced in the mirror, bared his teeth, smiled, posed, and then he started smearing gel on his hair and arranging it in peaks and kinks.

"Who's that?" he asked between tweaks.

I put my hand over the phone and hissed "Iain."

"What's he want? He's always ringing."

"Be quiet," I hissed again.

I didn't move to the mistletoe. I stayed exactly where I was, with my eyes open.

"Are you there?" said Iain. "Are you ready?"

"Yes," I lied.

"This is for you."

Kisses down a phone line, kisses at the wrong time in the wrong place, kisses from someone who is not your husband that are delivered in the presence of your son… such kisses don't work.

I felt deprived.

Friday 19ᵗʰ December

Janina Lemon is away. Janina Lemon is away.

I am on page three of the features section—in the place reserved for Janina Lemon. I am impossibly proud. At the end of my piece it says in italics *Janina Lemon is away.*

I am beside myself with excitement. Thank you KayWh for forwarding my piece, thank you Daphne Vicars for printing it. Thank you Janina Lemon for being away.

Janina Lemon is away!

Saturday 20ᵗʰ December

Nina rang me yesterday morning to say well done on Janina Lemon being away (as a media babe she understands the significance of this). We talked about my impending TV appearance and about what I was going to wear.

Later this afternoon, when I was getting dressed in preparation for driving down to the TV studios in Derby, I couldn't remember what Nina had said about clothes—except that she had mentioned my stripey shirt that I sometimes wear with her old navy trouser suit she gave me last year. So I fished them both out of the wardrobe and put them on.

I was still pumped up with glory from Janina Lemon being away that I wasn't even a little bit nervous when I arrived at *Midshires TV*. I checked in at reception and then sat and waited in the foyer for someone to come and collect me.

Pretty soon a man bashed his way through the door at the side of the rear foyer, pushed through the security barrier and said "Mrs Howe?"

I got up and turned round and he said: "Oh shit."

"Sorry?"

"Shit, shit. You're wearing stripes."

Then I remembered what Nina had said about the shirt—Whatever you do, mother, don't wear your stripey shirt. You can't wear stripes on TV.

So much for Janina Lemon being away. My columnist-in-waiting halo dropped to the floor and shattered.

"But what can I do?" I asked.

"Shit."

"Is there something I can do?" I asked again.

"Come on. We'll see if someone has something to fit you."

He took me through the barrier and down the corridor to the make-up room, where Nicola, the weather girl, was getting ready for her evening slot.

"Thank God," said the producer. "Nicola, do me a favour. Look after Mrs Howe, I'm running late. Find her something to wear instead of those damn stripes, and show her the make-up."

"Bloody hell, Dave, I'm busy doing my own. Anyway, there's no make-up for guests, apart from an ancient pot of powder. And the powder puff is positively skanky. Am I expected to share my-?"

But Dave had already buggered off.

Nicola sighed and looked me up and down and said "What size are you? None of the presenters is bigger than a size 10."

Some woman somewhere in the backroom wastelands of *Midshires TV* had her pale pink T shirt ripped from her back.

I had to wear it.

I HATE pink.

The TV appearance was fine. Wearing a borrowed pink T shirt and Nina's trouser suit made me feel like someone else entirely, which helped.

So now I can do TV. Carol Vorderman had better watch her p's and q's.

Sunday 21st December

Trend conscious Nina told me on the phone that this year feathers and crystals are *in* for Christmas trees—she can stuff that. I dressed my monster tree with all my favourites: two fairies, six angels, a sun, six stars (home made), two tiny Santas, a Czech decorated egg, a Canadian fabric moose, eight miniature parcels, heart baskets made by Nina when she was nine, a Happy Christmas modelled in Fimo by Sam when he was eight, and a cotton wool snowman eight inches tall, which Dan made at nursery school.

I used no tinsel (Nina should give me some trend points for that) and I hung 140 lights on it (static white—more trend points.)

The only problem with the tree is that I have to keep the curtains shut when I want to turn on the lights. Otherwise Mrs Mountain or some other village nosey parker will shop me to the media police.

Monday 22nd December

I got a parcel from Iain in the post this morning. I've sent him an especially tasteful card but no present. I had spent ages trying to think of something suitable and failed. Then

I'd forgotten all about it...

I opened his parcel on the spot. I didn't want to open it in front of the assembled hordes on Christmas morning.

Inside the jiffy bag were two wrapped presents—one big and boxy, one small and knobbly. The big one was a hairdryer! Nicky Clarke—whoever he is. Does Iain think I don't possess a hairdryer? Is it a hint?

I opened the little parcel. It was a Christmas tree decoration—Wallace and Gromit on a gold thread. Sweet, but an odd choice from a minimalist architect. I went to hang it on the tree.

I stowed the hairdryer safely upstairs and was coming down again when Richard appeared at the front door, to give me a lift down to Bakewell for last minute shopping.

My list was leeks, spuds, apples, clementines, celery, tea, and yet more mincemeat.

His was candles, paraffin, ibuprofen, kaolin and morphine, bandages, sutures and sick bags. He likes to be prepared.

from: kate wensley
to: sally howe
subject: xmas lunch

hi daise

champman and pesto just decided they want ikea
meatballs for christmas lunch

giovanna's shopping page not sure
a/ if ikea sell meat balls outside restaurant
b/ whether andy would stand another trip to ikea
if they do

personal suggestion of solving problem by going

252

to ikea for christmas lunch met with mother-has-finally-lost-it looks

best suggestions, love giovanna

Tuesday 23rd December

Richard popped in, apparently just to give me a giant air freshener.

"What's this for?" I asked.

"I thought it would be nice to put it in your loo—on Christmas Day. I wanted everything to be pleasant for Pippa."

"But why so we need one *this* big?" I asked.

"With all the heavy duty farting that goes on in there I thought you needed something with teeth."

from: kate wensley
to: sally howe
subject: last post

hi daise

bought tinned meatballs in gravy for dry run of christmas lunch for champman and pesto

tinned meatballs less appetising than pet food

all four cats refused to eat left-overs

on pesto's instructions had to ask phil down the road where they buy their meatballs as pesto had eaten good ones at their house

they get meatballs from ikea

personally suggested that could maybe have
meatballs some other time, perhaps after christmas
in conjunction with outing to ikea sale

pesto said—fuck that

personally suggested we should make our own

idea vetoed by champman's disgusted-of-matlock
face

therefore family trek to ikea—
aragosta got up from sickbed to accompany

pesto and champman each had meatballs in ikea
restaurant at 4pm (then felt sick but blamed
that on tinned lunch)

got polka dot cups and saucers in passing so
journey not entirely wasted

now have giant pack of ikea meatballs in freezer
compartment

champman may be going off idea as someone has
told him meatballs made from kangaroos
- it may have been me

best swedish traditions, love g

Wednesday 24th December

I went to Chatsworth to pick up the organic chicken—
looking like the sad ghost of a sad ghost. I hadn't cleaned off
my eye make up properly last night and also hadn't renewed
it this morning. I'm sick of trying to keep up my glam image
so my viewers and listeners won't be disappointed.

I left the house at 8 am, expecting to be the first woman in the shop and to be able to slip in and out unobtrusively. But the queue for the meat counter was already half way to the door and everyone was looking chi-chi, as they usually do in Chatsworth Farm Shop. Even the turkeys looked chi-chi: not handed over in plastic bags but presented in royal blue boxes stamped with the Ducal Crest.

When I got home Sam said that Iain had phoned from Brighton to wish me happy Christmas.

"Is he after you, Ma? Doesn't he realise you're happily married?"

I waited for Sam to go out before I rang him back.

Christmas Day

Too full and fat.

The family meal was a triumph: and for once the veggies didn't complain about the "stench" of burning flesh.

But unbeknown to me until it was too late, every time Pippa or Sam went into the kitchen during the afternoon and evening they gave Chomsky a meaty treat. "He's only a little cat," they said. "He doesn't get many treats" they said. "You wouldn't begrudge Chomsky a piece of your chicken, would you?"

It's odd not having Gus in bed tonight to conduct a thorough debriefing of the day. I've realised—now that he's not here for the first time in over 30 years—that he's my Christmas shadow. He can express all the grim feelings about the season that I deny or repress.

The last big family Christmas he hid in the kitchen reading his Christmas book, *Emotional Intelligence,* while I sat with the kids and their assorted partners round the dining table, with glasses of champagne, wearing party hats and pulling crackers. The only way we could persuade Gus to come in and pull his personalised cracker was to tell him that Chomsky was eating it. After that he went back to the kitchen with his book, only putting it down when I carried in dirty dishes. He's a stalwart washer upper.

But maybe he wouldn't want to do a debriefing if he was here tonight. The last time we had a Christmas houseful he said "Can we not discuss it? This Christmas has been a severe challenge to my pessimism. The whole thing has been far worse than I imagined it could be."

New Year's Eve

The whole of the festive season sends Gus into a spiral of gloom—as it does for some people—with New Year as the culmination, so New Year's Eve is usually a non-event here.

"Why on earth would I want to welcome in the New Year? It'll just be more of the same," is the kind of thing he says.

I remember last year showing him a news report of research about optimism: the results showed that being an optimist lengthens one's life.

Gus just said "What an excellent reason for not being an optimist."

He has always been appalled at my high expectations, while the blackness of his outlook creases me up. Oh how I love his quirky Eeyore ways.

"Do you want to write to someone on Death Row?" I asked him one New Year, after seeing an advert in *The Big Issue*. I thought it might cheer him up if he thought he was doing something positive.

"We're all on Death Row. It's just that some of us aren't in cages."

If Iain were here he wouldn't be oozing darkness. He'd be cracking open the champagne and kissing me at midnight.

January

Thursday 1st January

Career rundown—I've still not heard from Abigail Ferrers—the agent who wanted to see all of my manuscript—but I've had seven pieces in *The Recorder* (one of which was when *Janina Lemon was away*), one in *Hearth and Home*, two local radio slots, one regional TV appearance, and one aborted 'showing' on national radio. Kate seems to think that the festive media frenzy will bolster my image so that when I do get the book published it will be more likely to sell.

But what's the point of preparatory publicity for a novel which—judging by the lack of response from A.F—is too weak to be published?

I ought to be thinking about writing more pieces. I'd far prefer writing a column to being a novelist, anyway. Columnists are better paid and have a bigger readership.

Iain rang tonight to wish me Happy New Year.

"I'm so sorry I haven't rung earlier than nine o' clock, but to be honest we've had a bit of an emergency here today."

"Has Becky had the baby? I thought it wasn't due till the end of the month."

"Nothing as happy. My mother fell down Bec's spiral staircase. She's broken both her legs."

"Your poor mother!"

"She'll be all right. She's a tough old thing. But at her age it will be a long haul, a long time till she's up and about. And ages before she can cope on her own. Bec's insisting she'll have to stay here once she's out of hospital."

"That's very generous. What a nice daughter you have." Obviously brought up well.

"Which means it will be a long time before I have an excuse for going up and down the M1 again, and with Bec eight months pregnant, and my mother to visit in hospital, well…" he trailed off.

What a bummer.

"That's a shame."

"I don't suppose you're planning on coming down to London this month are you?" he asked, perking up. "I could come up on the train and meet you. I could take you for lunch at the RIBA in Portland Place, we could do a couple of exhibitions, we could go to the OXO tower for dinner."

"I've got nothing planned, but it's a possibility." How novel to have a man in tow who is neither allergic to London nor to dining out in style. But do we have to go to the bloody OXO tower?

It's been very nice having Sam at home for the Christmas holiday but I'm beginning to want my space back. Sam hasn't mentioned when term starts. I'll ask him about it tomorrow.

Friday 2nd January

I asked Sam when he was going back to Leeds, and he said he wasn't ever going back! It's the penultimate term in his final year and he's jacking the whole thing in! (I know Bodmyn Corner frowns on exclamation marks but I think those two were called for.)

"But why?" I asked.

"Because I've just found out that my degree course is funded by Excorico—those multi-national assholes are giving whacking funding to the ecology department."

"And?"

"Really, Ma. I can see who keeps you up to date with what's going on: Dad. Don't you listen to the news now he's not here?"

"Don't be so damn cheeky. Of course I do—I watch Jon Snow and Alex Thomson on Channel 4."

"Well you should know that Excorico are the bastards who are wrecking the swamps in Belonia."

"But Sam," I protested, "You'd be throwing away your degree. You only have two more terms and then you've finished. Couldn't you stay on just for two more terms?"

"No Ma, I can't."

"But this is your future, Sam. It's not as if you leaving the course is going to change anything. It's not going to stop the University from accepting funding from Excorico and it's not going to stop Excorico from their dodgy antics either."

"No, but if I leave I won't be implicated."

"But Sam—"

"I don't want any part of it."

Saturday 3rd January

Sam is still in bed and the house is quiet, but I can't write because I'm worrying about him.

I sympathise with how he feels. I even admire him for making a stand on the issue, I just wish either that he had found out about the Excorico funding after he'd been awarded his degree, or that he could think of some other way to make a stink about it. A way that didn't involve his throwing away two and a half years work and being landed with a student loan with nothing to show for it.

Why the hell didn't he tell me before Christmas that he wasn't going back? At least then I would have had several weeks to persuade him to think again. Now there's not much time at all—his exams start at the end of the month.

Just when I could do with Gus he isn't here. It's bloody annoying not being able to talk to him about stuff like this. It's too hard being grown up on my own. I need Gus here to be grown up with me. All I can do is write to him, and email Daniel, in case he's thinking of paying Gus a visit.

Monday 5th January

I'm working on a piece about sharing a house with someone who rants, i.e. Sam. At least he doesn't get up until one o clock so I have all morning for the writing of such a piece. The rest of the day I creep around the house in trepidation because of the habit he has of pouncing out and asking me what I think about what he's just heard on the news. It's a bit like living with a mini-Gus, but without the sympathy, the humour or the balance. Bloody hell I never thought I'd hear myself missing Gus because of his balance—Gus, the man who's given up his home comforts to spend a freezing snowy winter holed up alone in a hand built log cabin on the treacherous slopes of the Rockies.

Sam never slips out of rant-mode. If I leave my desk and slip into the kitchen for a quick coffee, there he is, munching his way through a mixing bowl full of chocolate cereal as he devours *The Recorder*.

But the cereal eating is merely a front. Before I can even switch on the kettle he has launched his first heat-seeking harangue.

"The bias in this reporting is so blatant it's laughable. Why do you get this right wing rag, Mother?"

I hate it when he calls me "Mother" in that tone of patronising distaste. And where does he think he got his left-leaning genes from? Does he equate me and Gus with Margaret Thatcher and Tony Blair?

"Actually, *The Recorder* has a balanced readership," I said.

"Have you read the editorials?"

"No, I don't bother with those. I read the columnists, though. That's what I want to be when I grow up—a columnist."

"Why do you want to spend your days polluting your mind with trivia? Why don't you write about things that matter? All your articles—the ones I've seen—have been about domestic nothings."

"Thanks, Sam. I'm overwhelmed by your support. Heart-warming, it is."

Tuesday 6th January

I have been invited for drinks at *The Recorder*. KayWh has sent me an invitation in the post. I can't believe it. I'm invited to drinks at *The Recorder*!

The letter says "Please join me and the leisure section team for drinks on Thursday January 29th at The Power House, Wapping Wall at 7 p.m. Very much look forward to seeing you there. Kay Wharton."

Sam saw me open the letter and asked if I'd got my novel accepted, my smile was so wide. I have been unable to do anything all day on account of hysterical excitement. It's fab. It's brill. If KayWh has sent me an invitation it must mean she sees me as a regular contributor. Maybe she has invited me down so she can see me in person and offer me a column. Do people get offered columns at drinks parties? Do they? I've emailed Kate and asked her what she thinks.

```
from: kate wensley
to: sally howe
subject: cool

hi daise

don't know about likelihood of column offering—
it's possible—is one of their regulars
emigrating?

whether or not—so much excitement—have been in
state of sympathetic palpitation all day—keep
feeling breathless and panicky that have nothing
to wear, then realise it's okay as it's not
actually me

why are they having drinks? do you think it's a
belated christmas party? maybe new cool is to
have them at end of jan

re: your wardrobe—I (as editor of deep water
shopping page) can't help feeling that they (as
London hacks) may all be terrifically disappointed
if you (as rustic contingent) don't turn up in
your barbour jacket

what is the power house?

best cool, best cool drinks, best cool drinks at
wapping, love giovanna



from: sally howe
to: kate wensley
subject: re:cool

Hi Giovanna
The Power House is apparently a power station
```

turned into a gallery and a restaurant—très London, très trendy, n'est-ce pas? I'm fed up with all this post-industrial architecture turned urban chic. Why can't they have it somewhere pretty?

My researcher (aka Nina) rang up the place for me and told them she had been invited to the party and wanted to know what type it is so she can decide what to wear. They said that the party is for 50 people and there will be finger food.

Nina is impressed that they are having a party when there is still a recession in the media with lots of redundancies. Maybe KayWh decided to have it in January so that lots of bods would have the flu and that would keep down the numbers.

Love and best,

Daisy

Wednesday 7ᵗʰ January

Now the nerves have set in.

Also the realisation that my wardrobe contains 95% denim and 5% smart.

As a first emergency step I have taken my blue linen trouser suit to the cleaners, but I really must go shopping and get something to wear with it, if not an entire new outfit.

But now I have an excuse to meet Iain in London. I could meet him for lunch and spend the afternoon with him before the drinks party, which would be nice in its own right, but would also serve to calm me down.

I rang him.

"You wouldn't like to come to the actual party as well, would you? As my partner? It would be so soothing having you there," I said. Soothing having him at the party, but exciting afterwards.

"I'd be honoured. Truth be told, quite apart from the

treat of spending the evening with you, it'd be fascinating to meet all the journalists. I've got a feeling I did my degree with the guy who writes the property section."

Thursday 8th January

Wendy is away and I had to go to Sheffield on my own to find something to wear with the suit. Not a wise move to go without it but it was still at the cleaners and I couldn't wait.

I started the search at John Lewis—mainly in the hopes that the atmosphere would calm me down a bit. No sooner had I alighted from the escalator onto the women's clothing floor than I was seduced by a Patsy Seddon see-through blouse in crushed silk and viscose with a wonderful extravagant pattern on it. It sounds revolting but is extremely glam, and also tasteful, and amazingly seems to suits my figure perfectly.

Sam was surprisingly tactful when I got back—maybe because he is keeping a low profile so I won't try to persuade him to change his mind about going back to Uni. His comments were definitely on the restrained side, but he couldn't resist saying that the blouse might be more suitable for Kylie Minogue or Louis XV.

Saturday 9th January

I got the suit back from Sketchley's and the blouse doesn't go. But I am still head over heels in love with it.

```
from: sally howe
to: kate wensley
subject: see through blouse

Hi Giovanna,
Please give urgent fashion advice.
```

I have bought a divine see through blouse (good provenance—Patsy Seddon.) Only problem is, it doesn't matter WHICH bra I wear under it, it doesn't look right. What are people supposed to wear under see-through blouses when they have only one titty (sorry, but on some occasions that word is unsurpassable) and when that one titty points downwards?
PLEASE ADVISE.
Nina has issued me with strict instructions not to wear my aged rainbow hippy boots. She also thinks the blouse is OTT for a drinks party in London Press-land—more suitable to be worn with velvet palazzos round the Christmas Tree. I don't care—I love it and am going to wear it with Calvin Klein denim (Daniel's cast offs.)
Love and best
Daisy

from: kate wensley
to: sally howe
subject: go sexy

hi daise
fashion page is working in the dark here—not having seen The Blouse -
visible underwear is big this season—go for it but if you chicken out of bra-as-showpiece go for flesh colour
best bras, love giovanna

Monday 12ᵗʰ January

Now I have the drinks party wardrobe sorted I am back at my writing, even with Sam being home.

He and I have evolved a kind of routine. I have a working breakfast so I can start writing straight away. I write all morning. He gets up at one o'clock and he has his breakfast while I have my dinner. We sit there and I try to read the paper. A mistake: I should read it in the loo like Richard does.

Before I can even open the features section—Sam has the news—he accosts me with "What do you think of what that fascist Blair said last night? Have you seen this report?"

"No dear, you have the news."

I get stuck into an article on autism, and have just reached a critical point in the highly technical discussion on aetiology, when Mr Paxman-Manqué interrupts with an outraged "Listen to this—"

I mark my place on the page with my finger, make eye contact so he thinks I'm listening, nod several times and say "Mmm, quite." If he's talking about genetically modified crops or global warming it's OK, but if he's talking about balanced ecologies I find my eyes straying to an upside-down advert for £22 fares to Venice.

I finish reading the autism article, and move on to the niceties of Janina Lemon's whimsy, only to be jarred by "You should see this about Cutworth's profits."

Of course I am pleased I have a son who thinks deeply about important issues.

But when I'm ironing there is something ineffably galling about someone in their dressing gown parking themselves with their feet up in front of the ironing board, wanting to debate the rights and wrongs of modern silk production methods.

And if I pop into the sitting room to consult a reference book, and find him supine on the sofa watching *Fight Club*, I'd rather not face a barracking on the censorship of screen violence.

He needs to get down to the Jobcentre, that boy. Unfortunately the one in Bakewell has just closed down. Now the unemployed are supposed to ring a helpline, or get onto the internet. I worry about my phone bill. Or I will do when he actually starts to look for a job.

"There's no point in looking now, Mother. Everyone is still recovering from Christmas," he said, when I mentioned jobs.

"You know, Sam, you could still reconsider going back to Leeds and finishing the course."

"You just don't get it, do you, Mother?"

Tuesday 13th January

Sam continues to rant.

At least the boy provides good copy. I wrote a cracking piece about him and sent it to KayWh.

I tried this afternoon—yet again—to persuade him to go back to Uni. He's missed the start of term but his exams for this semester don't start until the 26th so he still has time to do a bit of revision and go back for them.

I was wasting my breath.

Italian class resumed for the new term but the gritting lorry hadn't been to Goose Lane by the time *Neighbours* had finished and it was too icy to venture out on the roads. Bugger.

Wednesday 14th January

My piece about ranting Sam is going to be part of a special issue on the boomerang generation, this coming Saturday. They were looking for another point of view and mine is it. Yes.

Meanwhile, my own personal boomerang has taken up with some new age travellers and eco-warriors who are living in the wood at the bottom of Stoneymoor Edge. He could do worse than hang out with them.

He says the eco-warrior contingent are about to go off to a protest site in Tadcaster to swell the numbers, as it has been threatened with eviction.

One of the travellers is six months pregnant. I bet she's longing for a nice warm bath. I told him to invite her down for one. Lying in the bath and eating chocolate was the only thing to get me through pregnancy. The only thing to recommend pregnancy itself is feeling the baby kick.

Nina doesn't share my views—she likes being pregnant. But she wouldn't be away from bathing facilities even for one night, pregnant or not. And she never goes anywhere without three sponge bags full of toiletries.

Thursday 15th January

Nina and Tim are away in Egypt the week of the party— wouldn't you just know it?—but they say I'm welcome to stay in their flat. They're going to stay at a hotel on the Red Sea which has its own luxury spa. Nina is going to have gentle massages and pedicures while Tim goes snorkelling in the sea. She says the spa has its own wine cellar, Indian restaurant and film library. It's all right for some. Gus and I didn't have the money for such fripperies when I was 21 and pregnant with her, but then I suppose if you're an elderly *primagravida* you need all the pampering you can get.

I've decided to go down to London on the Wednesday teatime, the day before the party. That way I can leave all my stuff at Nina's and have a good night's sleep before I meet Iain in town on Thursday morning. Iain's going to catch the late train back to Brighton. He needs to be on hand in case Bec goes into labour—why do children always get in the way?

Sam heard me booking the train and asked me how far I would be prepared to travel just for drinks with an editor with me paying the expenses, and I decided that the limit is probably Eastern Europe (Prague?). I can imagine what Gus would think of me going all the way to Wapping for drinks—and the budget required for the trip. He wouldn't go to drinks *next door*.

Sam's friend Clover arrived at tea time for a bath. I offered her a bar of Fair Trade Co-op Chocolate, but she declined. She stayed in the bath for an hour and came out looking like Red Clover (ha ha).

She was very smiley and sweet. I wonder if she has a partner, or if she has her eyes set on Sam as a potential father. No telling.

Friday 16th January

It was snowing today. Those poor eco-warriors. They'll be freezing to death in their benders.

Richard popped in and stayed for a coffee. We talked about this and that and not very much. I had the feeling that he wanted to ask me something but couldn't bring himself to do it.

Finally he got up from the kitchen table to go home and walked towards the door. Then he turned round and said "I didn't leave my Swarfega here when I moved out, did I? I can't seem to find it at Pippa's."

"I haven't seen it," I said.

"And talking of Swarfega," he said, and paused.

"Yes?" I said.

"Talking of Swarfega, Pippa and I are having a bit of a problem. Well, it's Pippa. And as you're about the same sort of age, I thought you might have a suggestion."

"Oh that," I said. "Gus and I find KY Jelly works just fine."

271

Saturday 17th January

There are four pieces about the boomerang generation and mine is second one down. Hooray!

Iain rang tonight to say how much he'd enjoyed my piece and we had a nice long chat. I was lying on the sofa in front of the fire feeling relaxed.

"What I want to know is" I said, and then stopped—maybe the question I was asking was a bit too personal.

"What?" Iain said. "Go on—what do you want to know?"

"Well, when you're so obviously eligible—why hasn't some woman snapped you up?"

"To be honest I've been on my guard," he said. "So, you think I'm eligible, do you?"

"What do you mean, you've been on your guard?" I asked, feeling embarrassed.

"A few years ago a friend of mine lost his wife and even before the funeral there were women lining up, jostling for position with quiches and clinches. Until then I had no idea that unattached women could be so hands on at a time like that."

"Sounds pretty disgusting."

"And then there's my Magic 8 ball."

"Your what?"

"Didn't you see *Toy Story*?

"I hate animations," I said.

"Buzz Lightyear used one, but if you didn't see it, never mind."

"Hang on—did you say Magic 8 ball? Is that the American oracle thingy—a plastic ball that you shake and ask questions?"

"Yes. Serena brought me one back from a New York shopping trip once."

"But what's it got to do with predatory women?"

"For the first two years after Serena died I didn't even notice other women. Now if there's a woman I like, well, truth be told, I ask my Magic 8 ball if it would be a good idea to follow it up. So far the ball's always given me the same answer: *My sources say no*. That is… until the last time I asked it."

Of course I was dying to know when the last time he consulted it was and what the ball said, but I didn't ask.

Does it matter? Could I take seriously a man who believes in such twaddle?

Sunday 18th January

I was lying in bed this morning day dreaming about the drinks party and trying to think of some opening gambits for conversation as I am completely useless at small talk, and I was just musing on Thurber cartoons and wondering about the advisability of quoting from my favourite—*I love the idea of there being two sexes, don't you?*—when I heard the front door slam.

"Sam?" I shouted, sitting up.

No answer. Surely Sam would still be in bed, wouldn't he? He'd been up at the crusties' camp last night. Or was he just returning?

"Sam," I shouted again.

Still no answer.

I heard the gravel crunching on the drive, and I would have leapt out of bed if my arthritic knees and ankles had allowed it. But they are always impossibly stiff in the mornings. I hauled myself up and out and stumbled across to the window and was only just in time to see Sam climbing into the passenger seat of a big yellow van, an old and rusting yellow van. Where could he be going so early?

I pulled on my dressing gown and went down to the kitchen for a cup of tea. I picked up three socks between the front door and the kitchen and then found the airing rack was at half mast and empty. Last night it had been full of Sam's washing. I yanked it back up and tied the rope, and switched on the kettle. On the work surface next to the fridge was a note from Sam.

"Bojangles has given me a lift in his van. Will ring later. Love Sam."

Had he gone off with them to the protest site in Tadcaster?

If so, I felt faintly pleased he is taking some kind of initiative. OK, he's refused to go back to Uni, he's chickened out of looking for a job, but at least he's now doing something positive, and not just standing on a soap box in my kitchen lambasting the world.

Monday 19th January

I rang the agent and didn't even get the bloody assistant this time, just his voicemail. I left him a message with my number and a request for him to ring me back. He hasn't. *Che sorpresa*.

I also rang Sam, as he hasn't rung me. His phone was switched off so I left him a message.

Why does no-one want to talk to me?

Tuesday 20th January

Maria was in a frenzy at Italian class tonight. One of her daughters is in labour with her first child and Maria obviously can't think about anything else. I wonder if I'll be like that when Nina starts her contractions.

We were supposed to be learning about booking hotels and flights and buying train tickets and everything to do with travel. But Maria said she'd rushed into the travel agents just before closing tonight to get some materials, and they said they hadn't any spare Italian brochures, and sent her away with a handful of stuff about North Sea Ferries. So we learned how to book a cabin for an early spring break in Amsterdam. *Mama mia*!

Wednesday 21ˢᵗ January

Gus's monthly epistle arrived.

I can't believe it. Arnie says winter is just beginning.
I have found an alternative track across the mountainside to avoid passing his house as he always tries to lure me in.
In any case, I haven't come half way around the world to be polluted by twentieth century socialising.
My average day is as follows:
Stay in bed as long as possible. Get up. Stoke fire. Eat soup. Stoke fire. Collect wood. Eat more soup. Stoke fire. Go to bed.
Some pioneer.
Though I do think a lot.
Bird list
Blue Grouse
Pygmy Nuthatch
Great Horned owl

Too cold. Hope you enjoy your trip to the Great Wall of Wapping, although why you should want to go beats me. Take care, Gus
ps Daniel came to see me to tell me about Sam. It's a bugger.

But full marks to him for his principles. We can't have done
everything wrong as parents.

Well thank you Gus for your help. Is that all you have
to say on the matter of Sam? I thought you'd at the very
least send me an apposite quote from the big T. On the other
hand I know there's nothing he could do to persuade Sam to
go back to Uni if he were here—you can't tell a 20 year old
anything.

Gus is obviously feeling bad spending so much time in
bed. As for the trip to London—he has no inkling of the
significance.

A career launching party in Wapping is not the only
reason to venture south of Watford.

Thursday 22nd January

I went into Sam's bedroom to look for stray teaspoons
and baking bowls this afternoon as I seemed to be short
in the kitchen, and I noticed that his telly and stereo had
disappeared—why would he need those on a protest site? Or
has he taken them to sell?

Friday 23rd January

How long should one wait for a putrid agent's assistant to
respond to phone calls? As long as it takes for a fetid agent to
read a manuscript? Three months? I hate the lot of them.

And no-one round here has any consolation to offer.

Last week when I moaned about the agent Sam said I
should have written something worthwhile, something
political and hard hitting.

"You shouldn't be wasting your time on mind-numbing fodder for the masses."

At least Richard tried to be sympathetic.

"Why don't you forget the agent and publish it yourself? You could get a hundred copies printed, give them to friends and family and sell any remainders at the village fete. And I'm sure Billy-the-Kid Bathgate would mount a display in the post office. You know how he feels about you. Mounting a display of your books would be second best to mounting you of course, but—"

"Richard! Don't be disgusting! What *has* come over you lately?"

That Pippa is a bad influence.

Anyway, who wants to self-publish? What I want is for someone *in the trade* to think my work is worth publishing.

Even Wendy doesn't get it.

"Don't worry about the novel, Sally. Your pieces in *The Recorder* are great. Everyone thinks they're funny. I can never understand why you haven't got them all framed and hung on your wall."

Of course I haven't got them framed and hung on my wall. Having them framed on your wall makes them into an unusual achievement that you may not repeat. You can bet Janina Lemon doesn't have her columns hung on her wall.

Wendy talks crap sometimes and I can't take her seriously when she's doing her Dolly Parton look—a look that does her no favours—vintage green suede with lacing, and embroidered cowboy boots in red.

I emailed Kate for sympathy. She's the only one who has even an inkling.

Monday 26th January

There is still no response from Abigail Ferrers, Alistair Daltry (her assistant) or even the chirpy switchboard girl at *Pigs-R-Us*. I am getting to the stage when I would even be happy with a polite rejection.

Tuesday 27th January

I had hot sweats all night last night. That's the third night in a row. I think it's due to nerves about the drinks in Wapping, but it could be related to afterwards with Iain. The acu-doc's budget has been cut and it's six weeks since I've seen him. I'm desperate for his magic needles to calm me down.

Re: the drinks—I have to keep telling myself that KayWh is having a party and that's all it is. Who cares that she is an editor? (i.e. God) All I have to do is go along and be friendly—like at other parties. If it all turns ghastly and I am completely tongue tied I shall throw myself on the mercy of the man who writes the Q&A etiquette column and ask him the etiquette of drinks parties.

Re: afterwards with Iain—reasoning isn't relevant.

Wednesday 28th January

```
from: kate wensley
to: sally howe
subject: a day ahead
```

```
hi daise
have spent all day thinking of you in london,
wondering what time drinks were, wondering if
```

```
you were sitting down for drinks, or standing
up, what exactly you were drinking, what kaywh
looks like etc etc
this was whilst visiting bakewell for thistle's
special dog food.

then coming down a6 had sudden thought that today
was not the 29th
am suffering from terminal confusion—due to
fatigue or untimely menopause

will be even more confused tomorrow as I'll be
doing a re-run of today
re—how many ice cubes has daise got in her drink
at this moment  etc etc

some friends from bradford are coming to see us—
need to clear comatose teens from public areas

will expect detailed report of tomorrow—when are
you back?
have a wonderful time,
best vodka gimlets, love g
```

Friday 30th January

So anyway, there I was this morning, standing waiting
for Iain in the foyer of the National Portrait Gallery wearing
THE BLOUSE, wondering why the hell he was three
quarters of an hour late, when my mobile beeped.

A text from Iain:

```
Sorry, sorry, sorry. Domestic crisis. Can't come.
Will phone tomorrow. Good luck for tonight. Love
Iain. xxx
```

What bloody crisis? Had he got a speck of dirt on his
wellingtons? A broken down hairdryer? Gus would never
let me down at the last minute like that. But then Gus would

not have entertained the idea of coming anyway. He'd only come to London for me if I was dying.

I spent the day on my own, getting more and more nervous, and then at 6.25p.m. I was standing on the platform of Kings Cross tube station with a complex and lengthy tube route to The Power House all planned out when the lights went out, and there was an announcement saying "Will all passengers evacuate the Metropolitan side of the station" (where I was). Thinking it just a little local difficulty I followed the herd up the stairs and thought "Oh bugger I'll have to re-plan my route with a longer journey," but I couldn't see the stations on my tube map in the dim emergency lighting, as columnists-in-waiting attending chi-chi drinks parties do not wear £1.50 reading glasses off Chesterfield market.

I got to the Northern line and there's another announcement—"Will all passengers please evacuate the station—we cannot guarantee your safety—there has been a power surge." I rushed out of the station thinking "Hell's teeth what do I do now—it'll be £25 to get all the way out to Wapping and anyway all the taxis will be full."

At that moment a bus went by with Whitechapel on the front—which I remembered was somewhere on my tube route to Wapping. Your fearless and intrepid correspondent jumped on. I asked the driver to tell me when we got to Whitechapel. He said, trying to be helpful, it's the stop before the last. Mmm. Very helpful.

I managed to get a seat near the front downstairs so I could potentially ask the driver if we were there yet, and then my mobile beeped. It was a text message from Nina all the way from Egypt (isn't technology wonderful?) saying "Good luck. Be sensible. Remember what I told you." I texted her back "I am on a bus to Whitechapel but no idea how far it is." She texted back "Ask the driver."

The bus only crept along and I kept looking at my watch

the hands of which were moving faster than the bus. People were continually jumping on the bus and asking the driver "Are you going to King's Cross?" and he kept saying "No, Whitechapel." Eventually another passenger—as fed up as me—stood on the platform and as soon as someone got on he said in a loud voice "Whitechapel, we're going to WHITECHAPEL."

When I got off in Whitechapel it was pissing it down. I had no idea where Wapping was from there. The streets were busy but with not a taxi in sight. Eventually one came along with its lights switched off. I flagged it down anyway and miraculously it stopped.

The driver said "I'll take you if it's on my way home."

He was not going past Wapping, but I begged him to take me there.

The good news is that I got to the drinks party half an hour late.

Well, 50 people might have been invited, but only 20 turned up, and I was the only freelancer.

A flunkie took my coat at the door and showed me to the area set aside for *The Recorder* people. I wandered over and as no-one greeted me I made for the eats table and whilst grabbing some foccaccia and some olives and cheese, I tried to strike up a conversation with a tall forty-ish bloke also filling a plate. He responded, but I sensed he was thinking "Who the hell is this old bird?"

Then a smiley woman came up and said "Is it Sally Howe?"

It was the one and only KayWh. She was friendly and welcoming. As to looks, she was pretty, petite, sweet, was wearing a blouse and skirt, little make-up, altogether nice, and then I looked down and she was wearing those pointy shoes and standing in a ballerina pose—yuk!

I told her how pleased I was to be invited to the party and

she took me over to meet some of the staff.

They were mostly all sitting down, and I took a seat at a table with the countrywoman (who was more attractive than in her photo), Venetia (shopping page woman), Anthony the deputy editor who sometimes emails me, and Jack Norton (the man who edited the ranting piece).

Apart from the country columnist and the fashion columnist, everyone else was staff—plus the secretaries and sub editors. All the big names were absent. Everyone was very friendly bar the fashion columnist—she was obviously envious of THE BLOUSE.

Anyway, I did some ace networking—got some suggestions for publishers for *Fast Work*, a contact on the Grauniad (excellent!) and just meeting them all was nice.

After an hour or so KayWh stood up and said "OK, OK, OK" very loudly, and "Can we have a bit of hush?" and everyone gathered round her clutching their drinks.

"I'd like to take this opportunity to say thank you to everyone for all their hard work, and to say how much I will miss you all. And to wish those of you who are staying on with the new set-up, to wish them the best for the future."

"Is she leaving?" I asked Anthony who was standing next to me.

"We all are."

"What do you mean?" I said, aghast.

"Don't you know what the party's about?"

"Isn't it a belated Christmas party?" I said, bewildered.

"It's a farewell party. Farewell to the leisure section. This week's the last issue."

The leisure section is finishing and next week *The Recorder* has something called *Arts Review*.

Bugger, bugger, bugger.

KayWh—the only editor in the known universe to like my stuff—is taking early retirement. Some of the staff are staying on with the new *Arts Review*. Anthony said he was. And he said I could send stuff in to him as long as it was artsy. What? I don't do artsy.

Bugger, bugger, bugger. If the leisure section is finished then so am I.

I have to face my failure. My career is in tatters.

Saturday 31st January

Too fed up to write. Anyway, people who aren't writers don't keep writer's journals.

Later:

Iain rang.

"I'm so sorry I let you down, Sally."

He'd been all ready to go and catch the train when Bec had suddenly gone into labour with contractions only five minutes apart and he'd had to organise an ambulance whilst babysitting Cosmo, whilst tending to his mother who is now out of hospital. It had all been such a whirlwind of activity that he hadn't been able to call me and let me know. Hmph. Hasn't he heard of multi-tasking?

"Gosh, you did have your hands full," I said. "Is it a boy or a girl? How's Bec?"

"A boy. Milo. 8lbs 3 ozs. I knew you'd understand, Sally. Being a mother."

"Of course."

"So tell me everything. How did you get on at the drinks party? What did you wear? How did you do your hair? Did they offer you a column?"

He sounded as though he really cared.

I filled him in on what happened in Wapping, not a blow by blow account, just a two sentence summary. I wasn't in the mood.

"You don't sound your usual perky self," he said.

"Well, would you be if your career hopes had just been definitively stomped on?"

"Of course. It's very disappointing. What can I do to cheer you up?"

There was nothing.

February

Sunday 1st February

I'm going to give up writing. I'm going to become a photographer. No-one goes on for ever, not even Jane Bown.

Monday 2nd February

Iain has sent me some flowers. The biggest bouquet I have ever seen. It's all white apart from the ferns. Multi-headed lilies, roses, daisies and gypsophila, all wrapped up in spotty cellophane and tied with a big white paper satin bow. And he's also sent a card in the post. It's a print of a fab oil painting of Venice by Ken Howard. He's written the message in a beautiful italic script in black ink. (A Parker Fountain Pen with an italic nib, I bet.)

"So sorry to have let you down. The beauty of the evening light playing on the Grand Canal is as nothing compared to the warm redeeming sunshine you have beamed into the frozen wasteland of my life. Multo amore, Iain."

His message made me squirm with embarrassment. I know what he's telling me is sweet, sweet, sweet, but oh dear, why does it read so sentimental violinsy, so Florid Trev from Deep Water, so *Woman's Weekly* cosy-toes?

I have two men writing to me and neither gets it right.

I put the flowers in the sitting room and I buried the card

in my jumper drawer. Then I rang Iain to thank him, but his phone was switched off and I had to leave a message.

As far as my writing is concerned, I'm going to pick myself up, dust myself off, and start all over again. But how can I get my pieces published? I've tried sending stuff to other papers before—the same stuff I sent to *The Recorder*—and they haven't responded. Either they are completely closed to outsiders, or my voice is a *Recorder* voice, and doesn't fit anywhere else.

The novel is my best bet. If I get it published it may not earn me much money but I suppose it could be seen as the start of a career. Maybe Abigail Ferrers is stuck in traction after a ski-ing accident and is so behind with her work that she's not been able to read my script, and when she does she will think it's a corker. Some hope.

I couldn't even go to Deep Water tonight for a bit of morale boosting, because it was snowing hard and I thought I'd end up stranded in Matlock Bath.

Tuesday 3rd February

I am sick and tired of the London-centric media. We had nine inches of snow here last night and today no-one could get to work until dinner time, from Derby right up to Leeds, and yet there was no mention of it on the national news. If a sprinkling of snow stops a commuter train in bloody London, the whole of the British Isles gets to know about it.

```
from: kate wensley
to: sally howe
subject: deep water drift
hi daise

yesterday's deep water ranks depleted by
weather
```

not-an-american arrived at nine o clock—he had
spent half an hour putting snow chains on his
car and once he reached the main road found there
was no snow so had to stop to take the chains
off again

paul was in polar explorer mode—had travelled
three miles on foot
(dedication or what?)
think he was itching to get feedback on latest
piece—an alien romance
(new genre of year?)
  noticed he hitched ride back with not-an-
american

performance janet read chapter one of her new
project—also a romance
she referred to it as mills and boon with
pulsating and panting (do they have an erotic
stocking section?)
not-an-american defined it as top shelf
paul thought it was top hole

florid trev rang to say he was coming but
never arrived—perhaps lost in blizzard of own
adjectives

best glacial melt love giovanna
p s extreme climbers meeting in room next door
called off—due to snow

Wednesday 4th February

Pigs-R-Us returned the first three chapters of my book—
three months after they asked to see the whole manuscript—
with a standard rejection from smelly AF.

And why haven't they sent me back the full manuscript?
They are *so* unprofessional.

I have found three more agents in *The Writer's Handbook*, and sent them all a submission. It took the whole day.

Thursday 5th February

Nina rang up tonight. She was talking about maternity leave and about when she's going to go back to work after having the baby. She said she'd seen something in *The Guardian* about it costing £326,000 to raise a child in London, what with nannies and private education—what piffle. She is starting to worry. She and Tim are thinking of moving north to cut the expense.

Friday 6th February

I was too fed up with my lack of success to be able to write this morning, and too fed up with Bodmyn Corner to consult him for tips.

Saturday 7th February

Nina has sent me that piece about the £326,000 children. It makes me want to vomit. If raising children is time consuming, expensive, stressful, and wipes out your libido— why do any of these people submit to such traumas?

I told Iain all about it when he rang.

"Well not everyone's the same," he said.

"How do you mean?"

"I mean, some parents think state education isn't good enough. And they think private education is worth a lot of sacrifices—including having to go out to work to earn the school fees, rather than spending time with their children.

And if women are going to keep their careers going, then there's often no way round employing a nanny."

"Is Cosmo down for Eton, then?" I said, facetiously.

"Actually Hugh, my son-in-law, has him down for Winchester—his alma mater."

Oh my God.

"What about primary school?" I asked.

"I said I'd chip in to send him to a nice little pre-prep round the corner from where they live."

"You've surprised me, Iain. I didn't know you had these views."

"It's not important. Hey, I've thought of somewhere else in Italy you must see. Let's talk about our trip."

We talked about Lucca and other little hill towns and so moved into safe territory again. When I put the phone down I realised we'd been rattling on for forty minutes.

Sunday 8th February

I hate February.

Today's property page had photographs of half a dozen houses, all on sale at the same price, including a studio flat in Camden and an eight bedroom detached house with twenty acres in deepest Northumberland. Urbanites reading the feature would no doubt think—along with Nina—that they ought to consider decamping from London. They don't realise that living in the country in spring, summer and autumn may be heavenly, but there is a price to pay, and it's not the one printed on the property page. The price is February. The grey days, the looming mists, the dripping rain, the faded grass, the inescapable mud and the long dark nights: I hate them all.

Tuesday 10th February

It is a situation steeped in irony that as soon as Gus went to the Rockies and I had an empty house with time and thinking space to write, Richard came to stay, and as soon as Richard moved out, Sam came home and filled up the space, and now that Sam has disappeared and I have an empty house I am too discouraged to write.

Does my inspiration for pieces only come when there are people here annoying me?

Wednesday 11th February

When Wendy came round this morning she was dressed in a sharp city suit of perfectly tailored pinstripes, with a silk scarf in a black and white geometric design.

"What are you today?" I asked. "Personal-assistant-to-the-MD?"

"Do you mind? I finally got my Diploma in the post this morning so I thought I should start looking like a professional astrologer."

"What?"

"Don't tell me you expect me to wear a batik head scarf and gold hoop earrings and to have a crystal ball clanking in a carpet bag? That is so cliché."

"Maybe that's why I've failed as a writer," I said, "thinking in clichés." I moaned on about my stalled career and then went on to carp about the weather.

"I'm pissed off with February too," she said, slipping off her impeccable high heels and making herself comfy on the sofa. "We should go away for an early spring break to cheer ourselves up. How about Amsterdam?"

So I fished out the brochure about P&O cruises from

my Italian folder, and there was a special offer: a round trip with two nights on a luxury North Sea Ferry and a day in Amsterdam for £57.

We have booked for two weeks time, so now at least I have something to look forward to.

Thursday 12th February

Iain rang today.

"How's it going up there in Derbyshire?"

"Crap. It's crap in February."

"You sound as bad tempered as that woman in the Thurber cartoon—*I said the hounds of Spring are on Winter's traces—but let it pass, let it pass!*"

"Well maybe the hounds of Spring are out in Brighton, but it's so cold here they're still cowering in the kennels."

"Do you like dogs?" he said.

"They'd be all right if they didn't bark. Do you?"

"I prefer cats, to be honest. Another thing we have in common. I wish I was up there with you, I could maybe cheer you up."

"I bet you'd rather be in Italy. How can you bear to be over here in the winter when you could be there?"

"Truth be told, it's more who you're with than where you are."

I wondered if that were true. Yes, up to a point. But where was that point?

"It's funny you should mention Italy," he said. "I'm off there tomorrow. I have to sort out a few things at the old homestead."

"What about the family?"

"Hugh has taken some paternity leave so I'm free for a while. Plus my mother is mobile now. I'll be taking her home when I get back."

I told him about the trip to Amsterdam and he asked me if I would bring him back some cards from the Van Gogh gallery. It's uncanny: he wanted three of the peach tree in blossom and that's one of my favourites, too.

"We must get together when I get back, bella. Do you mind if I call you that?"

"I wouldn't mind, except that Jeremy—that man in my Italian class who's chasing me—he calls me that."

"In that case, arrivederci, sunshine."

Richard called in today for a coffee. He asked me what was happening with my writing, and I had a good old moaning whinge about it. He tried his best to cheer me up.

"You ought to buy yourself a treat to brighten up your life."

"Like what?" I asked.

"Well, I like wall plugs," he said.

"Wall plugs? Wall plugs?"

"They're colourful, you get a lot for your money, and they're very useful."

"Thanks for that, Richard. Tell me," I said, trying to change the subject, "how are you and Pippa getting on?"

"Wonderful! Superb! She's a first-rate woman. But I'm feeling a little tense."

"Why's that?"

"I'm on the prowl for a nice new tool. It's a very dangerous time."

Friday 13th February

A letter from Gus:

I have had to make a concession—I made a temporary move to the main cabin, because the shingle system was sadly not windproof. In the gales and temperatures here I was in danger of not waking up. I feel sullied by this need to compromise, but I haven't completely sold out—I'm still cooking on the fire and using kerosene lamps. Arnie (who is enjoying the luxury of a chair, now, when he visits) keeps coming round for a chat and "to kill some time." He is obviously unaware of what Thoreau said—you cannot kill time without injuring eternity. Arnie keeps saying that the snow will be here till the end of March, which means I shall be leaving just as the snow does.

Sorry to hear things didn't work out for you at the Recorder shindig. Never mind—it's something to have been invited. Perhaps you should have framed the invitation and stayed at home.

Bird list
Black-capped chickadee
White breasted Nuthatch

take care Gus

Poor Gus. Although, if I were feeling unkind, I could say that he's made his cabin and he ought to be freezing in it.

But I am sick to death of his scanty letters. His letters have been so unlike what he's like in real life I sometimes wonder if he's had his neighbour Arnie writing them for him.

Tuesday 17th February

Iain rang from Italy but I was out.

Thursday 19th February

Fantastic news. Surprising news. Sam has gone back to Uni. He went last month in time to take his exams.

How do I know? Did he ring? Did he write? Not on your nelly. I found out from Clover when she came for a bath.

I was surprised to find her standing on the doorstep. I thought she was in Tadcaster.

"Come in, come in. I thought you and Sam and the others had gone to Tadcaster to support the protest," I said.

"Oh no, I didn't fancy it, and Sam didn't go either."

"Is he staying with you, then?" I said, feeling panicked. I mean—I like the girl, but Sam's too young to be a father.

"No. They gave Sam a lift back to Leeds. Bojangles persuaded him that it'd be more of a statement, like, if he sat his exams and got his degree, like, and then refused to accept it at the ceremony thing. If he told the press, like, beforehand, he could make a statement, get some coverage. More effective protest. What d'you think?"

I didn't tell her what I thought. I didn't want to scare her off.

So the boy has done his exams. Now I have to wait till the end of June and head him off at the pass.

Friday 20th February

I'm too fed up to do anything, even writing. So fed up, I watched *Neighbours* at dinner time and the same episode again at tea time.

Monday 23rd February

Still fed up. Watched *Neighbours* twice again. Feeling very ashamed.

Tuesday 24ᵗʰ February

Double *Neighbours*.

Wednesday 25ᵗʰ February

I did nothing productive today apart from pack for the trip to Amsterdam—one overnight bag.

Let's hope the trip gives me a boost, and when I come back there's a letter from an agent waiting for me. I've given Richard all the details of the trip, the times of sailing, where I plan to go, even down to my cabin number, just in case someone rings and offers a six figure contract for my book. He promised to check my answerphone for me.

Thursday 26ᵗʰ February

Just seeing Wendy in her French fisherman look cheered me up—wide leg navy sailor-style trousers with navy and white stripe, Guernsey style jumper with shoulder buttons and matching woolly hat, plus authentic French navy espadrilles (though why she won't freeze to death with no socks I don't know) and a bait bag with a strap across the body.

And going somewhere different in the car—even driving through Lincolnshire in February in the rain—perked me up a bit. Then, when we arrived in Hull, Wendy and I found that we were booked onto the biggest ferry in the world, *The Pride of Hull*. It was new and neat and clean, and our en suite cabin was simple, but it had little touches that I wasn't expecting, such as bedside lights, cotton sheets, and real glass tumblers in the bathroom, not tacky plastic ones made misty with a million scratches. How modest are my needs. How little it takes to please me.

We dumped our stuff in the cabin, and Wendy took off her hat and rolled up her trousers. She wanted to put on a little off the shoulder fun t-shirt that says—*All the nice girls love a sailor* ("I got it especially from the McArthur Glen shopping outlet south of Matlock—it was only £6")—but I persuaded her not to. We went upstairs to what was optimistically called the Sunlounge Bar.

We bought pre-dinner drinks and sat down on the side of the bar overlooking the dock and the lights of Hull. Hull is not pretty, but it has to be more interesting on the fag end of a wet Thursday afternoon in winter than the view on the other side—the North Sea, grey and seemingly limitless. The music they were playing in the bar was a sixties compilation, and when *A Groovy Kind of Love* came on I thought of Gus, and a tear dropped in my spritzer: that was always our song.

After drinks we sauntered down to find something to eat, and opted for the set price meal in the buffet restaurant, because it was cheaper than the à la carte. It turned out to be great food but there was low spot at the beginning of the meal when we dithered over our choice of wine and the waitress looked us up and down—two grey haired fifty-something women—and suggested sweet white. We gave her a look of disdain and ordered the driest we could find.

"What about that for stereotyping?" I said. "Admittedly our faces are lined, but hasn't she noticed my writerly plait, specifically grown to make me stand out from the flock of menopausal crows?"

"It's your fleece that's the problem," said Wendy.

"But turquoise is one of my colours. Anyway, for some reason my hot flushes have deserted me, tonight."

"Fleeces are the new shell suits," said Wendy. "The sniffy young madam has obviously got you pegged as an old woman with no taste."

When we booked our ticket two weeks ago, the cinema on the ferry had been an added attraction. Unfortunately, they were not showing the new Julia Roberts and we had to make do with an old Harry Potter. The sound was sludgy and the seats had low backs and when your head is reeling from a cocktail of Pinot Grigio and a strong spring tide you long for something to rest your head against. We bailed out of the film before the end and Wendy lurched cabinwards while I went to reception for an explanation of an announcement about "adverse tides."

Friday 27th February

At six this morning a Dutch woman woke us over the loudspeaker to tell us about breakfast. I forgave her for waking us up so early, because she had the most mellifluous voice I have ever heard, like elderflower cordial on an August afternoon, and her faint continental inflexion combined with the English dipping cadence at the end of her sentences gave her an air of sadness. In terms of attractiveness, she was the Charlotte Green of North Sea Ferries.

There was a scheduled coach waiting at the dockside to take us all to Amsterdam but Wendy took so long trying to decide what to wear that we nearly missed it. In the end she could see I was at the end of my tether and just draped a pashmina over the French fisherman's outfit to make it her "lighthouse-keeper look."

We walked towards the Van Gogh Museum alongside canals the colour of black coffee, soaked by rain dripping from a grey sky, popping into a café on the way—not for a joint—but to scoff exquisite cakes with our earl grey tea. As we passed by the red light district I saw a man in a trenchcoat with a dark floppy fringe—a man who looked just like

Jeremy—loitering with another man outside a bookshop, and I hurried Wendy on. But it couldn't have been him. It would have been too much of a coincidence.

Once at the museum, we were overwhelmed by the paintings. It was like golloping down a box of Belgian chocolates all at one sitting. I felt as though we should have spaced out the viewing over the course of a week. Around every corner we were faced with more, and still more pictures that I have known for so long but only seen as flat prints.

I got up close to see the brushstrokes and was reaching out to touch the thick daubs of paint when Wendy caught my arm and yanked me back, saying "Sod it, Sally, I know the Dutch are laid back, but don't push it."

In one of the galleries she started to whistle *Starry Starry Night* and I had to shut her up.

"You don't have to shout at me—all you need to do is point it out gently. I've told you before, I don't know I'm doing it."

Back on the ferry in the evening we avoided the sniffy waitress in the buffet, and went to the calm and quiet à la carte restaurant, where the waiter was friendly and funny, and no-one offered us a bottle of P&O Blue Nun.

A force seven gale was lashing the side of the ferry by the time we left the restaurant, and Wendy was looking decidedly green. She was gripping the handrail and edging her way along like a geriatric sloth. I felt fine. I escorted her back to the cabin, but wasn't ready for bed, so I took *The No.1 Ladies Detective Agency* to read in the Sunlounge Bar.

I thought I'd managed to find a quiet corner, but the place soon filled up with several groups of riotous drinkers. The one that settled in my corner was a hen party. I was finding it really hard to concentrate on my book, because of all the inane comments flying around. I found myself wishing I'd brought my writer's notebook with me to write down some of the dialogue, but then I remembered that juicy dialogue or no juicy dialogue, the writing game was lost.

Just at that moment someone leaned over my shoulder from behind and said "Ciao bella."

So it *must* have been him I saw in Amsterdam. What was *he* doing on the trip? The same as me, I expect. Having an early spring break with the destination courtesy of Maria's handouts from Italian class.

"Jeremy! What a surprise!"

"Let me take you away from all of this," he said.

"I'm not in the mood, Jeremy. I'm feeling very low. That's why I'm here. It was Wendy's idea to cheer me up."

"Why, what's the matter?"

"My writing was going really well. I had loads of pieces published before Christmas, but just when I thought I was getting somewhere the bloody *Recorder* leisure section finished. She was the only editor who liked my stuff. Maybe she had a warped sense of value. Maybe all the other people in the know who have seen my writing see it for what it is—crap."

"But you write very well. I've read all your pieces in *The Recorder*. They're very funny."

"You've read them?"

"You don't think it's just your plait that turns me on, do you?"

"Oh."

He had found the way to my heart. If he had told me that he liked my writing all those months ago he might have stood a chance. Well not really, but you know what I mean. I looked at his wide smile and his shiny, floppy fringe and wondered if I'd misjudged him.

"You mustn't lose heart and give up, *bellissima*," he said. "I'm just wondering if I can help you with getting published. I don't know any journalists but I do know someone who works at Harper Collins. My brother's just got married again—his new wife is an editor there."

"Really? Could you ask her to look at my novel?"

"I can certainly ask her. But you'll need her contact details yourself. My filofax is in my cabin. If you want her email address and her phone number—her direct line—you'll have to come and get it."

"Couldn't you go and fetch it?" I said. I might have been fed up, but I was still in touch with my common sense. "Surely I don't need to go to your cabin with you," I said. "Do you know that Thurber cartoon, Jeremy?—a couple in a hotel lobby and the man is saying to the woman—"

"*You wait here and I'll bring the etchings down*."

It was Iain! I whisked round in my seat. There he was, standing behind me.

"I thought you were here with your friend Wendy," said Jeremy. "I didn't realise *tuo marito* was here as well."

I whizzed round again. "My husband?" I said puzzled. Then I remembered that back in the autumn at the showing of *Il Postino* I had pretended that Iain was Gus. I swivelled round again—all this turning was making me feel dizzy— and winked at Iain and very, very slightly inclined my head in a gesture to indicate Jeremy.

"How do you do," said Iain. He put his hand on my shoulder and leaned forward to shake hands with Jeremy. "Are you going to introduce us, darling?" he said to me, tenderly tucking a strand of my hair behind my ear.

I introduced them, and after a couple of minutes of meaningless small talk Jeremy excused himself and left the bar.

"Iain!" I said. "What on earth are you doing here?"

"Aren't you supposed to say *thank you, Iain, for saving me*, and *how lovely to see you* and things of that nature?" he said, smiling, and sitting down at the table.

"It is lovely to see you—of course it's lovely to see you. And thank you for saving me from the predations of Jeremy, but what *are* you doing here?"

"Well," he said, examining his trousers and flicking a barely perceptible bit of fluff off them, "it stems from my telling Bec about you. Truth be told, I was a bit nervous of how she was going to react—you know what some children are like about their parents' new partners—but she said she was pleased I'd found someone to make me happy again. And then she said 'What are you doing sitting on my sofa telling me about her, Dad? Why aren't you with her?'"

My heart lurched a bit when he said "new partners." I grabbed the edge of the table with both hands.

"Sally? Are you all right?" he said.

"But how did you find out which sailing we'd be on?" I asked, fumbling for something to say.

"I rang Richard. Then of course, wouldn't you know, the ferry was booked on the outward trip so I had to fly to Schipol and catch it on the way back."

Fancy flying out to Holland just for the pleasure of a return sailing to Hull with me. I was bowled over by his extravagant gesture. But there was something that was disturbing me, and I couldn't put my finger on what it was.

"Well, I couldn't be more surprised," I said weakly.

"And pleased, too. I hope. To be honest, I wondered if you might think it an intrusion."

"I—"

"Sally. Why don't you come back and share some champagne in my Club Stateroom? I'm in this ridiculously luxurious cabin—it's the only one that was left when I rang to book. It's so much more civilised there. We could sit and have a quiet drink away from the rabble. I've got a mini-bar, a sofa, a television. We could watch a late film. *Top Hat* is on."

Top Hat! He'd never told me he liked Fred Astaire.

"Well—" I dithered.

"Coming?" he said, getting up.

I was just about to answer him when a skinny blonde girl sitting opposite me—one of the hen party—got up from her seat, edged her way around the table, and then lurched sideways and retched, spraying vomit all over my hair.

One of her friends jumped up and said "I'm really sorry," and then she grabbed her friend by the arm and said to her "Maddy, come on, I'll come with you to your cabin," and dragged her away.

"Why don't you come with me to mine?" said Iain, as I gingerly fingered the sick in my hair. "You'll be needing a shower," he said. "And my Stateroom Cabin has all the niceties. Including a hairdryer and a bathrobe."

I knew that Wendy and I didn't have a hairdryer in our cabin. I said yes.

I had a shower, and as my clothes smelled rather iffy I pulled on the Stateroom spare bathrobe. When I came out of the shower Iain was standing waiting, playing with a hairdryer.

"Gosh, that's posh for a ferry accessory," I said. "Fancy— a Toni and Guy hairdryer." His cabin must have cost a fortune.

"No, it's mine—a travelling one. Come here and let me give you a blow dry."

Once my hair was dry I lounged on his sofa drinking champagne, eating a banana from his P&O Stateroom fruit bowl, and watching *Top Hat*. Iain was sitting next to me and getting closer by the tap dance.

"I'm so glad I came," he said. "Maybe my Magic 8 ball was right after all."

"Did you ask it about me?"

"Of course," he said. He put his arm round my shoulder

and gave me a kiss on the cheek. Soft.

I turned my head to face him. "What did it say?" (I had to ask.)

"*Signs point to yes*." He kissed me on the lips. Not so soft, more sort of purposeful.

At the end of the kiss, I pulled away and smiled at him—why the hell was I feeling so nervous? I turned back to the film. It had reached that scene where the hotel flunky is telling the Fred Astaire character that Signor Bellini pays all of the Ginger Rogers' character's bills, and buys all her clothes, and supplies all her niceties—"And her niceties are very nice."

And I flashed back to Iain in the bar saying his Stateroom Cabin had all the niceties, and now he was supplying them to me.

"Sally," he said, interrupting my thoughts. "I'm so glad I found you. I feel—now—that I have a future again."

"Pardon?"

"A future that's not solely tied up with my grandchildren."

"What do you mean?" I said, unfurling my legs from under me and sitting upright.

"I mean *you,* of course. When I was out in Padua, I started ringing up hotels for our trip round Italy. I've been booking dates in May. It won't be too hot and it will give you April to sort things out with Gus."

"Gus?" I squeaked. "Sort things out with him?" My voice had gone peculiar. It's a wonder I got any words out at all. My throat felt so tight. It was like in one of those nightmares when something awful is happening and you're so petrified you can't scream for help.

"Sally? Are you all right? You've gone dreadfully pale. You're not seasick, are you?" he asked.

"No, no." I grabbed the arm of his Stateroom sofa, and

pulled myself up to my feet. My legs felt shaky. He'd been booking actual dates? Those things printed in black and white on an actual calendar?

"Where are you going?" he said.

"I'm being horribly selfish. I've just remembered Wendy. Poor Wendy. She was really, really sick and I've just left her to get on with it. I ought to go and check on her. See if there's anything I can do."

"She'll be all right. She'll just want to be left alone won't she?" said Iain, taking my hand and squeezing it.

"I must go and see. It's miserable for her."

"OK, I'll come with you," he said.

I went back in his bathroom, took off the bathrobe and pulled on my vomit-laden clothes. All the time my mind was going bananas.

When Iain had started to talk about new partners, and his future I'd felt a slight catch in my head, but then dismissed it. But with the mention of Gus and April and sorting things out it was as if he'd sloshed me with a bucket of briny. There was no sense at all in my head—I was just soundlessly screaming *noooooooooooooo*. How could I possibly leave Gus? How could I leave my life with him?

"Sally? Are you ready?" Iain called through the bathroom door.

We left his cabin and walked down the long corridors towards my modest, non-Stateroom cabin with none of the niceties and no double bed. And as we walked it was as if I was outside myself and watching me walk, stumble more like, on automatic pilot.

We found Wendy asleep—in my bunk—in oversized baby blue winceyette pyjamas looking very Meg Ryan in *You've Got Mail* but ten times as groggy.

"There. She's fine. Are you going to come back to my cabin now?" Iain said.

Wendy stirred and turned over.

"Sally, is that you? God, I feel awful."

I stepped over to her, smoothed her fringe off her sticky forehead and covered her up with the sheet and blanket that had fallen on the floor.

"Who else would it be? How are you doing? Why are you in my bunk?—just out of interest."

"I'll move if you're coming to bed. I was sick all over mine. That's why I moved."

"Would you like me to get you anything? Do you want a drink of water?"

"Oh God, no. No. I'll only sick it up again."

"Sally, can I have a word?" said Iain, softly.

"Who's that in the doorway?" said Wendy.

"Sally, why don't you come back and sleep in my cabin?" said the man in the doorway.

Wendy hauled herself up onto her elbow and said "My God! Iain!" Then she flopped back down again and groaned.

I couldn't face any questions from Wendy. My mind was not in a fit state to conjure cogent answers, so I said "Wendy. You stay there. If you're sure there's nothing you want—I'll see you in the morning."

I grabbed my nightie and sponge bag and left the cabin.

Out in the corridor I looked at Iain and trembled. I was standing there under the stark fluorescent lights, shifting from one foot to the other and looking away from his face, staring at my left hand clutching the handrail. "Iain," I said, "How can I say this? I—"

"You still look pale, you poor thing."

"I—"

"Don't worry. I can see that all you need is a good sleep. You can have my bed. I'll have the sofa. Come on, if we don't get back we'll miss the scenes in Venice, and that bit when they dance the *Piccolino*."

Saturday 28th February

"I'll have the sofa," I said on the long walk back to Iain's Club Stateroom. "It's only fair."

"Fair, schmair, don't be silly. Of course you must have the bed."

We were back in time to see the last ten minutes of *Top Hat* but I can't remember anything about the *Piccolino* or the scenes in Venice. It must have been a hysterical reaction—blocking out anything to do with Italy. After the credits rolled up Iain got out some brandy from the minibar, and I wolfed down three. Normally I don't drink brandy.

We said goodnight with a quick peck on the lips and I got into bed. I could hear the gale worsening, and if this were a novel I would be saying that the gale wasn't as bad as the storm in my head, and that I spent all night with my thoughts and emotions churning, utterly unable to sleep.

But it's not a novel, it's my life, and as soon as I shut my eyes the brandies knocked me out.

I woke at ten to six the next morning. I turned over and caught a whiff of Iain's Dunhill after shave on the pillow and I suddenly remembered where I was and what had happened. I sat bolt upright. Oh God! What was I going to say to him?

Thinking that I had to sort out my head before he woke up, I pulled on my clothes and grabbed a blanket to keep me warm and crept past Iain asleep on the sofa, and out of the cabin.

I made my way out on deck and leaned over the side of the ferry in the grey dawn, looking at the turbulent sea.

I imagined life without Gus. It would be as bleak as an opencast mine. Worse. It would be like the North Sea in February—dull and flat and grey for the most part, but with the possibility of sickening gales and no Gus to lean on when they came.

My life would be devoid of meaning.

How it would ache.

A year had been bearable, all the time knowing he'd be coming back, but if he went for good? Wherever he was in the world, if he wasn't in mine, I'd always be wondering what he was up to, what was his latest fad, and feeling I was missing out because I wasn't there to share it or be annoyed by it.

I left the deck and as I walked back down to Iain's cabin, the P&O version of Charlotte Green announced breakfast over the tannoy. Her voice was so enchanting that I imagined men all over the ferry lying in their bunks, bewitched by her diction and howling when the next announcement came from the captain, who had a flat Hull voice.

When I got back, the shower was gushing—Iain was in there. I sat on the bed waiting to see him before I went back to my cabin. I couldn't do that awful woman-left-the-bed-in-the-morning-before-the-man thingy.

Iain is lovely. I've had a wonderful few months with him...he really is lovely. But I never thought things through. I was so flattered by his attention in the first place, and then so comfortable with him. And then, of course he's so damn attractive. But I've been out of touch with reality, living in an alternative world—with someone who likes going out to dinner and travelling. This whole year has been unreal. I've not let myself think about Gus and me. Our marriage. My life. In four weeks Gus will be home, and my real life will resume again. At least it will if Gus can be persuaded to forget about this ridiculous trial separation.

I looked around the room. There was a pile of neatly folded boxers and a T shirt on a chair, with folded socks perched on top. And oh goodness, had Iain been using the Stateroom trouser press?? Come back Gus with your mucky cycling clothes and your limp, worn jerseys covered in darns.

And there was the Toni and Guy traveller on the chest. Vanity, thy name is Iain. Come back, Gus, with your towel-dry bald head and side bits.

Iain stepped out of the shower and into the bedroom wearing a bathrobe, with a towel round his shoulders. I could see his bare feet. They were beautifully shaped, strong and bony with nice straight toes. That bit would have been all right, then.

He smiled and said "Good morning, sunshine."

Then he picked up the hairdryer and said "Bec gave me this for Christmas. I knew she'd notice if I didn't bring it along. Who the hell are Toni and Guy anyway?"

"They're two funky young hairdressers, I think."

"Oh. I thought they were the Italian version of Wallace and Gromit."

I said I was dying to put on some clothes that didn't smell of sick, but that I'd meet him later. Then I whizzed off.

I found Wendy feeling better, and about to get dressed.

"What's happened? What's Iain doing here? Tell me everything," she said. "Every little detail."

"I don't want to talk about it. I can't."

"Are you all right? You sound as though you're in shock."

"Look, I'll tell you later. I'll tell you tomorrow. You've just got to stay with me and not leave me alone with him until you drop us off at home. I'm still working out what I'm going to say to him."

"All right, chuck. Don't fret," she said, pulling on her navy and white knickers with the anchor-embossed elastic.

She finished dressing while I packed, and then we went to find a cup of tea. Neither of us could face breakfast, though for different reasons.

The ferry was supposed to dock so we could disembark at 8 o'clock but there was an announcement from the captain that the gale made it impossible to berth without tugs, and the tugs were busy with what he called "one or two incidents in the river." It sounded sinister, and the captain sounded stressed: the faint Hull inflexion in his voice had strengthened to make him sound like John Prescott. Having John Prescott as captain in a force ten gale is not reassuring.

Then Wendy and I realised that on our tour of the ferry we hadn't seen any lifeboats.

"Maybe they don't have them," said Wendy. "Maybe they give you a life jacket and leave you bobbing up and down in the briny while they wire for helicopters."

"Aha, this is when we cash in our menopausal chips," I said. "It would be women and children first, with grey haired women before young ones, and while we waited, our hot flushes would save us from hypothermia."

We had to sail out to sea again, and then back again. It took all morning, and we sat in the Sunlounge Bar with Iain, talking about nothing.

When the ferry finally docked it still took us two hours to make it ashore because the gale had damaged the pedestrian gangway. I left the ferry with a tidal wave of relief. I was still celibate, if only just. At least I didn't have going to bed with Iain on my conscience.

March

Monday 1st March

"So the thing is, Iain…" I trailed off.

It was Saturday. We were sitting in the kitchen after Wendy had dropped us off from the ferry trip. Iain and I were drinking coffee and eating lemon shortbread biscuits.

"Yes?" he said. "The thing is?"

"The thing is.." I stalled again.

"What *is* the bloody thing?" I could tell from his tone that he knew what was coming.

"OK…well…I'll tell you."

"Go on, then. Tell me." He sat back in his chair and folded his arms across his chest. His long legs were stretched out at the side of the table, crossed at the ankles.

"I like you very much," I said, running my finger round and round the rim of my mug.

"But?"

"I love Gus. I want my marriage."

"Oh."

"Splitting up is not the same as a year apart. And it's not just about leaving Gus. It would be leaving the last thirty years of my life. We have so much shared history. We'd have to sell the house, leave my garden, we'd be a broken family. I couldn't bear it. It would be such a waste to throw everything away."

"But it wouldn't be lost. You'd still have it. I still have all my years with Serena in my head, in my heart."

Having a dead (ex) partner is so very different from having a live one, but I didn't point this out. And now I've been forced to think about it I know that Gus and I are so inextricably linked that the only way I could separate myself from him is if one of us did die. For the last ten months I've been chuntering along in denial, my typical way of coping with unpalatable truths. I've been pretending—without knowing it myself—that Gus and I are not on a trial separation, that Gus is just away for a year as he originally planned and as I originally agreed. That's why, until Iain talked on the ferry about the future, I had not spent any time imagining life permanently without Gus.

"Sally?" said Iain. "I just said something and you haven't responded."

"I'm just not available, Iain. I'm sorry. I know I seemed available sitting alone by the fire. I imagined I was, in as much as I actually thought about it. I'm really, really sorry, Iain. I should have thought it all through before, before we could get to this stage." (A stage where he could be hurt.) "You took me unawares. But I'm not ready to leave it all, to throw it all away."

"Hmm," he said.

He just sat there looking at me. I shifted in my chair. I looked away, caught sight of the scorch marks on the cupboard and then looked back at him. He'd followed my eyes.

"Screwed that right up, didn't I?" he said.

I smiled. "Well..."

"Truth be told I've never held a blow torch before in my life."

"You're a devil with a hairdryer, though."

He laughed and used both hands to tousle his hair.

"Well, um, OK," he said, standing up and pushing his chair back under the table, and dusting biscuit crumbs off his chinos, "I think I'm going to make tracks. I thought I'd go round and see Richard, ask if he'll drive me to the station." He smoothed his hair.

"I can take you," I said.

"Don't worry. I'd like to see him before I go back down south. I don't know when I'll be in Derbyshire again." He reached the door and then turned round. "D'you know what the worst of it is?"

I got up. "No. What?"

"I'll never be able to trust the Magic 8 ball again."

After he left I had no energy to do anything apart from watch my video of last Friday's episode of *Neighbours*. Ah yes—*Neighbours*. I remembered when he first told me he liked watching *Neighbours*—I remember being surprised that there wasn't a fated clicking into place—a feeling that we were meant to be together—instead, when he said it, I'd felt a wave of disappointment.

I want a man who will keep me on my intellectual toes. Gus is like the eagle who stands for morality on the Muppets. And I love him for it. You wouldn't catch Thoreau watching *Neighbours*.

Tuesday 2nd March

Last night I was too shattered to go to Deep Water.

But I did write to Gus to put a stop to this trial separation lark. I have told him how I feel. But I'm not going to pin all my hopes on just one letter. Dreadful things can happen when letters go astray. Look what happened to Tess of the D'Urbevilles when Angel didn't get her letter that slipped under the doormat. I'm going to write to him every week until he writes back and says we're OK, firm and steady like we always were.

Wendy came round this morning at half past bloody eight.

"Come in, come in, you don't need to batter the door down," I said. "Where have you parked the Harley?" She was dressed as a biker—black leather head to toe.

"Sod it, Sally. I think I've waited long enough. I was impeccably behaved on the boat, and I've not pestered you with phone calls, and I've been *dying* to know what happened with Iain. I've been so beside myself with curiosity I've had to take Rescue Remedy."

Over breakfast I told her everything that had happened and not happened and she looked disappointed about the not happening bit.

I told her about Gus and me, what I know now—at last—to be true: however complicated, however much it tugged and strained, I wanted my life with Gus. Yes he drives me up the bloody wall, but he is the love of my life. He may be impossible, but somehow, next to him, every other man seems second rate.

"Explain again. Why not Iain?" said Wendy. "He's charming, attractive, sociable, relaxed, appreciative—and he lives how you like to live."

"I know, I know. But there's always a but in my head when I think of Iain. But whatever I feel about him—buts or no buts—it's Gus I want. I don't know what I can have been thinking about all these months—and you've been no help."

"There are plenty of other men around, you know," she said. "Just because you don't want Iain doesn't automatically mean you have to go back to Gus. There are plenty of places for women our age to meet men."

"Like where?"

"Like—do you remember those two blokes who wanted to share our taxi from Marco Polo airport the last time we went to Venice?"

"But I don't want—"

"And last Saturday in Waterstone's I got chatting to a very tasty bloke in Mind, Body and Spirit. Sod it, how come these leather trousers are so tight when I spent all weekend being sick?" she said, undoing the button on her waistband.

"Wendy. Listen to me. I am not going to live out your unconscious desires for a bit on the side any longer. I want Gus. I love Gus. How could I possibly let myself get into this mess?"

"But Sally—"

"Look," I cut her off, "we both know how annoying Gus can be day to day. I know he drives me wild and woolly, but the point is that when he chips are down, when I need him he's always there. He's a rock."

"So where is he now?"

"I know he's not here now, but he would be if anything was really wrong."

"What about the stuff he does that you're always moaning about?"

"At least I know about his faults."

"Yes, I suppose if you went off with someone else—Iain, for instance—you'd have to go through that long tedious process of adjustment to someone else's idiosyncrasies. The thought is so tiring. Who knows? He might be one of those obsessive collecting types. Didn't you say he gave you a Wallace and Gromit Christmas tree decoration? Just suppose, he might have a whole room at his house devoted to Wallace and Gromit memorabilia."

"Oh don't be so daft."

"But he is incredibly yummy, isn't he?" She unzipped her boots and pulled them off.

"And Gus is exciting and eccentric and funny and really, really interesting. After Gus, life with anyone else (even someone who looks perfect and behaves perfectly and whose name begins with I), it would just be so samey."

"But—"

"I'm going to get back with Gus. It's Gus I want. I've written to him to call off this stupid separation malarkey."

"I don't blame you, chuck. If I was married to Gus, I'd want to keep him too. He's an out and out sweetie."

"Thank you! And why have you not acknowledged this before?"

"Oh you *know* I love Gus. How could anyone *not* like Gus. Anyway, I knew Iain would be a flash in the pan. Remember a few months ago I said you had Uranus squaring your Venus? Well, the exciting changes that Uranus brings often don't last."

```
from: kate wensley
to: sally howe
subject: fame

hi daise

missed you last night
huge excitement—duncan got a letter from elodie
champion

film of deep water going out next wednesday as one
of the progs in the bbc4 'creatives' series

can't wait

best grotesquerie, love giovanna
```

Wednesday 3rd March

Gus will be home in four weeks. So even if he doesn't respond to my written entreaties to be reconciled he'll pretty soon be here in person and more accessible to persuasion. I know I can persuade him. He'll want us to stay together. He hates change.

Maybe if I agree to go to Australia with him it will show my commitment and my determination to make things work. I must buckle down and try to see the positive: make a list of all the good things about accompanying him to the bush.

I rang Wendy for encouragement.

"That's weird," she said. "I was just checking your chart. I thought you might end up having to go to Australia."

"Why were you checking?"

"I wanted to see whether I'd have to learn how to do email so I could keep in contact."

"So what did you find?"

"Well, from May onwards there's a lot of activity in your ninth house."

"What on earth does that mean? What's the ninth house?"

"The ninth house symbolises long journeys."

"Oh."

"But it's also the house of publishing."

"Publishing! So which is it? Travel or publishing?"

"Sorry, I can't tell."

"So much for your precious Diploma."

"Look—no-one could tell. Not even an experienced astrologer. It could be either. It could be both. The important thing is that you can't fight your transits. You have to go along with them, use the energy positively and optimise the experience."

"Like how, oh oracle?"

"Don't give up on the book, but you'd better sort yourself out for Australia just in case. We'd better go shopping. You'll need some shorts, a cossie, moisturiser and an attractive bush hat. The bush hat might be difficult. They don't suit everyone, you know."

from: sally howe
to: kate wensley
subject: help!

Hi Giovanna
Cheer me up. It looks like I'll be spending a year in the outback with Gus and no-one else. I've decided I need to watch *Neighbours* twice a day, everyday, and I'm going to get out Sam's old video of *Crocodile Dundee* and watch that to get me in the mood.
Have you got any other suggestions?
Love and best,
Daisy

from: kate wensley
to: sally howe
subject: film therapy

hi daise

never mind neighbours, strongly advise following for background study:

a/ muriel's wedding

think edgy neighbours with abba soundtrack and marital obsession theme (sub)urban locations—feel the heat—grab the accent

b/ picnic at hanging rock

for crinolines read shorts

c/ priscilla queen of the desert

big on outback, bus travel and evening dress—
pack the ping pong balls

d/ kangaroo jack

location location location
kangaroo in bush in jacket pursued by arseholes

e/ australian vets in practice

useful suture terminology

reckon the above will set any girl up for a bush
year
I can lend you the films on video

best dingoes (missed that one out deliberately
by the way) love g

Monday 8th March

Poor Richard: the honeymoon period for him and Pippa
appears to be over.

I saw them down at Bakewell market this morning. They
didn't see me. They were standing on the other side of the
big greengrocers stall in the corner by Boots. I was on the
fruit side and they were buying veg. Richard was wearing a
humungous rucksack and standing sideways to the stall with
his arms folded, while Pippa chose produce, passed it to the
stallholder to be weighed and totted up, and then received it
back and loaded it into the rucksack. Twice Richard turned
round and pointed to items that he wanted—some purple

sprouting broccoli, and then fennel—but Pippa slapped his wrist and said in her Barbara Woodhouse voice, "They weren't on the list, pet. No they weren't. Now just turn to the side, will you, and then I can see what I'm doing."

And later, when I was making myself a bacon sandwich for dinner, he arrived at the back door looking wan. He was carrying two Chatsworth Farm Shop carrier bags stuffed full of something.

"Ooooh, that smell. It's months since I had a bacon sandwich," he said longingly.

"Come in, come in. Smells are free. What's in the bags?"

"It's my *Screwfix* and *Wolfcraft* catalogues. I've come to ask if you'd mind if I stored them here?" he asked.

"I'd really rather not, Richard. There's enough rammel in this house already."

"Rammel? These aren't rammel. I thought at least *you* would appreciate their significance, even if Pippa doesn't."

"Sorry. I was using the term loosely. Of course they're not rammel. I meant—well—why can't you keep them at Pippa's? I don't understand. Surely she knows how you depend on them?"

"She knows I get most of my supplies from them, but that's it. And she says she's working towards a paperless house."

"What do you mean? Doesn't she have any books?"

"She has a dictionary and the complete works of Shakespeare and the Bible."

"Very Desert Island Discs."

"And her floral art manuals, and *The Complete Red Setter,* of course."

"But she reads paperbacks. I've seen her. She always has her head in a Mary Wesley or a Jilly Cooper."

"She does, but she only has one book on the go at a time. When she's read it she either returns it to the library and borrows another, or if it's not a library book she donates it to Oxfam and then buys another."

"Do you mean to tell me that the only books she has in the house are the ones on that single mahogany shelf in her hall?"

"Yes. According to Pippa, books are untidy. And they harbour dust. And since she bought her computer she's trying to banish paper from the house, as well. That's why I've come to ask if you'll give these sanctuary."

"You poor thing. Would you like a bacon sandwich to cheer you up?"

"Would I? Do Screwfix do next day delivery?"

He sat down and I gave him my sandwich, and flung some more bacon under the grill for me. As soon as he'd wolfed down his sandwich he started moaning about Pippa again.

"She objects to me keeping the catalogues," he said. "Even inside my bedside table, behind a closed door. I've tried to explain. I've tried to tell her—they're reading matter for every mood and every season. When I'm feeling low they're a comfort. And when I'm feeling upbeat they offer enchantment, a frisson of excitement. There's a world of treasures in there."

"I know, Richard, I know."

"They're a way of spending money without spending money. It's like Thoreau said when he was looking at farms and wondering whether to buy them—what was it? Oh yes—*I never got my fingers burned by actual possession*."

"Not you as well!"

"What?"

I shook my head. "Never mind," I said.

"And this paperless idea," he went on, "she wants me to buy my DIY supplies from a website she's found."

"What's wrong with that?"

"They don't tell you the brand names of any of their goods, so you have no notion of what to expect. Is it an innovative clamp that you might expect from *Wolfcraft*? Or a classic design that will last forever from—"

"Yes, yes, I get the idea."

"Anyway, *Screwfix* have served me faithfully all these years. I don't want to change to another firm."

"You must stand up to her, Richard. Be assertive. Start as you mean to go on. She'll respect you for it, you know."

Tuesday 9th March

Maybe I can't be a columnist but I could have a problem page. I have even impressed myself with the success of my advice.

Richard and Pippa walked by the house today with the dogs when I was standing doing the ironing in the dining room bay window. I waved and so did they, and then as Ellie and Emmie dragged Pippa off down the lane and out of sight behind the escallonia, Richard gave me a broad grin and made a thumbs up sign. Both thumbs.

Wednesday 10th March

At least Billy Bathgate still loves me even if agents and publishers don't. He tried to pinch my bum again in the post office today. I was too quick for him, though. I could see it was coming and took a swift sidestep. Nice footwork. Fred Astaire would have been proud of me.

I was buying an airmail letter to write to Gus and some tins of spaghetti hoops.

"I hope Mr H is going to be home in time for the happy event?" said Billy Bathgate.

"I don't think either of us will be, actually," I said,

thinking he meant the arrival of Nina's baby.

"Och, won't you be Maid of Honour, then?"

"Pardon?"

"Young Pippa has asked me to order all the bridal magazines I can get my hands on."

Young Pippa? *Young* Pippa? The woman's the same age as me, dammit.

"Oh, the wedding. I'm not sure. I don't think the date's been fixed. I thought you were talking about the arrival of my daughter's baby, our first grandchild."

"Och, a baby in the family. That'll be nice for you. Put a spring in your step. Make you feel young again."

The cheek of it. How old does he think I am? I am thinking of taking my custom elsewhere. I shall transfer my allegiance to checkout Ron in the Co-op. He's a better packer than Billy Bathgate. He always stands the bottles upright in the carrier bag.

Putting the spaghetti away in the cupboard I noticed the scorch marks—again. Those scorch marks will always be there to remind me.

Thursday 11th March

I had two rejections today. Four still outstanding, plus one of the originals that I sent to an agent in the autumn. They're unspeakable, the lot of them.

Friday 12th March

from: kate wensley
to: sally howe
subject: deep water sodding programme

hi daise
just to let you know the news from the tv guide

elodie's bloody deep-water-on-tv gig only going
to be called blank page
what sort of a creative bloody title is that???
blank bloody page
apparently supposed to stress unlimited potential
open to creative writer
why didn't they just call it writers (on the)
block?
best blank screens love g

Saturday 13ᵗʰ March

Richard and Pippa invited me for a meal this evening.
I knew that I was the only guest so I thought it would be
informal and I didn't change out of Sam's old sweatshirt
and my jeans. What was the point when the dogs would be
slobbering over me all evening?

As I stood on the doorstep waiting for someone to answer
my knock, I could hear Pippa saying to Richard, above the
baying of the hounds, "No of course you can't wear that.
We're entertaining and you must go and change. Yes you
must."

She opened the door and I could see Richard in his bib
and brace retreating up the stairs, dragging his safety-booted
feet.

Pippa had her hair scraped back into a barely-possible
chignon. She was wearing scarlet lipstick (which didn't do
her any favours) and gold blob ear-rings as big as cherry
tomatoes, a pink cashmere sweater with a low scooped
neckline, all set off with a chunky pearl necklace tied in a
knot.

She ushered me into the sitting room and plied me with
sherry and roasted cashews while we waited for Richard. I
noticed a neat pile of *Friends* videos on the shelf above her
telly. Maybe the woman has hidden depths.

The meal was a joint effort. Richard had made some potato pancakes and Pippa had stuffed them with curd cheese, mushrooms and spring onions. Not bad.

The conversation glanced briefly at Sam and Gus and the health of Nina, then the blessed dogs, of course. Then there was a two second reference to my writing, before it settled for the rest of the long evening on their wedding plans. They still have not set a date. Richard wants me to be there, so he is trying to steer Pippa towards June next year. She, on the contrary, wants this September.

"It will be a shame if Sally and Gus can't be there, of course. Yes it will. But we could always go to stay with them in Australia for our honeymoon."

Pippa on her honeymoon: God give me strength.

"Australia would be rather pricey, sweetheart," said Richard, bless him.

"But it will be early spring. The climate will be lovely. Yes, lovely."

"Will the dogs be all right in the kennels for three weeks? I mean—it wouldn't be worth going for less than that, would it?" I said.

That was the clincher.

Australia was out.

Pippa went on and on about the wedding. Apparently her first husband—who died ten years ago—had insisted on a small wedding at the registry office, and she is determined to go to town for this one, so to speak.

Richard is indulging her in spite of the cost. Or maybe he thinks she is going to pay for it all. Who knows?

Or maybe he sees the wedding as a symbol of the start of his new life as a homemaker, and the bigger the wedding the more secure he feels in the permanence of the marriage. That's it. That's definitely it.

I really think I should be an agony aunt.

Sunday 14ᵗʰ March

from: kate wensley
to: sally howe
subject: local news

hi daise
have just come across following in peaks and
dales advertiser—along with hugely poxy but
thankfully blurred pic -

it says -
local creative writing group riverside writers
will be appearing on bbc4 next wednesday in a
fly on the wall documentary programme entitled
blank page
filming took place back in september and the
programme features the writers—all of whom are
local people
current group leader bridget fellowes said
everyone enjoyed the experience—we can't wait to
see ourselves on screen
if the programme is a success there may well be
a follow-up series

o my

bj group leader?? can't wait??? a follow
up???

best watch this space love giovanna

Monday 15ᵗʰ March

Two weeks and two days until Gus gets home. I wonder
why he hasn't replied to my letter.

I had a horrid dream last night, about him and the

redhead. They were on a desert island building a palm tree hut, and Sue Lawley was interviewing them for *Desert Island Discs* and when she asked them what book they wanted to add to the Bible and Shakespeare they both said *Walden*.

Tuesday 16th March

Deep Water is turning into a media circus. Last night's meeting was pole-axed by the press photographers, not to mention hysteria from all the new participants drawn in by the publicity. Who can fill a blank page with all that going on?

Kate brought her Australian videos to for me to borrow. I shall watch one a night, after I've taken my capsule of cod liver oil. I started after Italian tonight with her home-taped *Australian Vets in Practice*. Richard would like the Land Rovers.

I wonder if I'll ever get used to the accent. It's much broader than on *Neighbours*. The more dust there is, the twangier the accent becomes. It's particularly pronounced when they say things like "We've got a joey here with testicle problems."

Wednesday 17th March

When I watched the programme tonight it reminded me of the first time I watched *The Office*. To say that the embarrassment was torture doesn't come close. It was excruciating to see the Deep Water ensemble from an outsider's viewpoint. I was sitting there with eyes screwed up, squinting at the screen, my fists clenched in claws, my arms tense, and my toes scrunched up in my slip-ons. It was only when Performance Janet came on that I laughed and relaxed and began to enjoy the thing, and then all too soon it was over.

Thank goodness there's just the one episode. And thank goodness it was on BBC4 and that no-one will have been watching it.

Thursday 18th March

Did I say no-one would be watching it? Angelina was. I haven't heard from her since last August except for a Christmas card, but she rang me this morning, when I was out thank goodness. This is the message she left on the answerphone:

"Hi Sal-gal, Angelina here. Amazed to see you on the box last night. Had no idea your funny little group was going to be on. Archie was channel-hopping between the golf and the news and there you were! Are they coming to film you again? Wondered if you'd like me to come up to one of your meetings and give a talk on Mills and Booning? Give me a ring. Bye."

Friday 19th March

I'd just settled down tonight to watch tonight's film in my Australian season when Pippa and Richard knocked on the door. They were walking the dogs but just outside my house the heavens had opened and they wanted to borrow an umbrella. They ended up staying and watching the film. It was *Picnic at Hanging Rock*. Pippa took a shine to the picnic baskets. "They have some similar ones in that new gift shop in Bakewell. I shall put one on my wedding list. Yes I will."

Saturday 20th March

Tonight I watched *Muriel's Wedding*. Brilliant.

I'm passing it on to Pippa and Richard for wedding plan tips.

Sunday 21st March

I had the most awful dream about Gus last night. I was meeting him at the airport (it is in fact only 10 days until this happens for real). Anyway, there I was standing at the international arrivals barrier, waving to him and calling his name, and he completely ignored me. He walked right past me and out of the airport and I turned and followed him and when I got to the door I saw him climbing up Ayres Rock which had materialised outside the airport. He was getting higher and higher, further and further, into a dusty Australian sunset, and there was a tiny figure struggling up madly behind him, and I realised I was watching myself, desperate, trying and failing to catch him up. I woke up gasping for breath, sweating and dripping in a hot flush from hell.

Tonight, in spite of this, I girded my loins and continued my year-in-the-bush desensitisation programme by watching *Priscilla, Queen of the Desert*. If the film is anything to go by I need to go to John Lewis immediately and bring home the contents of the whole of their make up department, not to mention three miles of sequinned chiffon for Gus.

Monday 22nd March

A very surprising day. Abigail smelly Ferrets rang me at ten this morning. Fancy an agent ringing me. Fancy an agent being at her desk at ten on a Monday morning.

"Abigail Ferrers here, of Balls and Ferrers literary agents." She sounded posh. She also sounded as if she was on very good terms with herself.

"Yes?" I said.

"Am I speaking to the Sally Howe who was on the *BBC4 Blank Page* last week?"

"That's me."

So, real people as well as Angelina, had watched the programme. Not that A-smelly-F counts as a real person.

"You had tremendous presence. I'd like to sign you up. Represent you. I understand from the programme that you've written a novel?"

"Yes. You've seen it," I said.

"No. Can't have. I would have spotted your potential."

"Actually," I said, "you rejected it." *And you never returned my manuscript.*

"Couldn't have. My assistant goes through the slush pile. Not me. He sometimes misses talent. Whatever—a novel can easily be knocked into shape. It's the marketing that's important. And you have style. The over fifties are the next big thing, and from what I saw last week, you've got it. *It.* Do you follow?"

I told her I'd think about it. Yes I did. (Gosh, I'm beginning to sound like Pippa.)

I told her I'd think about it. I didn't immediately say yes, because she sounded so horrid.

And I'm glad that I did, because when the post arrived at 10.30 there was a letter from another agent—one I wrote to in February—who asked to see more of my writing. She thinks I have an original voice! And she thinks I have potential! Unfortunately, she also thinks that—"judging from the synopsis, this novel has serious weaknesses." She sounds like an Ofsted inspector. I don't care: I have an original voice.

Stick that up your jumper, Abigail Ferrets.

The third thing that happened today—why do things always happen in threes?—was a phone call from the producer of Johnny Hazlewood's phone-in programme at *SWISH Radio*. They want me to go on a phone-in about creative writing classes, this Thursday.

Deep Water was double its normal size tonight. Everyone except Kate and me had brought along "friends." It was manic. If it carries on like this I shan't be missing anything when we go down under.

What I *shall* be missing is Elodie Champion coming to film an entire series of *Blank Page*. She rang Duncan on Friday night and said there'd been such a good response to the prog last week that she'd been given a contract for six more episodes. She wants to start filming in May.

I watched *Kangaroo Jack* when I got home. Puerile drivel but the bit swimming in the waterfall looks like my kind of thing. Wendy's right. I must get a new cossie.

Wednesday 24th March

It's only a week until Gus gets home. One week. And he still hasn't replied to my letter. It's worrying.

Last night I had another dream about meeting him at the airport. This time I was waiting at the arrivals barrier and I spotted Gus and started waving and then a man behind him started waving and calling my name and it was Iain, and Gus was swivelling his head from Iain to me and back again and I didn't know where to put myself. Then I woke up. These stupid airport dreams are driving me to distraction.

I've realised that if we do go to live in the Australian bush I could write pieces about it. Kate told me about a teacher friend who was having a year off to go travelling, and she blagged a column with the *Times Educational Supplement* about educational differences around the world, so I started trying to think of who I could blag a column from.

I was looking through my folder where I keep all the clippings of my pieces, to cheer myself up, and to remind myself that I can write stuff that people like, and seeing the bit *Janina Lemon is away* reminded me that KayWh isn't the only editor who liked my pieces—the features editor of the Monday to Friday *Recorder*—Daphne Vicars—also likes my stuff. She printed the very first piece I had in, and she gave me the Janina Lemon spot. Why hadn't I thought of her before?

I emailed her and told her about the (possible) Aussie trip and asked if she would be interested in a monthly column. I thought that asking for a weekly one was pushing it.

Thursday 25th March

I feel like an old pro. I really enjoyed the phone-in today. Johnny Hazlewood was very friendly, and it was altogether enormous fun. It certainly helps knowing from the outset that the subject up for discussion has nothing to do with sheds and what the Howe family does or does not do in them at Christmas.

Talking to callers about creative writing is so much easier. It's a doddle. I was on air for thirty minutes—admittedly there were some musical interludes—and I fielded five calls.

The last caller was Mrs Mountain. Does she see it as her mission in life to follow my every media movement? She had rung about the Riverside Writers group that she'd seen mentioned in the paper. "I'd like to attend, but no-one can tell me when and where the meetings are held. Could you please give me details?"

I was on air being nice Sally Howe. I couldn't refuse.

Kate and I will have to form a breakaway group—Open Ocean. Except that I shan't be here, dammit.

When I got home there was a message on the answerphone from Daphne Vicars. She'd be in the office until seven—could I ring her back?

I did. And it was great news. As well as features, she said that she also edits the Saturday Magazine, and I could have an occasional column in that—along with colour photos. How did that sound?

Friday 26th March

It's not just Daphne Vicars who likes me. I am *everyone's* favourite person. The *SWISH* producer from yesterday rang to ask if I'd be available for three months, beginning in May.

"I'm not sure." I didn't say it looked as though I'd be very much *un*available. I wanted to see what she was offering.

"Oh God, I hope you'll say yes, Sally. Johnny Hazlewood has been on the waiting list for a hip replacement and now he's got a date in May. I'm hoping you'll agree to be his stand-in. Phone-ins—three afternoons a week."

"Really? How amazing. When do you need to know by?"

"The end of next week—April 2nd. If you can't do it, my assistant wants to have a go, but between you and me, I don't think she's got what it takes. She's not old enough. So many of our listeners are pensioners."

Oh my.

Saturday 27ᵗʰ March

Another bloody stupid dream last night about meeting Gus: it's obviously playing on my mind. Last night I dreamed I was at the airport and Gus leaped out of a giant chocolate Easter egg, waving a laptop. I tried to get close to him but a horde of *Hearth and Home* photographers swooped in front and shoved me aside. I eventually managed to push my way through the men and the flashing cameras and I asked him what all the fuss was about, and he said he'd just got a six figure contract from the Thoreau Foundation (is there such a thing?) to write an account of his year in the Rockies.

What a relief it will be when he gets home for real next Wednesday; I'll stop dreaming all of this rubbish.

When I was getting washed this morning I did a stupid thing. I glanced in the mirror. I was horrified to see how tatty my hair was, but even worse, how old and faded I looked, just like the grass in the fields, which still has it's winter colouring. In a few weeks time the grass will have its new spring brightness and be a beautiful vivid green, but I shan't get my summer colouring of a lightly tanned face until June if I'm lucky. And Gus is coming home in four days. I don't want him to walk through the doors from customs on Wednesday and see me standing behind the barrier and wish he was coming home to someone else.

Sunday 28ᵗʰ March

I went to have my hair cut yesterday—at the place in Sheffield that Wendy and I call Pricey Paul's. It's the same style as always—long with a fringe—but it feels sharper, there's no doubt about it, and he showed me how to twist it up and put it in one of those clips with fronds of hair spilling out the top. Having it in a plait may be writerly, but having it up suits me better.

Monday 29th March

Thank God. Last night, the airport dream was innocuous: Gus walking towards the arrivals barrier being pulled by Pippa's dogs.

Two days until he's home. Yippeee!

When I'd bought my fruit and veg at Bakewell market this morning, I was walking along while re-arranging the stuff in my basket and I bumped into a sandwich board on the pavement for the Tuscany Tanning Studio. Not being keen to court skin cancer, I have always spurned such places, but this felt like a sign. And there's no point in having signs if you don't follow them, even if you don't have your swimming cossie with you. So I did: I went in and had my first ever tanning session, so that I'll look better when Gus arrives home.

It was fun. And it was wonderfully warm. The only thing I didn't like about the experience was *Radio Peaks-n-Dales* blaring out in the sunshower cabin. I didn't like the DJ's choice of music. Radio 4 would have been preferable and so much more soothing. I could have listened to *Woman's Hour*. If they want to attract the grey pound they should think of such things. They could even have special pensioner sessions three afternoons a week and time them to coincide with the Johnny Hazlewood (or Sally Howe!) phone-in programme.

As I left, I bumped into Mrs Mountain in the doorway. Surely she wasn't going in for a tan? Mrs Mountain in that tiny cabin? She'd press up against the bars and come out looking like a char grilled steak.

I walked back along the river in the direction of my car and met Richard throwing bread to the ducks. He'd persuaded Pippa to have a lie-in while he went to the market.

"I've just been to the optician's to check out some new frames," he said. "Pippa says these are dated. I can't think what she means. Glasses aren't a fashion item. They're the ultimate in functionality—a tool for improving vision," he said.

"I think Pippa's right," I said, though I found it uncomfortable to be agreeing with Pippa on matters of style.

"Anyway, new frames are far too pricey. They don't know what to charge. A multi-position aluminium ladder would be so much cheaper."

"What?"

"Uppertown Tools have got some on special offer. They're half the price of the glasses frames Pippa wants me to have. There's a display outside on the pavement. I had to cross over the road to avoid looking at them—the ladders. You can have so much more fun with a multi-position ladder than with a pair of bifocals."

Tuesday 30th March

The dreams have stopped, but I am still sleeping really badly—I'm so excited that Gus will be home tomorrow. And today I got a letter—at long long last.

The winter is easing. Thank God. Snowed up for three weeks. It's been long and hard. Looking forward to being somewhere warmer.
Have finally got out and down the hillside and collected my mail. I don't understand your letters. I never thought we were on a trial separation. I thought you were just overwrought and blowing your top at the airport. Have wondered about your letter sign offs through the year, though. I seemed to remember you always signing All my love, not just love. Thought it must have been your hormones.

Dan has negotiated that the cabin can stay when I leave. This is great news—to pull it down would be to make me an accessory to 20th century disposable consumerism. I moved back into it when the wind subsided, soon after I last wrote. I didn't come half way around the world to walk past a jacuzzi on the way to the porch.

Dan suspects that there may be some end of lease issues due to kerosene lamp stains in the living room, but he's going to sort that one out too, don't worry.

see you shortly, take very good care Gus

ps almost forgot bird list

Three toed woodpecker

Mountain Chickadee

Thank God. Thank God. We're sorted.

Although I really don't know how he has the gall to mention the bloody jacuzzi.

And that comment "looking forward to being somewhere warmer"—sounds to me as if the bush is still ON.

But oh what a sweetie—he says "Take *very* good care." I can't wait to see him.

Tonight I had this email from Daniel.

```
from: daniel howe
to: sally howe
subject: dad
```

```
Hi Ma,

Dad safely loaded onto the plane. He seemed
relieved to be going home—bearing in mind his
general shell shock at being back in civilisation,
and also his dread of the impending air-travel.

I'm not sure he's still keen on the trip to
Australia. He said he couldn't wait to get back
```

to Derbyshire, and that he never wanted to be
away from you or Radio 4 again.
Lots of love,
Dan

Does this mean Australia is off? Or was Gus just traumatised by Denver and the airport?

Actually, his comment to Daniel tells me nothing. He *won't* be away from me if I go to Australia, and he doesn't have to be away from Radio 4 either because if we take my lap top he can listen to it on the internet.

Who knows what is going to happen to my career?

Will I be on the *SWISH Radio* Sally Howe phone-in three times a week? It's only poxy local radio, and it has nothing to do with writing, but a girl has to start somewhere.

Or will I be sending a column from down under—woo hoo a column (even if occasional)—to Daphne Vicars?

And will the agent like and sell my book—launching the start of a twilight career as a novelist?

Wednesday 31ˢᵗ March

I couldn't sleep last night. I am so excited. I can't *wait* to see Gus. In half an hour I'll be setting off to meet him at Manchester airport.

I have been awake since four. I gave up trying to sleep at six and had a shower and pottered downstairs for a cuppa. In the hall I was spotted through the window in the door by Billy Bathgate who was delivering the paper. He knocked.

"Good morning, madam," he said unctuously, handing me the paper. "Did you know your front path is flooding again? Should I be getting out my drain rods to assist?"

The drains again.

"Thanks for the offer, but Gus is arriving home today. He'll sort them."

Envoi

I stood there at the arrivals barrier opposite the open swing doors, at the end of the long wide corridor down to customs. I was holding *The Weight of Water* open and trying to read it, but I flicked my eyes so often between the page and the door from customs that it made me seasick so I shut up the book and put it away in my bag.

Half hour went by. Three quarters of an hour. Another half hour. I looked at my watch and checked the note I'd made and realised Gus's touch down was 3 p.m. not 2 p.m. Bugger.

I needed something to calm me down and perk me up at the same time and remembered my emergency Mars Bar. I squatted down and rummaged through my shoulder bag and found it at the bottom, stuck to my writer's notebook. I was easing them apart when someone loomed over me and said in a hopeless attempt at a Humphrey Bogart accent:

"Hey Babe, how's about coming back to my place and listening to Radio 4?"

I hugged his legs. Then, because my arthritic knee joints had caved in, I hauled myself upright by working my way up his legs like a body search in reverse. He grabbed me and pulled me up and hugged me—a warm giant bear hug. I sank into his arms and shut my eyes.

"Gus! Gus! Keep hugging, don't stop. It has been so long. So long. You must never, ever, do it again."

"Do what again? Creep up on you and make you jump? Proposition you in an airport concourse?"

"Go away for a bloody year, you fool."

I was crying. I couldn't help it. I was blubbering in huge snotty gulps.

"Thank God you're still here," he said into my neck. "Thank God I'm home."

We stood like that for ages. We stood like that until I got cramp in my left shoulder and he said "Hon, I need to put down my bags. I'm not getting any younger."

I loosened myself from his grip and stood a good foot away—I didn't have my reading glasses and I wanted to look at his dear, dear face: his honest hazel eyes, the three deep upright grooves between his eyebrows, his steady grin, his nice straight teeth, his thick grey beard, the curl in his hair that is always there behind his right ear. I licked him up. It was as if he'd come back from the dead.

"You look so handsome. You look so incredibly tanned."

He was smiling at me. He reached behind my head and touched the clip that was holding up my hair "What's with the headgear, Babe? Whatever it's for—it suits you having your hair dolled up like that. Makes you look like a bright-eyed pony."

"Er, thanks."

"But what's with all the gunk on your eyes?"

"It's mascara. I wanted to make myself look nice for you. Oh God, It'll have run with all that crying."

"You needn't have bothered, Hon. You're the best looking broad I've seen since the last time I touched down in this crumby two bit airport." He said all this in the Humphrey Bogart voice.

"Why are you calling me Babe and Hon? And why the accent?"

"You noticed."

"Of course I noticed, you fool."

"I thought it would make me seem more exotic and interesting. I've been nervous about seeing you."

"So you put on a funny voice? Most people alter the way they look—spruce themselves up."

"*Beware of all enterprises that require new clothes*," we said in unison. We linked our little fingers and each said the name of a poet—he said Brecht and I said e e cummings.

"So how was your flight?"

"I prefer not to think about it. Best forgotten. The worst kind of nightmare. Like being in the 21st century equivalent of the bowels of a slave ship. Hordes of unspeakably malodorous people rammed into unfeasibly small spaces—ugh!"

The same old Gus. I laughed.

"Lead me to the car. Take me away from this surging sea of horrible humanity."

"I'll just get you a *Times* from WHSmith—you'll have missed the crossword. Wait here. Don't budge an inch." I kissed him and rushed off.

When I returned he looked in horror at the paper I was carrying.

"What's that?" he said. "I thought you were getting a *Times*."

"You can only get it in tabloid now."

"A tabloid bloody *Times* is a contradiction in terms," he said. "Does it still have a decent crossword?"

"I expect so." How would I know? I'd been getting *The Recorder*.

"What else has happened that's awful, since I've been away? Has anyone important died?" he said, as we walked to the car park.

"Like who? Blair is still with us, unfortunately."

"Not bloody Blair—he's not important. He's a mere flake

of chaff. What about Tony Benn? Clare Short? Is Jon Snow still around?"

"All still here."

"Thank God for that."

We reached the car and piled his bags in the boot. He got into the passenger seat and said: "Take me home, Hon."

I got in beside him and took my writer's notebook out of my bag. "I just need to write down *Hon* before I forget it. I just need to find the page for new expressions to use in dialogue."

"How wonderful to be home," he said, stretching out his legs and putting his arm along the back of my seat. I flicked through the pages of my notebook and at the same time I reached out and laid my hand on his thigh, feeling the smooth firm muscle beneath his jeans.

"So how's the single life been working out for you?" he said, stroking my neck and exploding my concentration.

"How's it been working out for you? Is that American?" I said. "I must get that down as well. Have you got any more?"

"No idea. You're the listener. I'm the one who talks." He looked at his watch. "Come on. If the traffic's OK we'll have time to get back and have some hootchy-cootchy and—"

"Hootchy-cootchy? Oh—another one for my notebook."

"As I was saying, you psycho-writer—we can have some hootchy-cootchy and you'll still be in time to watch *Neighbours*."

"Oh Gus. I haven't seen you for a year. Do you think I care about bloody *Neighbours*? I want to talk to you, I want you to tell me *everything*."

"But I've pictured it in my mind's eye—one of the things I've looked forward to," he said. "Me lying on the sofa and you watching your half hour of undiluted preposterous pap while I disparage it from behind *The Times*."

"OK then," I said, "pap and sofa it is. I suppose *Neighbours* will start to break you in for when we go to Australia."

"Who said anything about Australia?"

"Oh come here, prat-face. Give me another hug to keep me going until we get home."

Acknowledgements

Thanks for sharing the joke, and for being great publishers:
Anna Torborg and Emma Barnes, and all at Snowbooks.

For comments and suggestions on earlier drafts, heartfelt thanks to:
Marion Chapman, Maureen Sandler and Liz Goulds, and other Scarthin Writers and Wirksworth Writers; Laura Longrigg, Broo Doherty and Clare Alexander; Chris Huntley, Christine Poulson, Sue Price and Kath Sharman.

Thanks to Jeff Connor, Natural Resources Specialist, Rocky Mountain National Park for bird information; to Ruth Barcroft for information on local radio; and to Lisa Dransfield for her welcome at BBC Nottingham.

Warm thanks for the encouragement, patience and support of The Woof family, the Hepworth family and the Willis family; Inge Bates, Annie Blindell, Ruth Carter, Dot Course, Pattie Delfosse, Chris Huntley, Maria Longwright, Christine Poulson, Sue Price, Mary Scurfield and Christine Shimell.

Special thanks to Dave Hepworth.
And a sad goodbye to Chomsky.

Permissions

Every effort has been made to contact copyright holders of material quoted in this book. However, the publishers would be delighted to receive corrections, clarifications or omissions and will acknowledge these in future editions of this work. Please e-mail permissions@snowbooks.com with any correspondence.

The publishers acknowledge the use of quotations and extracts from the following:

An die Nachgeborenen by Bertolt Brecht
I'm Alright by Loudon Wainwright III
Top Hat, produced by RKO
Cat's Cradle by Kurt Vonnegut
Walden by Henry David Thoreau
Men, Women, and Dogs by James Thurber
Published and Proud by Sue Hepworth
and several of Sue Hepworth's articles, which originally appeared in The Times.